the
WORLD
UNDONE

To Estelle,
It was such a
pleasure to meet yuu
today and share our
"book table"
Best wishes,
Mary

the WORLD UNDONE

MARY DRIVER-THIEL

CRUZO

PINE LAKE PRESS
Lake Forest, IL

PUBLISHED BY PINE LAKE PRESS
LAKE FOREST, IL

ISBN 978-0-9886568-0-2

Cover design by Lynn Bell
Monroe Street Studios
http://www.MonroeSt.com

Book design by Nathan Everett
Elder Road Books
ElderRoad@comcast.net

Author photo by Robert Tolchin.

Cover image by Irina Reznichenko, courtesy of Getty Images.

To my husband, Jerry,
and my daughters, Betsy, Sarah, and Kate,
whose love means the world to me.

the WORLD UNDONE

1
SYLVIA

*E*XCEPT FOR THE neon *Miller* signs festooning the lower level windows and the wooden placard out front that read "Stone's Throw Tavern," the drab little place was no different from dozens of other dreary dwellings waiting in the late spring sun for the tourist season to begin along the Michigan coast. A simple clapboard structure, its paint was worn to dusty gray from the constant lake winds. Plain white curtains laced the second story windows.

Sylvia had found her way to Stone's Throw more easily than she expected. From a small, unpaved parking lot across the street, she surveyed the building, beguiled by its very ordinariness. The entire town of Cedar Beach might be a little shabbier, a little quieter than the fly-specked resorts strewn along the Eastern Seaboard where she had grown up, but its familiarity resonated.

Still, it wasn't the place that Sylvia had traveled so far to see; it was Callie. Callie Collins. After a decade of fantasies, daydreams, and nightmares, it was hard to believe the real Callie was so close. A small part of Sylvia's heart understood there was more than one motive for what she was about to do. On the surface, she had always told herself that finding Callie would be a lark, something fun to do, something that would prove how clever she was. And it would definitely piss off her mother. Their mother. Sylvia smiled to herself imagining for a moment the gossip that would fly back home in Teabury when everyone learned that Anne Bennett's perfect little life was as fucked up as everyone else's. Sylvia's smile faded, though, when she took the thought a step further. An unexpected wave of trepidation diminished the bravado and curiosity that had brought her here. Only a few yards away from someone she had waited years to meet, Sylvia's resolve weakened, and for the first time, it occurred to her that maybe it hadn't been such a great idea to come rushing out here. It wasn't that she cared how Callie might *feel* about being tracked down; it was more that she had never considered how Callie might *react*.

Ten years ago, when Sylvia had first learned about Callie, she had had a visceral response: first the trembling started, then her heart had raced, and sparkles formed at the edge of her vision. Those same sensations overwhelmed her now, leaving her slightly faint, so that she was afraid she wouldn't be able to walk the fifty yards to the tavern's front door. The memory of her twelfth birthday teased itself into clarity.

It was on that day when Sylvia had gone uninvited into her parents' bedroom, something she knew was expressly forbidden. Her mother had often said that no good came from snooping and, at least about that one thing, Anne Bennett had been telling the truth.

Sylvia's parents were supposed to have arrived home in time for her birthday. They had been away for over a month. This time, their excuse had been that they were looking at marble samples in Italy. For six weeks. Sylvia hadn't understood why they needed new marble in the front hall; the stuff that was already there looked perfectly fine. Still, they had promised to return by Sunday. On Saturday morning, when the housekeeper announced that her mother was on the phone and wanted to speak with her, Sylvia had known what would happen.

"Surely you don't mind, do you, darling?" her mother had said. "After all, we can celebrate your birthday any time. Why don't you think about what you'd like to do, and Daddy and I will see you next week."

Sylvia remained polite as she responded, mimicking the cool, refined pitch of her mother's voice, but after she had hung up the phone, she ran straight to her bedroom and slammed the door hard. Hard enough, she hoped, that the sound would ring throughout the house. She sat for a moment on her bed, relishing the hot anger as it smoldered and grew in her, until it leapt to life like fire. If her parents couldn't be bothered to spend time with her, she could still spend time with them. She was never allowed to enter the master suite without invitation, but if they could break promises, so could she.

She drifted down the long upstairs hallway and silently entered the room, careful to close the door quietly behind her. She caught the scent of her mother's perfume blended with the aroma of furniture polish. Not surprisingly, the dark wood of the dressers gleamed, and the mirrors sparkled. But the chill of the room wasn't masked by beautiful fabrics or sun-colored paint. She crossed to a small bookcase containing four volumes on floral arranging and two on architecture. A set of matching guidebooks to Europe and the Far East took up the top shelf. The bottom shelf held only a couple of copies of *Town & Country* and an old *Wall Street Journal*. Scattered about the dresser tops and on the walls were the things that her parents had collected from their trips around the world—Russian lacquer boxes, Japanese fans, African sculptures, watercolors from the Mediterranean. These were the things her parents valued, the things they kept close.

In the alcove between the bedroom and the bath, there was a vanity table on which sat two small lamps with crystal-beaded shades, two bottles of perfume, and an empty blue and white Wedgwood box. Sylvia picked up the perfume bottle labeled *JOY*, removed the stopper and sniffed the contents, curious to know what joy smelled like. She'd splashed a bit on her neck, spilling some on the pristine glassed surface of the table. The drawers of the vanity held only tissues, and an assortment of lipsticks, eye shadows, and mascaras. There were a few pieces of costume jewelry, but none of the good stuff. Sylvia wondered where her mother kept the diamond necklace, the brooches and bracelets and rings so laden with heavy stones that they dwarfed her mother's delicate, birdclaw hands.

On the opposite side of the alcove were the closets. Each of her parents had a walk-in closet. In her mother's, perfume covered the slight mustiness of absence. Clothes lined the two longer walls. Formal gowns and dresses, encased in protective plastic, hung along one side; skirts, slacks and blouses were tiered on the other, each item grouped according to color. A rainbow of sandals, ballerina flats, and heels were perched toes-up in custom-built racks. Any disruptions in the regimented order indicated items that were currently traveling with her mother. At the far end of the closet, beneath a lighted mirror, several drawers were built directly into the wall. In the larger drawers, Sylvia found sweaters. The medium drawers held scarves and hair bands, and the smallest drawers were filled with velvet boxes, each containing its own treasure. It was to these that Sylvia gave most of her attention, pawing through the pearls, gold chains, bracelets and dozens of earrings like Aladdin in the cave of the Djinn. She slipped a strand of pearls around her neck, clipped on a pair of chunky gold earrings and looked in the mirror. It startled her to see the image of her mother's face in her own ice-blue eyes, high cheekbones and straight, narrow nose.

She looked again in the drawer of scarves, carelessly rummaging through the carefully folded silk. Beneath several layers, her fingers tapped against something solid. A book. The black cover was embossed with gold lettering: *Tristan*. Caught between two of the pages were three stems of dried lavender and a delicate gold chain necklace with a wine-colored stone that dangled like a bookmark fob from the center of the story.

Casually flipping through the pages, Sylvia found a slim, plain envelope tucked inside the book. It was addressed to Miss Anne Charles, which had been her mother's name before she married Henry Bennett III. Lifting the flap, Sylvia removed the single sheet of paper. It took her a few minutes to comprehend what she was seeing, even though the words at the top of the page were quite clearly printed: Certificate of Live Birth. Baby girl. Father: unknown. Mother: Anne Charles, age 18. The certificate was dated June 26, 1979, ten years before Sylvia's own birthday.

CℜED

NOW, SYLVIA FOUND herself sitting across the street from the drab little tavern that her half-sister called home. Maybe all those fantasies she had spun over and over in her mind, the scenarios of sisters reunited, were stupid. Maybe this wasn't like a Shirley Temple movie or Little Orphan Annie. Maybe it had been a mistake to come here. Her hands were damp now, leaving a sheen on the steering wheel.

For nine years, her mother's secret had been Sylvia's secret, too. It had become her talisman. Every time she had been ignored, slighted, or made to feel unworthy, she soothed herself with the knowledge that the day would come when she would find her half-sister and bring her back home to Teabury. In all those years she had told no one of her plans, and her mother never suspected a thing.

She reminded herself that this undertaking had required time, patience, and money. She had invested too much of herself to walk away now. It would be the worst thing she could do.

As soon as she turned twenty-one and had access to her trust fund, Sylvia had hired a private detective. Tom Harvey's office was in Danfield, a down-on-its luck town on the outskirts of Providence.

An hour's drive from her home in Teabury, it was close enough to be practical, yet far enough from home to be discreet. Harvey spent six months and a substantial amount of cash searching before he finally called with a name—Callie Collins—and an address for the tavern in Cedar Beach, Michigan. That had been three days ago. Too excited to consider all the possible consequences, Sylvia had jumped on a plane.

She had told her fiancé, Pier, that she was going to Chicago to visit Jen Gardner. That was only half a lie, and exactly the same line she'd given to Jen when she announced her impromptu visit. The two had been best friends since their boarding school days, when they reigned as the most popular and most outrageously behaved girls at stuffy old Farmington.

Arriving at Jen's apartment late on a Thursday night, she confessed the real reason for her trip while she and Jen ate Thai takeaway from cardboard containers and shared a bottle of wine.

"You have got to be kidding," Jen said. "First off, I can't believe this is your mom, of all people, that you're talking about. She's like, Mrs. So-Totally-Perfect."

"Unless you happen to be one of her kids."

"Okay, so she's not Mommy-of-the-Year. But she puts on a pretty good public face, you must admit."

"Whatever." Sylvia routinely dismissed compliments to her mother. "So, I need to drive over to Michigan. Any chance I could borrow your car for a couple of days?"

"Yeah, no problem. It just sits in the parking garage all the time, anyway. Take it for as long as you need." Jen hesitated. "Maybe I'm being a chicken-shit, but are you sure you want to do this? It's pretty intense stuff you're messing with, and your mother isn't someone I'd want to piss off."

"That's exactly the point. She doesn't have any idea I know about Callie, let alone that I've actually found her. And she won't know until I'm ready to spring it on her. I'm thinking the rehearsal dinner might be a good time to introduce Callie to everyone."

Jen's eyes widened. "Holy shit. You're planning to have your secret half-sister just show up at your rehearsal dinner?"

"Sounds like fun, *n'est-ce pas?*"

"Sounds like big trouble."

"Oh, come on, since when have either of us ever been afraid of a little trouble?"

"Okay, but don't say I didn't warn you," Jen added, handing over the keys to her BMW.

☾☙☽

SYLVIA SAT BACK in the leather seat of Jen's car and watched the mid-afternoon sun play off the tavern's weathered siding and dance with the young summer leaves in the breeze from the lake. At the end of the block, she could see the deep blue water of the lake just beyond a collection of ramshackle docks and rickety marine paraphernalia. This inland coast had a familiar summer resort atmosphere, but seeing the sun sink over water to the west was disorienting. Everything here felt off-kilter. At home, where the sun *rose* over the water, she had been so sure she would know exactly what to say to Callie. In this place where even the sun was in the wrong place, she felt completely lost. Clearly, she hadn't really thought things through. Maybe it would be better to turn the car around and drive away.

The only person besides Jen who knew what Sylvia was planning was Tom Harvey. She had never worked with a private detective before. It was quite exciting. The guy looked like a private eye—tall, dark, and even moderately handsome for as old as he was, though he was definitely a little rough around the edges. He had been matter-of-fact, almost dismissive, that first day when she walked into his office, but as time went on, he had called her more and more frequently to discuss details. She'd met with him several times in the course of the investigation, twice at a wine bar in Boston where he claimed to have one of the waiters under surveillance. He bought her drinks and asked a lot of questions that didn't seem relevant to the case and, after a while, she began to wonder if his interest was purely professional. Not that she minded. She'd never admit it, even to Jen, but she thought Mr. Harvey was cute. For an old guy.

Sylvia worried that Tom would be disappointed in her if she didn't follow through and meet with Callie, but so what? She shouldn't care what Tom Harvey thought; he was the hired help. She had paid his fees and owed him nothing more, not even an explanation. She should drop this whole ridiculous idea.

She put the key back in the ignition, but a sense of regret rose within her so overpoweringly that for a moment, she found it hard to breathe. She looked again at the tavern across the street. What was it like to live there, she wondered? How long had she indulged in fantasies about her half-sister? Now that the reality was in front of her, she felt a certain obligation to follow through, to learn who her sister was, what her life was like. This tavern, or bar, or whatever it was, was so different from the house in Teabury where Sylvia had grown up. From Tom's investigation, Sylvia knew that Callie had purchased the property a few years earlier, and that it was her home as well as her business. Tom had also told her that Callie was married to a man named Brad Collins, and they had a son, Ethan, who was five years old.

Still reluctant to get out of the car, Sylvia rummaged through her purse, deciding to reapply her lipstick, knowing full well it was a stall tactic. Pulling down the sun visor so that little lights came on around the vanity mirror, she examined her face. She had her mother's honey-blond hair, high cheekbones and almond-shaped blue eyes, but Sylvia's face was not as sharply angled. As she studied her own features, she tried to remember from high school biology which genes were dominant: brown eyes over blue? Thick eyebrows, or delicate arches? What traits would Callie have inherited? Which features, if any, might they share? With the little mirror framing only her light blue eyes, Sylvia shivered. Her eyes were a bit too much like her mother's eyes.

Her mother was beautiful. Of that there was no doubt. She was also intelligent and reasonably accomplished, at least in social graces. But she was not an easy woman. The effort required to be rail thin, perfectly coiffed, and elegantly dressed at all times consumed her. Frequently out of town and always too busy, Anne Bennett was either bored or irritated on the few occasions when she and Sylvia spent time together. Sins of the fathers, or in this case, the mother.

Flipping the visor mirror closed, Sylvia grabbed her purse and forced herself out of the car. If she didn't go in that tavern right now, the moment would be lost. She would never find the courage to try again, and then she would never forgive herself. It was time to make good on a promise she had made, a promise to put right a situation and, in the darkest part of her heart, to settle a score.

⊂જ⊃

THE QUIET, FURTIVE DARK of any tavern in daylight hours heightened its seedier qualities. The interior of Stone's Throw was no exception, with its sweet-musk scent of liquor, old and new, and the harsher odor of ancient cigarette smoke. A Muzak version of Lennon's "Imagine" played softly from unseen speakers. In the dim light, a man and woman, hunched protectively over their bottles of beer, occupied two stools at the bar, which spanned the length of the right side of the interior. A grungy fellow whose gray hair protruded wildly from an orange hunting cap sat at the far end of the bar. Even from a distance, he looked as if the air around him smelled of old grease and body odor.

Across from the bar was a dining area, large enough for only a dozen tables, one of which was occupied by an elderly couple.

They watched Sylvia with the chary quality of people unused to strangers. Behind the bar, a man in his mid-thirties polished wine glasses, sliding each of them stem up into overhead racks. His hair was thick and dark, combed back in a style that was almost, but not quite, trendy. He wore wire-rimmed glasses, and despite his slightly thick features and a short, stocky build, he was nice-looking.

"Afternoon," he said, glancing up from the glassware. Maybe it was her imagination, but Sylvia could have sworn she saw him do a double take.

He moved to the end of the bar so that he was only its width away from her. "What can I get for you?" he asked, his head cocked slightly to one side as though he were trying to work out a puzzle.

"Uh, I'm not sure," she replied, wishing she'd stayed in the car. She hadn't thought about ordering a drink, and here was Brad (this must be Brad, she thought) asking her what she wanted. What she wanted was her sister, but what she asked for, in a quavering voice quite unlike her own, was, "Maybe a Coke. No, wait, I'll have a cup of tea."

"Tea?" Brad raised an eyebrow.

Stupid. That was so stupid, she thought. What kind of an idiot comes into a bar at four in the afternoon and orders tea? She really should have stayed in the car.

To his credit, the bartender swallowed any sarcastic comment he might have been tempted to toss out. "Okay, I can do tea," he said. He hesitated, then added, "Anything else?"

"Umm, is Callie here?"

"Yeah," he nodded, but his tone took on a guarded quality. "She's in the back. You want to talk to her?"

"Please," was all Sylvia could manage to whisper.

He tossed the polishing cloth into a shiny stainless steel sink and, without a word, ducked out the opposite end of the bar, through a set of swinging doors set in the far wall, vanishing to an unseen area. Callie would be there.

Sylvia's imagination followed him behind the doors where she could see the two of them talking. He would begin by saying something like: "Callie, there's someone out front asking for you."

And she would casually reply, "Who?"

Then she would see the look on his face and ask, "Is something wrong?"

"I don't know," he would say, "Just go out there. By the way, she wants some tea. Do we have any tea around here?"

Sylvia's heart began pounding. In seconds, Callie would walk through those doors, and the two of them would have to offer each other some sort of greeting. Sylvia would have to explain why she had asked for Callie by name. "How do you do?" and a handshake seemed cold, but an embrace wouldn't be right, either. What did one do in such circumstances? Physical contact was out of the question. Sylvia had been brought up understanding that well-bred people regarded public displays of affection as extremely vulgar. Even within her own tiny family unit of three, affection was awkward. Anne and Henry Bennett were not the hugging type. The closest they ever came to demonstrating emotions were those times when they returned from long trips. Her father would pat the top of her head, saying, "Good to see you, dear," and her mother would say, "I have a such a headache after that wretched plane ride." And then both her parents would drift to the music room, which had less to do with the highly-polished grand piano than with the fully stocked bar.

In Callie's tavern, Sylvia glanced at the rows of bottles behind the bar. Her reflection, trapped amongst the collection of liquor bottles, reminded her how often she sought solace in their seductive depths. But liquor was a con artist, trading temporary peace for the truth, and truth was a commodity that had been too rare in Sylvia's life. She had learned early that guarding secrets and evading truth, more often by omission than outright lying, was a reasonable, necessary and highly regarded social skill. Sylvia glanced at the swinging doors through which the biggest lie of all, the best-kept secret, would walk in a matter of seconds, and once again the desire to bolt from the bar almost overwhelmed her. Then the doors opened, and when Sylvia met the eyes of the woman approaching her, she knew there was no turning back.

It was not surprising that Brad had done a double take. Callie's hair was a shade or two darker than Sylvia's, she was taller by three inches, and leaner by twenty pounds, but there was no mistaking the two for blood kin. The recognition of each in the other was like a flash of lightning in the room.

Instead of slipping behind the bar, Callie walked around its perimeter. When she drew closer, Sylvia saw a close facsimile of her own features, but Callie's skin was weathered, its texture coarse, and lines were visible at the corners of her eyes and mouth. The most startling difference, however, was in the color of the other woman's eyes. Later, Sylvia would know they were a deep brown, but in the dim light of the bar, they looked nearly black. Callie cradled a thick white mug in her hands, but instead of putting it down in front of Sylvia, she nodded toward the tables in the dining area.

"Let's talk over there," she said, heading to a far corner of the room. Sylvia slid off the bar stool, following obediently. She was aware that the elderly couple had stopped eating, and both of them watched intently as Callie placed the tea mug on a table, then sat across from Sylvia. An awkward energy pulsed in the room.

"So. What do you want?" Callie asked. She pinned her eyes on Sylvia, eyes that, despite the color difference, challenged with the same intensity as those of their mother.

"My name is Sylvia Bennett—"

"I know who you are," Callie interrupted. "The question is,

why are you here?" Her tone was direct, but not unkind. "I'm pretty sure Anne didn't send you."

Only minutes ago, Sylvia had assumed Callie would be the one to be surprised when the two of them met, but now it was Sylvia who was thunderstruck. She was stunned silent as she realized that not only did Callie know her birth mother and half-sister by name, she apparently also knew something about Anne's personality.

"Don't look so shocked," Callie said. "It's not that unusual these days for adopted children to find out who their birth parents are."

"I, umm…I guess I hadn't thought about it. I mean, I hadn't thought that you might already know about us."

"Well, obviously I do."

Sylvia struggled to find words. "How long have you…well, did you—"

"Let's start with you first," Callie interrupted. She leaned both elbows on the table, crossing her arms in front of her.

Sylvia summoned her courage and met Callie's gaze. "I decided I wanted to find you, so I hired a private detective."

"Guy with a mustache? About forty?"

"That sounds like Tom."

"Yeah, he was in here a couple of weeks ago. I kind of wondered who he was, what he was doing here. We don't get that many tourists this time of year." Callie paused, reached into the pocket of the hooded sweatshirt she was wearing and pulled out a pack of Marlboros. Without asking permission, she lit one, blowing the stream of smoke sideways out her mouth.

"The smoking ban was supposed to go into effect a couple of months ago," she said, waving the cigarette casually, "but things change slowly around here."

She took another deep drag, then flicked a quarter inch of ash into the glass ashtray that sat between the salt and pepper and the sugar caddy. "So this Tom guy, he was spying on me?"

Sylvia thought it sounded awful when put that way. "No. Not really. It was more like he wanted to be sure he'd found the right person before he called me. Tom's like that. He's really thoughtful, and he does his job well. I'm sure he just wanted to be certain he wasn't sending me on a wild goose chase or into some tacky biker bar."

"I see." Callie took another long pull on the cigarette.

Too late, Sylvia realized that the "tacky biker bar" remark might have been insulting, so she tried to cover herself by adding, "This is a really nice place."

She looked around the room, noticing the large photos of sailboats on the walls, the fresh paint, the well-scrubbed hardwood floors. Obviously, this tavern was clean and well cared for, definitely a cut above the average small town roadside bar. "How did you come up with the name 'Stone's Throw Tavern'?"

"Because it's a stone's throw from the water. Saginaw Bay."

Okay, Sylvia thought, that made sense. From Callie's tone, maybe it should have been obvious. Sylvia had seen the shimmering blue from her car, and assumed it was Lake Huron, or Michigan, or whatever. Geography had never been her best subject. She tried to picture the "mitten" of Michigan in her head and decided that the water between the thumb and hand of that mitten must be Saginaw Bay.

Callie blew an angry stream of smoke out the corner of her mouth, and Sylvia felt as if she had ventured physically and emotionally into unfriendly territory. She fished around for something safe to keep the conversation moving. "So, Tom said you've been here about four years."

"That's about right." Callie stubbed out the half-finished cigarette. Again, she crossed her arms protectively in front of her chest and leaned back in the chair. "But you still haven't told me what you're doing here. Like I said, I don't think Anne Bennett sent you. What's the deal?"

Sylvia thought about saying, "I've wanted a sister all my life and it took me years to find you." Then she considered, "Because you're the only person I can think of who might actually make me feel like there is someone on this earth who can share with me all those things that families are supposed to share." Closest to the truth would be, "Because you're the best revenge ever on our bitch of a mother who thinks she walks on water." Instead, all she said was, "It's a long story."

Callie glanced around the bar. "It's four in the afternoon. We're not busy. I guess I can spare a minute or two." She nodded at the white mug. "Is that tea still all right, or would you like something a little stronger?"

"The tea is fine," Sylvia replied, taking a quick sip. Stalling for time, she took a packet from the sugar caddy and emptied it into the bitter drink. She took a deep breath, as though she was about to begin speaking, but hesitated, not knowing how to start. Callie wasn't what she had expected. Though not exactly rude or unfriendly, there was an edge to her that Sylvia hadn't foreseen. And she certainly hadn't foreseen that her own existence would be old news to her half-sister.

"You've known about me for *years?*" she said, finally managing to break the brittle silence.

Callie shrugged. "Yeah. A couple, maybe three." She tapped another cigarette out of the box, put it to her lips, then changed her mind. "Jeez, I really need to quit this filthy habit." She put the cigarette back in the box. Folding her hands on the table between them, she leaned in toward Sylvia. "Look, it's not anything personal. It's just that I don't consider Anne to be my real mother. My real mother is the woman who raised me."

"I understand," Sylvia said. "I just…it's just that I had no idea, and I've been wanting to meet you for a long, long time."

"Really? Why is that?"

Sylvia couldn't quite read Callie's tone. It implied more than just curiosity; there were also definite hints of bitterness and sarcasm. Choosing her words carefully, she said, "I always thought I was an only child. Then I found out about you." Her voice caught, which surprised her. Perhaps it was fatigue or tension, but amazingly, tears began to brim in her eyes.

Callie rubbed the spot between her eyebrows with two fingers. "I'm sorry. I'm sounding like a total bitch." She looked at her half-sister, offering a small but sincere smile. "I'm glad you're here. It's nice to meet you."

"Thank you." Sylvia's response was softer than she intended, but the effect was pleasing. Callie seemed to relax a bit.

"So what else did this Tom fellow tell you about me?"

"Not much. I know you grew up in Ann Arbor, you're married to a man named Brad, and you have a little boy, right?"

"All true. Brad's the guy at the bar. You've already met him. And Ethan—our son—is running around here somewhere. He's a good kid, but he can be a handful at times."

"He's five?"

"Your detective did a good job."

Sylvia didn't reply. She held onto the tea mug with both hands, bringing it close to her face, feeling almost as if she could hide behind it. "Okay, now it's your turn. How did you learn about me?"

"I had a little help, too," Callie began. Then, when she saw the look on Sylvia's face, she added, "but not from some Magnum, P.I. guy." She ran her hand over her hair, smoothing her French braid in a gesture that Sylvia found eerily similar to the sort of gesture their mother would make.

"It was Kevin, my brother—he's adopted, too—who got most of the information," Callie said. "He's a computer geek; there isn't anything he can't do or find with a computer. A few years ago, he hacked into some files to find his own birth parents, then decided that as long as he was at it, he might as well find information for me, too. "

"So you knew about us, but you never tried to get in touch with us?" Sylvia asked as she took a second packet of sugar from the caddy on the table, shook it, torn it open, and poured it in her cup.

Callie's face hardened. "Let's just say I had a lot to think about."

The two women regarded each other for a moment. Then Callie broke the silence by asking, "Why now? What brings you here now to look for me?"

"That's part of the long story." It was a story that Sylvia wanted to tell well enough so that she could take Callie with her back through the years, back to the world in which she, Sylvia, had grown up. She wanted her to understand exactly what it was like to be Anne's daughter, so she began by telling her about the house.

Sylvia's home in Teabury, Connecticut, the house in which she had grown up, was by anyone's standard, magnificent. Built in the 1920's by one of the kings of the shipping industry for his bride, the rooms of Sylvia's childhood home were a testament to lavish spending: glistening marble hallways, winding staircases, long, polished wood floors reflecting the light of crystal chandeliers. But aside from Sylvia, there were no children there. Living room, dining room, day parlor, library, music room, family room, sunroom, kitchen, breakfast room, butler's pantry—each room was beautifully decorated and totally unsuitable for child's play. On the second floor, in addition to seven bedrooms, four baths, and a master suite, her parents had provided her with a playroom. The third floor was the servants' quarters, but Sylvia was not allowed to go there. She respected that rule mostly because she truly feared the housekeeper, Mrs. Dent, who oversaw life in the house with terrifying authority. It was a relief when, at thirteen, she finally had escaped to boarding school.

"You had a housekeeper?" Callie asked.

"Present tense—have a housekeeper. Except for boarding school and college, I've never actually moved out. I keep planning to, but the timing never seems right. Anyway, there's Mrs. Dent, and a cook, and then there's Mr. Tandy, who's kind of a combination gardener, handyman, and chauffeur. Mother and Daddy travel a lot, so he and Mrs. Dent take care of the house when they're away. Tandy's ancient, but I guess he likes working for my family because he's been with us forever. He used to work for my grandparents before they moved to Florida. Now he lives in an apartment over the garage. When I was a kid, he drove me to and from school every day. All the other kids had moms waiting for them in the parking lot. I had Mr. Tandy."

"That's wild. You had a chauffeur drive you to school every day?"

"It wasn't like I had a choice," Sylvia replied. A defensive tone had crept into her voice. "My parents have always traveled a lot, and even when they are home, they have stuff to do. Flossie—she's the cook—is my favorite. When I was a kid, she would let me pester her while she worked. She taught me how to make scrambled eggs and the world's best grilled cheese sandwiches, which are still the only two things I can cook. She's pretty cool, and Mr. Tandy is okay, but Dent's a total bitch. Always has been, always will be. She and my mother get along perfectly."

Callie sat back in her chair, tilting her head to one side. "So am I supposed to feel bad for you because most of the time you just rattle around this huge house with only a bunch of servants to keep the princess company?"

Stung, Sylvia said nothing. She picked up one of the empty sugar packets, gave it a couple of vicious twists, then tossed it down on the table like a miniature gauntlet.

"Maybe I shouldn't have come here," she said. She started to stand up.

"Wait," Callie said, "I'm sorry. That was uncalled for."

Sylvia wanted to leave, but if she left now, there would be no coming back.

"A big house is just a big house," she said, trying to choose her words carefully. "If there's no one else there, it's just a lot of empty space, like living in the middle of nothing. Now, of course, it's not so bad; I have friends, a job, and I come and go as I please. But when I was a kid, I was usually alone. My chief form of entertainment became snooping, which is how I found out about you. It was, oddly enough, on my own twelfth birthday. I was messing around in my mother's closet, trying on her jewelry, checking out her makeup. I found a copy of your birth certificate in one of the drawers."

"That's how you found out about me?"

Sylvia, her lips pressed tightly together, only nodded.

"Did you ever say anything to your—um, our—mother about me?"

"Are you kidding? No. She has no idea I know about you. Certainly, she has no idea that I came out here. I've kept her little secret. Then last fall, I hired Tom to find you."

"So what happened all of a sudden last fall that made you decide to hire a detective?"

"Two things. I had the money to hire a detective, and I got engaged."

"Congratulations, but I don't see what that has to do with finding me."

"Well, Pier—he's my fiancé—has two sisters and they are both going to be in the wedding. I got to thinking that I'd really, really like it if my own sister would stand up for me, too. I want you to be there. I want you to be in my wedding."

"Whoa—wait a minute," Callie sat back in her chair, a scowl of annoyance on her face. "That's not going to happen," she said.

Sylvia put her hands on the table, literally reaching out to Callie. "Please, Callie? Please say you'll think about it. The wedding isn't until October, so that gives you plenty of time to make plans, get used to the idea. You could stay at the house, and I'd pay for your flights and everything. Please? It would really mean a lot to me."

"You have to be joking. How do you think Anne would feel about having me show up all of a sudden? Have you considered that?"

Sylvia gave an exasperated little snort and rolled her eyes. "I don't really care what she thinks. It's my wedding and I can do what I want."

"Sorry, kid. The answer's no. Even if I was inclined to go visiting, which I'm definitely not, I sure as hell wouldn't choose your wedding day. You'll have enough on your mind, and I'm not interested in being the bombshell you drop. Besides, as you can see, I have a family of my own and a business to run here. I can't just waltz off, especially during the tourist season."

"Please?" Sylvia was begging. "It would just be for a day or two. And I told you I'll pay for anything you want. You can bring Brad and your son with you, too. And we can hire people to run this place while you are away."

Callie pushed back her chair and stood up. "It doesn't work that way around here. Like I said, it was nice to meet you, but I need to get back to work." She started to turn away.

"Wait," Sylvia said, rising from her seat. She had to give this her best shot, but when Callie looked at her with an all-too-familiar scorching glare, all she could say was, "I'd really like to have you there. Won't you at least think about it?"

Callie shook her head and walked away.

2
CALLIE

THE MOMENT CALLIE heard herself say that there was nothing to think about, she knew she was wrong. After Sylvia left the tavern, when Brad asked if she was okay, and later, after more of the regulars had drifted into the bar and she got busy pulling beers and fixing baskets of burgers and fries, she owned up to the fact that there was a lot to think about. She'd been caught off guard. Looking back, she remembered exactly when that detective—Tom, wasn't it?—had been in here. She'd had a funny feeling at the time that he might have something to do with her birth mother, just one of those intuitive moments that only became clear in hindsight. Life was busy, other things had taken over, and she'd forgotten all about it. Until now.

She flipped a couple of pre-formed burgers on the griddle, scraped a pile of golden onions to one side, and lined two more red plastic baskets with squares of waxed paper. She wondered if she'd ever see Sylvia again. Probably not. She was surprised to feel a pang of regret, but reminded herself that refusing to consider Sylvia's offer wasn't her decision. Nothing about her real "family" had ever been her decision.

"Hey, Cal, you got those burgers yet?" Brad called out from the half-open swinging door.

"Yeah, in a minute. Tell Clancy to keep his shirt on; he wants 'em cooked first, right?"

Norm Clancy was one of the regulars. He came in every Tuesday and Thursday at five. He always drank three Buds, and ordered two burgers with grilled onion, no pickles, and fries. Callie flipped the burgers again, mashing them flat against the griddle with the spatula. Clancy's life was simple: eat, sleep, and work. And not much work since he retired last year from his job at the post office. He had no family that Callie was aware of, and lived alone in a small apartment building across town. As she scraped his burgers off the griddle, she wondered what it would be like to have such a simple existence. Boring? Sure. But no surprises, either. No half-sisters wandering unexpectedly into town. No long-lost birth mothers who didn't want to be found. No brothers who couldn't leave well enough alone.

Callie had seen the look on Sylvia's face as she'd explained why she'd come to Michigan. Maybe, she, Callie, had been the lucky one. The little that she did know about Anne, the woman who had given birth to both of them, seemed to have been confirmed by Sylvia: she was cold, possibly cruel, neglectful at best. Callie couldn't imagine being raised by such a person. Maybe she had been wrong to shut Sylvia down, to be such a bitch. But what else could she do? There was no way she was ever going to set foot in Teabury while Anne was still there.

She carried the burgers out to Clancy, and took food orders from two other tables. At least they had some customers; business had been slow over the winter months, which was normal, but the bills kept increasing. Just yesterday, the accountant had called again. He wanted to meet Monday morning to talk about the last couple of P&L statements. He'd been cagey on the phone, refusing to say what the problem was, just that he needed to talk to her.

On her way back to the kitchen, she gave Brad the drink orders for the new tables, then decided to dash upstairs to check on Ethan. He was pretty self-sufficient for a five-year-old, but this morning, he'd complained that his head hurt, so she'd let him stay home from kindergarten. Alyssa, their part-time waitress and babysitter, had watched him during the day, but she'd left an hour ago, and Callie hadn't looked in on him since.

The apartment on the second floor of the tavern consisted of two small bedrooms, a bathroom, and one large room that was truly a living room: it was where she, Brad, and Ethan spent all their time when they weren't working at the bar or asleep. At the top of the back stairs in the kitchen, a door opened directly onto the living room. To the left of the door stood a trestle table cluttered with half-folded laundry, newspapers and junk mail, a Frisbee, and a bird's nest that Ethan had found in the street. One corner of the room held an old desk and a five-drawer metal filing cabinet, which served as their "office." Along another wall, cinderblock and plank shelving held an ancient television, across from which sat an equally ancient brown corduroy sofa and a scratched up old coffee table.

Callie could see the minute she reached the top of the stairs that Ethan was asleep on the sofa. His baby blanket, dubbed "Gunky" for obvious reasons, was entwined in his arms, his thumb was in his mouth, and his face, pale against the dark sofa, held the unique sweetness of a child in slumber. The coffee table was littered with coloring books, crayons, and assorted plastic cars. Ethan was crazy about cars and trains. Callie smiled down on her boy, resisted the temptation to touch his brow, reaching over instead to pick up a plastic Thomas the Tank toy wedged between the sofa cushions.

Ethan was never sick. Normally, he ran circles around both Callie and Brad all day long, falling asleep between nine and ten at night and always up and going by seven in the morning. Alyssa had taken him to the park for two hours after school yesterday;

he was probably just overtired. Most days, he had the energy of a football team and an appetite to match. She was sure that as soon as he woke up, he'd rush into the kitchen and begin pestering her for a burger and fries while she was trying to take care of customers.

Satisfied that he was fine, Callie blew a kiss to her son and went back downstairs. In a part of her mind so guarded that the thought was almost subconscious, she wondered for the millionth time how a woman could give her child away. She rarely let such thoughts rise to the surface, but the feelings they evoked rippled like currents deep in a river.

In her left hand, she still clutched the food orders she'd taken before going up to check on Ethan. One of them was for a bacon cheeseburger. The bacon had to be nuked, doubling the prep time, so she had to hurry. Brad was in the kitchen when she returned. "Hey, babe, we've got four more at table six wanting food," he said, depositing more orders on the counter. "Time to hustle."

"Coming right up," she said, glancing at the stack of orders, calculating the most efficient way to get all the food cooked and served. Ethan's supper might have to wait at the rate they were going, but she wasn't going to complain about a busy night. They could sure use the money. She had never forgotten, though, how tough it had been for her as a kid, when it seemed like the whole world got fed first, and then when you were too tired to care, someone might sling a plate of leftovers at you. Callie wanted Ethan to have it better than that, and she figured most of the time he did, but when things got busy, she worried he'd get short shrift.

Twelve cheeseburgers, seven chicken sandwiches, and half a dozen pounds of fries later, Callie and Brad were alone in the bar. It was after midnight, and the last of their customers had drifted out half an hour earlier.

"Ethan okay?" Brad asked, as he began to sort money and charge slips at the register.

"I guess," Callie answered. "I checked on him a little while ago when I finished clearing up the kitchen. He was still on the sofa. Out like a light. I can't believe he didn't even come down for supper." She finished wiping down the last of the tables and tossed the wet towel into a hamper behind the bar. "It's not like him to sleep like this," she added, settling on one of the bar stools with an after-work shot of Jack Daniels.

"Does he have a fever?" Brad asked, looking up from the stack of merchant copy receipts.

"No." Callie lit a cigarette, inhaled deeply, then blew out the smoke in a thick stream.

"Kids sleep a lot when they're growing," Brad said. "I bet that's all it is. He'll probably wake up at frickin' five in the morning wanting pancakes." He turned his attention back to the charge slips.

Callie sipped the whiskey, savoring its smoky harshness, and kept quiet while Brad finished the tally and generated a master receipt from the bar computer.

"I guess that must've been the sister, eh?" he said. He bundled the money and slips in a neat stack. "She sure looks a lot like you." He handed her the computer receipt and put the zippered pouch that held cash and coins from the night's sales on the bar between them. Callie looked at the receipt, then put it down next to the pouch. It would be her first task in the morning to make sure the amount on the master receipt matched the cash and charge slip totals.

"Yup. That was Sylvia." She crushed out her cigarette and shoved the ashtray away.

"So?" Brad asked.

"So, what?"

"So what did she have to say for herself?"

"I don't know. Bullshit, mostly."

Brad gave her an I-don't-think-so look. He picked up her ashtray, wiped its contents into the trash with a paper towel, and set it back on the bar. He didn't say a word, but Callie could tell he was waiting. *Damn,* she thought, *he could do that.* He could pry stuff out of her, guilt-trip her into blabbing away about things she didn't even realize upset her.

"Okay. She said she's getting married. She wants me to stand up in her wedding."

"Yeah? When?" He sounded curious, more open to the idea than Callie expected.

"What do you mean, when? Who cares when? This is not something I'm going to do."

"Why not? She's you're sister. It seems like a reasonable request. You might even get a kick out of hanging out with her."

"No fucking way. Besides, you know the deal I made. I promised I'd stay out of her life."

"You promised The Bitch you'd stay out of *her* life. You didn't say nothing about the sister."

The Bitch. That was how Callie referred to her birth mother on the few occasions she was mentioned. Mostly, Callie tried not to think about her. Once upon a time, she had been sympathetic. When she was very young, she had made up stories about how poor her mother must have been, how young and desperate. All the years she was growing up, Callie believed only complete desperation would force a woman to abandon her child. Then, four years ago, when her brother, Kevin, provided her with the name and address of her birth mother, Callie decided to find Anne. She wanted to tell her mother that everything had turned out fine. Her childhood was good, the people who had adopted her were decent folks, and whatever the reasons were that Anne had had to give up her daughter, Callie understood. Only things didn't quite go the way Callie had planned.

"Look, it's late. I don't want to talk about this now." Callie picked up the receipt and money pouch. "By the way, did you put in that extra order with Gordon? The weekend's going to be crazy and Mom called to say Molly's in town, so we'll have about sixteen here on Monday."

The first weekend in May was now way over-scheduled. On Saturday night, the bar would be the venue for a surprise birthday party that Ron Garland, one of their regulars, was throwing for his wife. Sunday was the Walleye Festival, that annual spring rite in Cedar Beach, and half the damn county would end their day of fishing by hanging out at Stone's Throw. Monday, the day the bar was normally closed, Callie was hosting a fortieth anniversary party for her own parents. The three events required Gordon, the main distributor of food in the Thumb area, to make an additional delivery.

"The order's in. We've got extra liquor coming, too. Stan oughta be around with that sometime tomorrow. Do we have enough cash to cover this stuff?"

"I hope so. We'll have to pay Alyssa, too."

"You called Alyssa in?" Brad asked.

"Yeah, for both Saturday and Sunday. We'll need the extra hands for busing and KP, if nothing else."

It had been just over a year since Alyssa Linn had walked into the tavern looking for work. Her timing was perfect; Callie had had the flu all week and extra help showing up on the doorstep seemed like a miracle. Petite and energetic, Alyssa had plans to move to California, but she needed money and jobs were scarce. She claimed to have had experience tending bar and said she didn't mind sweeping the floor, cleaning the bathrooms, or hauling heavy boxes of supplies up and down the steep basement stairs. Callie had hired her on the spot.

Alyssa was attractive in an impish sort of way. In her mid-twenties, her heart-shaped face was framed by short, brown hair and her dark eyes, if a little on the small side, sparkled. She proved to be an efficient waitress when the tourist season was in full swing, and further endeared herself to Callie by helping to clean and organize the basement storage rooms without complaint. Ethan, too, was charmed by her. When business was slow, he followed her around the tavern like a puppy, and she tolerated his endless questions with good humor. Still, during the quiet winter months, it was hard to justify the expense of extra help. Callie kept her busy as best she could, often asking her to take Ethan to the park or the beach.

"I thought we weren't going to use her for a while," Brad said. Lately, he had been acting weird about Alyssa, griping that she screwed up orders and they really couldn't afford her. While it was true that Alyssa's wages cut a chunk from the budget, Callie had never seen her mess up an order. Plus, she felt a responsibility toward the younger woman. She was part of Stone's Throw, popular with the regular customers, and on busy nights, they did need the extra help.

"We're going to be swamped on Saturday and Sunday. You know I can't be doing all the cooking and covering the floor with so many people here."

"Maybe we can get someone else."

"That doesn't make any sense. Anyone else would cost just as much, maybe more. Besides, I don't have time to train someone new." Callie tossed back the last of her whiskey, pushing the empty glass across the bar. "I don't know why you've been so down on Alyssa lately. You ought to cut her some slack. The way I see it, this weekend we'll be making decent money what with the Garland party and the fishing festival. Paying her shouldn't be a problem."

Brad didn't reply. He washed and dried her shot glass, then flicked out the main light switch and together they went through the darkened kitchen to the back stairs leading to their apartment.

"Speaking of cash, Barry called this morning," Callie said. "He wants to schedule a meeting. Something about the last couple of P&L statements. He said it's not an emergency, just something he thinks we should be aware of."

"Like what?"

"I have no idea," Callie said over her shoulder, as she reached the top of the stairs. She went to the filing cabinet, unlocked the top drawer and tossed in the money pouch.

"Hang on, honey. Are you saying he's found some sort of problem?" Brad asked.

Callie huffed with exasperation. "I just told you I have no idea what he wants, and whatever it is, it can wait. I'm going to check on Ethan. Then I'm hitting the hay. I'm exhausted."

Brad came up behind her and began gently massaging her shoulders. Callie rolled her head and felt the tension release a bit. She melted into his touch, leaning against him, hoping that he would pick up on her body language. Even though she was exhausted, she wanted to make love before going to sleep. Whenever either of them felt stressed, they drew close to each other. No matter how long or crazy the day, at night in the quiet of their bed, they found peace in each other's arms.

3
SYLVIA

SYLVIA DROVE THE six miles inland from Cedar Beach to Oakton, the only town in Huron County large enough to have a Holiday Inn Express, where she'd booked a room for two nights. It had been a few minutes past five when she left Callie's, and she considered driving around a bit to see the area, but except for watching the sun as it set over the water, there didn't seem to be that much to see. Along the shoreline, the cottages and marinas reminded her of home, of the Atlantic coast, but inland, it was just long straight roads, flat fields, a farm house and barn standing in isolation every few miles. Once in a while, an intersection was cluttered with a gas station, a couple of worn-down houses, and a bar. Sometimes, there would be a small, weathered shop, its signage advertising milk, beer, and ammo. It wasn't an area that took kindly to strangers.

On her way back to the Holiday Inn, she'd kept her eyes open for someplace to get dinner, but the only options were Taco Bell, Pizza Hut, or McDonald's. She chose the latter and ordered a salad and fries from the drive-through. The evening stretched out before her as long and dull as the road she'd just been on, but she was used to keeping her own company. Usually, she preferred solitude to the fragile pleasantries of her social life at home.

In her hotel room, she set the paper bag of food on the coffee table, opened the window to counteract the smell of old cigarettes, and turned on the television to something that wouldn't require too much attention. She had a lot to think about. Callie might have dismissed her today, but Sylvia was determined to try again tomorrow, and Saturday, too, if need be. At some point in her life, she had learned the power of tenacity, and it had served her well. Getting to know Callie, bringing her back to Teabury for the wedding, was the key part of a plan that Sylvia had been working on since the day Pier proposed. She would not give up. Sitting on the edge of the bed, she pulled the plastic utensils and box of salad from the paper bag. The French fries were unappetizingly limp, but she ate several just for the salt. Callie would come around, she thought. She, Sylvia, would make it happen; otherwise, why was she sitting here in the middle of nowhere eating this gross food?

Picking half-heartedly at the salad, she thought about the events, the details that had brought her to this place. The irony was not lost on her. Anne and Henry Bennett had to be the most clueless parents on the planet. She wondered what they would say if they had any idea what their daughter was doing at this moment. She looked at her watch. Six o'clock. What time would that be in China? Probably the middle of the night. No doubt they were sleeping peacefully in some fabulous hotel, insulated from the harsher realities of life. Wrapped up in parties, travel, and the occasional philanthropic gesture, they knew little and cared less about their daughter. A couple of times, their lack of attention had been the subject of interviews conducted by earnest but ineffective counselors at Sylvia's various schools. Grade school had been moderately humiliating, but boarding school was worse. Not once in her four years at Farmington did either parent set foot on campus. Tandy drove her to and from school as needed.

Sylvia tried to combat the loneliness and frustration of their neglect by ambitiously searching for whatever she could learn about her elusive parents. Her explorations had started innocently enough in the year before she was sent away to boarding school. She was working on a paper for social studies in the walnut-paneled room her father used as an office. The books and materials she needed were spread across the large desktop, but her attention wandered. Analyzing the effect of the Industrial Revolution on American cities was not nearly as interesting as the array of desk drawers. Out of boredom more than anything else, she pulled open the middle drawer. Two fountain pens sat in a little tray. There was also a leather-bound calendar and a checkbook. She flipped through the calendar, but nothing much had been written in it. She looked at May 14th, which was her birthday. Nothing. She put the calendar back and took out the checkbook. A lot of checks had been torn from the book, but there were carbon copies showing to whom each check was written and the amount for which it had been written. Almost all of them were made out to the servants: Mr. Tandy, Flossie, and Mrs. Dent. It seemed to Sylvia that the household staff was paid very little. By contrast, the cost of the annual dues to her father's golf club was impressive, and there was one check payable to Neiman Marcus that was larger than all the servants' salaries combined. Sylvia returned the checkbook to its place and closed the drawer.

Later, her snooping expanded to the music room. In a lacquer box on one shelf, she found a short letter from the grandparents whom she had only met once when she was three or four, asking her mother to bring "the child" to their house in Florida for a visit. The letter was six years old. On another shelf, there were four old yearbooks from her Dad's prep school. When she flipped through the pages, she saw pictures of her father as a teenager. His hair was thick and dark and he was smiling. In one photo, he was on a stage, playing a saxophone, which she had certainly never seen him do in real life.

Next, she had gone to the liquor cabinet, toying with the various bottles on display, opening each one, sniffing the contents, examining the collection of odd-shaped, exotically scented decanters, and fingering the assortment of crystal glasses. The decanters were particularly fascinating: each had a sweet little label, like a silver necklace, to identify the potion inside: whiskey, vodka, gin, bourbon.

In the dining room cabinet, she found a silk-covered box that held a dozen silver knives and forks. They were smaller than normal cutlery, with intricate patterns etched into the blades of the knives and on the handles of the forks. She wanted to ask her mother why they never used these lovely things, but that was the trouble with snooping. It was impossible to talk about what she found without giving away secrets.

Eventually, she found her way back to the liquor cabinet. The beguiling, heady scents, sweetly pungent and clearly forbidden, lured her into another world, a place she could claim as her own. Sylvia discovered alcohol was an easy way to find diversion, seasoned with rebellion. There was escape, if not solace, in golden whiskeys, diamond-bright vodkas, and the sugar topaz of rum.

The liquor cabinet became the cornerstone of her years at Farmington. She smuggled enough of its contents back to school to gain status as the girl with the best stash of booze. She'd only been busted twice—once as a freshman when she was too naïve to know the system, and once senior year, when she just didn't give a shit. She'd been falling down drunk, puking on her shoes in the head-mistress's office that last time. It had cost her father a packet to keep them from kicking her out. All new chairs for the auditorium and a substantial amount for "growth and development" of the school's theater program was what it took for the Bennett family to keep the incident "our little secret." It was no wonder her parents wanted nothing to do with her.

Well, it was all about secrets, wasn't it? Sylvia closed the Mc-Plastic salad box, wadded the fries into the paper bag and tossed the whole mess in the trash. She hoped the maid service would come in early to remove it so the room wouldn't smell of stale food. She looked around at the drab beige walls, their monotone broken only by one ugly painting of a harbor scene hanging above the rust-colored sofa. The few times she had stayed in other hotels (for the occasional New York shopping spree), the rooms had been much nicer.

There had been one disastrous experience in Paris with her parents the summer she was fifteen. The third day they were there, while Anne and Henry were resting before dinner, Sylvia sat in the hotel bar and, with the help of several new friends, consumed eight bottles of Cristal champagne and $3000 worth of Ossetra caviar, charged to her father's account. Her parents had sent her home on the next available flight. It was the first and last time she had ever been allowed to travel with them.

With the window open, the room had grown cold, but at least the air was fresher. She found a coarse brown blanket in the closet and draped it, shawl-like, around her shoulders before settling herself on the bed to watch television. As she was scrolling through the list of pay-per-view movies, her cell phone rang. The little blue letters on its screen read: Tom Harvey.

"Hey, Tom, what's up?" she answered, feeling an unmistakable buzz of excitement.

"Hi, Sylvia. I was just calling to see if you had any trouble meeting up with Callie." Tom's deep baritone thrummed in her ear, eliciting a heady sensation of both safety and danger.

Keeping her voice as matter-of-fact as she could, she described her visit to Stone's Throw Tavern.

"Sounds like she didn't exactly welcome you with open arms," Tom said.

"Not really. I mean, she seemed friendly enough, but there was something else. She definitely doesn't have anything good to say about my—um, our—mother. It kind of makes me think maybe they already know each other. Like they have been in contact at some point."

"I doubt it. You're probably reading too much into her reaction. Think about it for a minute: Callie was abandoned by her. That alone is a good enough reason for some major resentment. I'm sure that's all there is to it."

"No, it was something more than that. It's like Callie knows something. I can't quite figure out why I think so, but I'd bet big money they have met, and maybe not that long ago. I tried asking her outright, but she ignored the question, and I didn't want to push the issue."

"So, now that you've seen her face-to-face is that it? Are you done?"

"Absolutely not. I'm going to hang around here for a couple of days, see if I can get to know her a bit. Maybe I can even persuade her to come to Teabury." Sylvia stopped short of telling him exactly what her plans were.

As their conversation wound down, Tom offered to pick her up at the airport when she returned home.

"Thanks, but my car is in the long term lot," she answered. "I'll be fine."

Later, after Sylvia settled herself in bed under all the available blankets, she couldn't keep from wondering what might happen if she had accepted his offer.

Intrigued by the man, she'd often thought about his personal life, what he was like when he wasn't being all professional and business-like. He was so different from anyone she knew. Last autumn, she'd found his name online when she'd googled "private detectives," and after a brief phone conference, she'd driven to his office near Providence. The first time she'd met him, he'd been wearing a striped, button down shirt. Not the kind her father or Pier would wear. It was definitely a cheaper style, more like something from J.C. Penney's than Brooks Brothers, but it looked good on him. His dark hair, in the first stages of going gray, was nicely offset by his slightly olive complexion, and his mustache was definitely sexy. In the months they had worked together, the anticipation of finding Callie had created a certain level of excitement, but if she were honest with herself, she had to admit that seeing his name on her phone display gave her a thrill that had nothing to do with finding her half-sister. She knew Tom traveled a lot, worked strange hours, and dealt with unsavory people on a regular basis. She wondered if he carried a gun—which would be very cool—or if any of his work was truly dangerous. Gun or not, the man looked as if he could take care of himself.

Pierson Kent IV seemed almost feminine by comparison. Conservative beyond his years, he was a walking preppy stereotype: oxford cloth shirt (most often pink), khaki trousers, tasseled loafers (no socks, naturally) and tortoise-shell eye glasses. His light brown hair, side-parted on the right, was neatly combed and never allowed to grow beyond the top of his collar. Moderately attractive, clean-shaven, and casually self-assured, he was the oldest child and only son in a family of five. His parents had provided him with every possible advantage and artifact relative to his place in society. In return, Pier had fulfilled part of his parents' expectations by doing tolerably well in top schools and securing a suitable job in the financial markets. Sylvia suspected that the Kent family was also quite pleased when he and Sylvia became engaged.

She pulled the blankets closer around her, trying to ignore their stale odor. It would be nice to get back to her own bed. Once she was home, she'd probably call Tom. Just to thank him for every-thing he had done. Better yet, she could stop in at his office to say hello and tell him more about her visit with Callie. Make it seem very spur-of-the-moment, even though it was an hour's drive from her house. Maybe she'd offer to buy him a drink.

She drifted off to sleep, enjoying that betwixt and between stage of consciousness when the mind free-falls through all its nag-ging puzzles and predicaments. Images of Pier and Tom and Callie and her parents and Pier's parents jumbled together. Something just under the surface of those images began troubling her, some-thing she couldn't quite figure out. She rose back into full wakeful-ness with the deep and disturbing sensation that she was neither as clever, nor as in control of events, as she believed.

CB&D

IN THE MORNING, the skies were overcast with the damp of a late spring drizzle. It chilled the air, blowing in through the window that Sylvia had left open all night. Shivering her way out of bed, she showered and dressed hurriedly. The Holiday Inn advertised a free breakfast buffet, and she needed coffee desperately. After last night's lousy dinner, she also needed something to eat.

In the dining room, the lights were too bright and the mu-sic—some tune from the seventies—was ridiculously disco, but the coffee smelled good. A young family sat at one table, a middle-aged couple at another. At a third table, three men close to Syl-via's age were looking through large manila envelopes of glossy photographs, occasionally chuckling and sharing comments. Syl-via chose a table in the far corner. Draping her rain jacket over a chair, she made her way to the "buffet," which consisted of a coffee machine, three pitchers of juice, a jug of milk, and a stack of min-iature cereal boxes. She took a mug from the stack by the coffee machine and filled it to the brim. Mug in one hand, she picked up a mini-box of Cheerios, which she decided to eat straight from the box rather than use the milk. The milk jug looked as if it had been sitting out for hours.

Feeling awkward, she settled at her table, sipped her coffee, picked at the Cheerios and glanced at the newspaper that someone had left behind. When the dry cereal made her mouth gluey, she decided to get a glass of juice. As she crossed the room, one of the young men with the photos stepped over to refill his glass. He smiled at her, said hello and offered to pour juice for her.

He was cute—blonde and blue-eyed with a sharp, intelligent expression and a friendly, open smile. Sylvia picked up a glass, held it out, and when he'd filled it, she thanked him and returned to her table. She tried to read the newspaper, but the groups of people at the tables around her made her acutely aware of her aloneness.

Trying not to be too obvious, Sylvia watched the three men with the photos as they gathered their belongings and put on their coats. The blonde guy slung a large bag of photographic equipment over his shoulder. He turned and waved to her as he left.

4
CALLIE

SOMETHING WAS OFF. For twenty minutes, Callie had been staring at the numbers in front of her trying to see what didn't add up. The problem was, however, the numbers did add up. Maybe not to the exact penny, but close enough so that whatever discrepancy their accountant, Barry, had been worrying about, it was too well hidden for Callie to spot. It shouldn't be this complicated, she thought. Frustrated, she pushed the pieces of paper around the desk top, twiddled the pen between her fingers, gazed at the picture of the French chateau on the calendar pinned to the wall and, in a brief moment of day-dreaming, wished she were there instead of here in her own life. Was that the sort of place she would be familiar with if she'd been raised by Anne Bennett?

Her thoughts were interrupted by the sound of footsteps on the wooden staircase leading up to the apartment. A woman's voice called cautiously through the open door, "Hello? Callie?"

Callie turned in her chair.

"It's me," said Sylvia, stepping inside the apartment. "Brad said I should just come on up."

"You're back?" Callie saw Sylvia cringe slightly at the sharpness of her words. "Look, I don't mean to be rude, but Brad shouldn't have sent you up here. I told you yesterday that I'm not going to play 'happy families' at your wedding, and we really don't have anything else to talk about."

The two women eyed each other. Then Sylvia said the one thing that Callie couldn't ignore: "Christ, you sound exactly like our mother."

"I guess that's not a compliment," Callie replied, wondering why she felt such curiosity at being compared to a mother who had tossed her out like some ill-fitting clothing purchase. *How else are we alike?* she wanted to ask.

"That all depends," Sylvia answered. She took two tentative steps into the room before adding, "I suppose if I were you, I'd want to know a few things about my birth-mother, and even about my half-sister. Don't you wonder what your real family is like?"

"Not really," Callie said, doing her best to ignore how easily her thoughts had been intercepted. "I have a real family." She nodded toward several framed photos hanging on the wall.

Sylvia stepped toward the photos, peered intently at them, then turned her gaze back to her sister. "Okay, fair enough. But I still think we have a few things to talk about."

Callie crossed her arms and regarded the young woman before her. Torn between resenting the intrusion and her interest in someone who was, aside from her son, her only blood relative, she was unsure how to react.

"Okay, come on in," she said, gathering up her courage and the clutter of paperwork on the desk. "I was about finished with this mess anyway." She picked up a coffee mug, drained the last of the contents, then nodded toward a couple of mismatched chairs next to the trestle table. "Have a seat," she said.

Callie pushed aside the pile of laundry and moved the stack of mail and magazines to her desk. "Sorry about the mess," she said. She was tempted to add, "I really ought to fire the maid," but she wasn't sure Sylvia would get the joke. She glanced around the apartment, trying to see it with Sylvia's eyes: one shabby room, flanked at the far end by two small bedrooms and a bathroom. The bathroom door stood open, a display of intimacy that made Callie cringe. Nearby, crayons spilled over the coffee table's surface and onto the worn carpet; Ethan had left coloring books and toys on the sofa.

"On second thought, I changed my mind. Let's go downstairs," Callie said, waving her coffee mug toward the door. "I need more caffeine."

In the tavern's small kitchen, Callie poured each of them a mug of strong, fragrant coffee. Ethan was sitting at a child-size table and chair in one corner of the room. From his slumped posture, Callie could tell he was not happy. "Hey, kiddo, what's going on?" she called to him.

He looked up glumly at his mother. "Daddy said I have to stay right here until I finish this stupid cereal." He pushed at the bowl in front of him.

Callie moved across the room to him, leaving Sylvia behind. "Aren't Choco Pops your favorite?"

"Yeah, but I'm not hungry." He put his head down on the table.

"You're not? You didn't eat dinner last night and you're not hungry now? What's up with that?"

"My head hurts," he murmured.

Callie frowned, put her hand on his forehead, and gently brushed back his soft brown hair. "I don't think you have a fever," she said. "Tell you what, why don't you take two bites? If you still don't want any more, you can go on upstairs and watch Saturday morning cartoons."

"Who's she?" Ethan looked at Sylvia.

"This is Sylvia. She's a…friend."

Normally, Ethan would take such an opportunity to shamelessly show off for a visitor or pepper her with questions. Instead, his head drooped, and all he said was a barely audible, "Oh."

"Honey, if you eat your breakfast, I bet you'll feel a whole lot better. Come on. Two bites, please."

Reluctantly, the little boy obeyed. Callie stood watching him, trying to be stern, but her expression was too soft to fool either of them. After two small tastes, Ethan put the spoon down. "Can I go now?" he asked.

"Put your bowl in the sink first. I'll be back upstairs in a bit."

With Sylvia following her, Callie went through the bar area to the dining room. Late morning sun shone through the windows, giving the place more the look of a café than a tavern. On one of the tables, there was a red plastic bucket with a dozen carnation sprigs ready to be placed in the small vases that went on each table. Brad was behind the bar setting up supplies for the day ahead.

"That kid finish his breakfast?" Brad asked, putting a stack of cardboard Miller coasters on the bar.

"Close enough," Callie answered. Brad nodded, then looked back and forth between the two women as if he were expecting a formal introduction. Callie pretended she didn't notice. She knew she was being ornery, but she didn't feel like playing hostess. Besides, Brad and Sylvia knew perfectly well who the other person was; they had obviously had a conversation before Brad sent her upstairs.

"I thought Alyssa was taking care of the flower vases," Callie said, nodding toward the carnations.

"Yeah, well, she hasn't shown up yet. When'd you tell her to get here?"

"Ten. Sharp."

"It's almost eleven. I'm guessing she's a no-show." Brad stepped out from behind the bar.

"That's not like her." Callie turned to Sylvia. "Alyssa's been working here since last fall. She's usually real reliable, so I don't know what's up, but if she's not here, it's going to screw up my morning. The tables haven't been set yet, either."

"Looks like you're stuck with the flowers, too," Brad said. "I still have to bring up a bunch of crap from the basement, and hook up a new keg. And Marge and Pete'll be through that door any minute."

"Marge and Pete are regulars," Callie explained. "They show up every Saturday at eleven on the dot for cheeseburgers and beer. They don't make us rich, but they're sweet old dears and this is their big outing for the week."

"I can fill the flower vases, if that would help," Sylvia volunteered.

Callie, surprised by the offer, didn't react as fast as Brad. "That'd be great," he said. The look he gave Callie was unmistakable.

"Okay," she said, not sure who she was most annoyed with—Alyssa for not showing up, Sylvia for volunteering to help, or Brad for accepting the offer.

From the supply cabinet, she gathered up a tray of clean cutlery, a stack of paper napkins, and a box of paper napkin bands. "Nice thing about carnations is they don't need water. Just stick 'em in the vase and you're done. But let's get the silverware done first."

She showed Sylvia how to wrap fork, knife and spoon in a thick paper napkin and secure it with red paper tape. While they worked, Callie began to talk about her childhood. "There were eight of us kids. Four of us were adopted: Maureen's a year older than me, then after me are the twins, Kevin and Bobby. They aren't really twins, not even related, but they're less than a year apart and they've always done everything together, so we call them the 'twins.' Kevin—he's the computer guy—is the one who gave me the info about my birth mother. Then there are four kids of Peg and Jack's own. Bill, he's the oldest of all of us, then Carrie, who's three years behind me, and Molly, the baby. She's nineteen now, off at college."

"And the fourth?"

Callie's expression changed. "There was another brother, Steve. He was killed in a car wreck ten years ago. Worst night of my life."

"I'm sorry," Sylvia said quietly.

Callie shook her head. "Hey, that's not something we want to think about today," she said, forcing a smile. She looked at the stack of wrapped cutlery.

"How many of these do we have?" she asked, changing the subject. "We don't need more than forty."

"Looks like we have thirty-six," Sylvia answered.

"Okay, a couple more, then we're done. Anyway, as I was saying, Peg and Jack Hanlon, they're the saints of the world. I mean, who the heck takes in four strays when they have their own kids to worry about? And it wasn't like they had a whole lot of money. They're just good people who felt like they could step up and take care of kids whose biological parents couldn't, or didn't want to, accept responsibility."

Callie, normally reticent with strangers, surprised herself by telling Sylvia about the small restaurant the Hanlon family owned near Ann Arbor. All eight kids had worked in the family business from the time they could carry a basket of the biscuits that were Peg Hanlon's specialty.

"We were only open for breakfast and lunch, but weekends were always chaos." She paused, grimacing. "Actually, they still are. Bet I haven't had more than a half-dozen Saturdays to myself in my whole life. As kids, we'd work all day in the restaurant, go to Saturday evening mass, and be back in the kitchen by five on Sunday morning." Callie gathered a handful of the sets of cutlery and gave them to Sylvia. "You can set one of these at each place once I get the mats down," she said, picking up a stack of paper placemats.

"Didn't you ever get a break? Go on vacation?" Sylvia asked, following Callie from table to table.

"Sure. Once a year, usually in July, we'd pile in the station wagon, and Dad would hitch one of those trailer campers to the back. We'd go to some RV park, eat peanut butter and jelly sandwiches for lunch and macaroni and cheese from a cardboard box for dinner. Mom and Dad would sit in aluminum patio chairs and listen to a transistor radio while we ran wild around the park. At bedtime, we'd all cram into sleeping bags in the trailer, or maybe the boys would sleep on the ground. Then the next morning, we'd go home because there was a business to run."

Callie watched her half-sister take in this information and tried to figure out what she might be thinking. Sylvia didn't look like the RV type. "Bet that's not what you guys did for family vacations," she said.

They'd finished setting out cutlery. Callie opened the packet of carnations and began untwisting the tangled leaves and stems.

"I never really traveled much with my parents," Sylvia said. "They took me to France once, but I was…well, let's just say I was left to my own devices and I got bored. After that trip, they just left me at home." She picked up one of the long-stemmed carnations. "If you have some scissors, I'll trim the ends of these."

Callie pulled a penknife from her jeans pocket. "You'll have to make do with this."

She watched closely as Sylvia opened the knife and began cutting stems with a fair degree of competence. Relieved that it was unlikely blood would be drawn, Callie noted the unhappy expression on Sylvia's face and wondered if she might have preferred camping in an RV park to traipsing around Paris by herself. Hard as it was to imagine what it would be like growing up rich and pampered, without a horde of people arguing over whose turn it was to take out the trash or who tracked mud on the kitchen floor, Callie didn't envy Sylvia her loneliness. One of these days, she and Brad would have to make sure Ethan didn't grow up as an only child.

"What do you do back home when you're not hanging around private detectives?" Callie asked, partly to distract herself from wondering when she and Brad would ever have either the time or the money to consider another baby.

"1 work for an event planner. Well, that's what she calls herself. Mostly, we organize weddings for her friends' daughters and Christmas parties for her husband's business associates."

"You get paid to do that?"

"Not much. But it's something to do."

They worked quietly for a few minutes, trimming the carnation stems and filling the flower vases.

"So tell me about the guy."

"What guy?" Sylvia asked.

"The guy you're going to marry."

"Oh. His name's Pier. I've known him since kindergarten. Teabury is a small town. Well, not small like Cedar Beach, but still we saw each other off and on over the years, and we kept in touch when we were away at school. After college, he moved to Boston. He's an analyst for a financial services group there."

"So how'd he pop the question?"

"He gave me his grandmother's ring for my birthday."

Callie glanced at Sylvia's left hand. "You're not wearing it."

Sylvia shrugged. "No. It's kind of…I don't know. Not really my style. First of all, I never wear yellow gold. There's something tacky looking about it. And I hate red, so a ruby is like the last stone in the world I would have chosen."

"I see."

"I mean, I get the whole family heirloom thing, but the ring is pretty ugly. I wish he'd asked me what I wanted."

"Why don't you try telling him what you want?"

Sylvia looked at her. "Maybe." She sliced through the stems of the remaining carnations with one deft motion of the knife. "Maybe I'm not sure what I want."

They finished filling the vases and had distributed the flowers to each table when the front door opened and a middle-aged couple came in. Callie was more than a little annoyed that Alyssa still hadn't shown up. They needed her this weekend.

"Hey, Marge, Pete. How's it going?" After greeting her customers, Callie turned again to Sylvia. "I have to get them sorted out. Thanks for your help here. You want a burger? On the house."

"No, thanks. I'm not really very hungry right now. But if it's all right, I'd like to come back for dinner tonight."

Callie hesitated for just a split second. "Yeah, okay. But I'll be too busy to chat."

⊂ℬℰ⊃

CALLIE WATCHED BURGERS sizzling on the grill and thought about Sylvia and all that had happened in the last twenty-four hours. She brought the heavy spatula down on each of the meat patties, squeezed out the juices, scraped up the brown bits, and smeared them on top of each burger. She'd been frying burgers on a griddle since she was twelve years old and recognized something steady and reliable in the task. It was a good time to think.

Sylvia wasn't like the image Callie had been carrying in her head for the past four years. All her life, Callie had constructed stories to explain and soothe away the rawness of rejection, but not long after Kevin dug up the facts, she had had to rewrite her stories. He had discovered that her mother was named Anne, and that she was married to a man named Henry Bennett, had another daughter, and lived in a huge house in Teabury, Connecticut.

Callie had found out the hard way that her birth mother was a block of ice; she had assumed that Sylvia would be an equally stuck-up little bitch. What she hadn't counted on was having her assumptions and emotions turned upside down by actually meeting her half-sister. She'd never talked with someone who looked so much like the face in the mirror. And Sylvia was a puzzle. On the one hand, she had an obvious sense of entitlement—how dare she practically command Callie to drop everything in her life for some frou-frou wedding? But there was also something vulnerable about her. She seemed a little lost. And what was up with the fiancé? Callie had the impression it was not a match made in heaven.

Flipping the burgers onto fresh Kaiser rolls, she topped them with cheese, sliced tomato and lettuce. Almost immediately, Brad came through the swinging doors. She marveled at his timing—he knew within seconds whenever an order was up, no matter how busy they got. The two of them were a good team.

"Alyssa's still MIA?" she asked.

"Yeah. No sign of her."

"You didn't say something to her, did you?"

"Like what?"

"I don't know. You've just been kind of funny about her lately."

"I just think we can't afford to pay her. Maybe it's not a bad thing she's not here."

"Are you kidding? There's going to be a bunch of people here tonight. How am I supposed to cook and wait tables?"

"Don't worry, we'll handle it." He lifted the tray of burgers. "Hey, these look pretty good. How about you make me one? Lots of onion."

"There's nobody else out there but the Watsons?" she asked, already knowing the answer. Brad wouldn't have asked for food if even one other table had been occupied.

"Nope."

The summertime tourists weren't back full force yet, and even though business would be brisk tonight, the lunchtime crowds were too thin. It had been a tough winter and their bills were staggeringly high. In the four years they'd been running this tavern, this was by far the worst the finances had ever been, not just for Stone's Throw, but for everyone in the area. The economy was sinking like a pig in mud, and unless they were careful, Stone's Throw would go right down with it.

She took another burger out of the freezer and let her thoughts return to Sylvia. It was pretty damn obvious *she* didn't have to worry about the economy. Jeez, what would that be like? Callie had never minded not having a lot of stuff, but it sure as hell would be nice to not toss and turn half the night worrying about bills. Remembering that she had a meeting with their accountant next week, she wondered what he had on his mind. Bad news, no doubt. Maybe something to do with taxes? She broke out in a cold sweat just thinking about it. *Absolutely no point in going there right now,* she told herself, refocusing her attention on Brad's burger. She put it on a thick slice of rye, topped it with Swiss cheese, tomato and mustard, and set it out on the stainless steel counter. Fifteen seconds later, like radar, he was back in the kitchen.

"Thanks, babe," he said, taking a mammoth bite. "Wanna take the bar while I finish this?" he asked with his mouth full.

Before she could answer, Ethan came up beside her. His face was paler than usual, and his eyes had an odd, glassy look.

"Hey, buddy, I thought you were going to watch cartoons," she said.

"I don't feel good," he said. He swayed a little, then suddenly vomited, splattering Callie's legs and shoes.

"Oh, Christ," Brad said, throwing the remaining part of his burger down on the plate. "Callie, get him out of here. I'll clean up this mess."

"I'm sorry, Mama. I didn't mean to do it," the child whimpered.

"It's okay, baby. Daddy's not mad at you," she shot Brad a look.

"Yeah, Sport, I'm not mad," Brad said. "We just don't want customers knowing you hurled in the kitchen. Bad for business."

Callie carried Ethan up the stairs, cleaned him up and tucked him into bed. She took his temperature, which was normal, and began to read him a story, but he fell asleep before she got to his favorite part. When Brad came upstairs a little later, Callie wondered aloud if they should call the doctor.

"Nah," said Brad, "it's probably just a twenty-four hour bug. Something he picked up at school, or maybe something he ate."

She raised an eyebrow. "Choco Pops on a queasy stomach was probably not the best idea."

Without health insurance, they needed to minimize trips to the doctor, and right now was not a good time to be running up extra bills. Callie decided Brad was right.

03800

SATURDAY NIGHT STARTED out hectic and got worse. Beth Garland's birthday party guests arrived an hour before they were expected, so Brad and Callie rushed to shuffle tables around to get them all seated together. Before she could take their drink orders, three more couples came in the door. By six-thirty the place was jammed and looked as if it would stay that way all night. Alyssa still hadn't shown up, so Callie was running like a mad woman from the kitchen to wait tables and back again. Food orders were stacking up, people were getting buzzed, then hungry, then cranky, and she had no idea how she and Brad were going to get through the evening without killing someone. Alyssa was first on her list.

Just before seven, she saw Sylvia standing at the bar looking ridiculously overdressed in a satiny black top and pearls. Brad, who should have been carrying beers to a six-top table, was putting a glass of some frothy, fancy drink in front of her. Callie walked up to them, shot Brad a nasty look and snapped at Sylvia, "Nice necklace, Hon, but shouldn't you be someplace else? Like maybe the Ritz?"

"Hey, Callie," said Brad, "calm down. She doesn't deserve lip from you."

"Yeah, well in case you didn't notice, we're really short-handed tonight. I'm trying to do eight things at once, and the place is up for grabs," she replied. Turning to Sylvia, she added. "I sure as hell won't have time to sit around chatting, so maybe you oughta go back to your hotel or whatever and order a pizza."

"Do you have another apron?" Sylvia asked. "I'll wait tables for you."

Callie was about to object, but Brad pulled an extra black apron from under the bar, tossed it at Sylvia and said, "You're hired."

5
SYLVIA

HER HANDS SHOOK as she tied the apron strings. She hadn't actually done any real waitressing before, but how hard could it be? All she had to do was write down what people wanted and bring it to them. No big deal. Only it didn't quite work out that way. She forgot to ask how people wanted their burgers cooked, what kind of cheese they wanted on the cheeseburgers, or if they wanted mayo, onions, tomatoes and lettuce. She couldn't figure out the computer, so she had to get Brad to key in her orders, and she had to run back and forth to the kitchen at least a zillion times.

Around nine o'clock, the three men Sylvia had seen at her hotel that morning walked in. When she finally got to their table to take their orders, the one who had poured orange juice for her said, "I know this sounds really lame, but haven't I seen you somewhere before?"

The other two men snorted, one of them saying, "Kowalski, can't you do any better than that?"

Sylvia, relieved to stand still for a few seconds, answered, "You poured orange juice for me this morning at the Holiday Inn."

Kowalski smiled again in the same open, friendly way he had that morning. His blue eyes sparkled and with his blond hair and light tan, he was the perfect blend of Midwestern farm boy and California surfer. "Oh, yeah. Right. I remember now," he said. "So you work here?"

"No. Not really. I mean, I'm just helping out. Just for tonight. I'm only visiting. A friend." She knew she sounded as awkward as she felt. "My, um…friend…owns this place and her waitress didn't show up tonight, so I'm helping out. Or at least, I'm trying to help." Sylvia made a face. "I might be the worst waitress ever."

Kowalski cocked his head to one side, appraising her. "You look okay to me. How about you bring us some cold beer and we'll let you know for sure? By the way, my name is Mike Kowalski, and these two reprobates are my cousins, Jeff and Peter."

"I'm Sylvia," she replied before rushing off to get the beer they ordered.

When she returned to their table, she remembered to ask if they wanted any food. Pete and Jeff ordered baskets of fries, but Mike leaned back in his chair, patted his flat belly with both hands and claimed he'd already eaten too much that day. He explained that he and his cousins had just spent the afternoon at a family reunion, loading up on Uncle Ray's pulled pork and Aunt Bev's potato salad.

"And don't forget the red cake," Jeff added.

"That was definitely my undoing," Mike said.

"Hey, no one forced you to eat three pieces," added Pete.

"Please don't remind me." Mike rolled his eyes. "It was fun, though. Good to get everyone together again. We all grew up around here, and our parents and grandparents are still here, but the three of us went off to find our fortunes in the big city."

"And did you?" Sylvia asked.

"Well…Jeff here did. He's a big time real estate guy in Chicago."

"And Pete's a banker," Jeff volunteered.

Sylvia noticed then that Jeff and Pete were both wearing the kind of clothes that Pier would choose—Lacoste shirts in navy and dark green, professionally creased khaki trousers, and shiny loafers without socks.

"So what about you, Mike?" Sylvia asked. She felt a little guilty standing around chatting with them when Callie was so stressed about being shorthanded, but Mike was really nice. Unlike the other two, he was dressed in frayed and faded blue jeans and a white cotton shirt that looked as though it had been washed a thousand times. Relaxed and casual without being sloppy.

"Me? I'm a lowly photographer," he said. "I have a small studio just outside of Ann Arbor. Portraits, weddings, the usual family stuff," he said. "I'd rather spend all my time doing more creative images, but there's a steadier income in the studio."

"That's so cool," Sylvia said. "I would love to be a photographer. My mother is pretty good. She travels a lot and has taken some great pictures on her trips."

Mike reached in his jacket pocket and pulled out a business card. "Here. This is me. There's a website you can go to and see some of my work."

Sylvia took the card, promising to check it out. She was about to turn away when he added, "In fact, tomorrow I'll be driving around the tip of the Thumb taking shots that I hope will eventually be part of an exhibit in a Chicago art gallery. There's a ton of interesting stuff out there, old farms and machinery, lighthouses, harbor towns, and some great stretches of coast line."

"That sounds wonderful. I bet you'll get some great shots."

"Why don't you come with me?"

"I don't think so, thanks," Sylvia answered quickly.

"No, seriously. I could lend you a camera." Mike looked like a small boy anxious to show off his favorite toys. "You can take some travel pictures of your own to show your mother."

"Sorry, I really can't." Showing her mother photos of this trip would be the height of irony.

"Oh, come on. These guys are going home, and it'd be a lot more fun if I had some company." Mike's expression was totally earnest, and there was a sweetness about him that Sylvia found very appealing.

"I can't just jump in a car with a total stranger," she said.

"We're not strangers. We've had breakfast together. Remember? I poured your orange juice. And besides, my folks have been coming to Stone's Throw since the day Callie opened the place. If you ask her, she'll tell you I'm trustworthy and upstanding," he said, adding a straight-faced salute.

Sylvia wondered if he might also be a little drunk. Why else would he make such a ridiculous offer? She tried to decline again, but he wouldn't take "no" for an answer.

"Okay, how about this," he insisted. "Tomorrow morning, I'll be in the Holiday Inn dining room for breakfast at nine o'clock sharp. If you decide you want to come along, meet me there." Using his left hand as a makeshift map for the state of Michigan, he pointed to the side of his thumb. "We'll start here on the east coast, then go up around the tip of the Thumb, find some lunch somewhere, and I'll have you back here by two or three in the afternoon. Scout's honor." He saluted again.

"I'll think about it," she said, smiling politely, but with no intention of accepting the invitation. "Right now, I'd better get back to work."

An hour later, while Sylvia was trying to balance four bottles of beer, two Cokes, three hamburgers, and a basket of fries on a small tray, Mike and his cousins got up to leave. He waved good-bye to her, calling out, "See you tomorrow!"

"Bye," Sylvia called out, trying not to lose the tray. While she served the drinks, she decided maybe she would ask Callie about the Kowalski family. Not that she was planning to take Mike up on his offer, but just to see what Callie would say.

Finally, when all the tables were empty and Sylvia had returned the last of the red plastic baskets to the kitchen, Callie said, "You did a great job out there, kid. Thanks. I guess you've earned that cheeseburger I promised you."

"I'm starving," Sylvia replied, realizing that it was true. She hadn't eaten since breakfast. "Can I get that burger medium well, please, with cheddar?"

"Fries?"

"Sure. I think I walked off at least five pounds tonight." Her feet and back hurt like hell, and her arms ached from carrying trays, but she felt good. She had done something new and had not made a complete mess of it. Pulling a bar stool up to the stainless steel kitchen counter, she also had a sense of being a part of this place, a part of Callie's world, even if it was only for one evening. It was not a feeling she was accustomed to.

"You got it." Callie put a burger on the grill. Sylvia watched her, and tried to imagine what it would be like to be Callie. There was a sureness to her movements, a strength and confidence about her that Sylvia envied.

Brad came in from the bar. "That's it. Five minutes to one, and the front door's locked." He walked over to Sylvia and handed her a wad of cash. "Here, this is what we would've paid Alyssa tonight, and I can tell you, she wouldn't have worked as hard as you did."

Sylvia remembered how much time she'd spent talking with Mike Kowalski and felt guilty all over again. She refused to take the money, insisting that it hadn't been work at all; she'd had fun. "I really didn't know what I was doing, and besides, I've been a pest here the past couple of days. Let's call it even."

A look passed between Callie and Brad. He nodded and put the money back in his pocket.

"You could do me one favor, though. Do you guys know any-one named Kowalski?" Sylvia asked.

"Sure. There's three families by that name around here. Two of the brothers, Ray and Pete, have farms out off of M-53, and there's another brother that works in Kinde."

"I thought I saw a couple of the Kowalski boys in here earlier tonight," Brad added.

"Must've been while I was back in the kitchen," Callie said. She turned to her half-sister. "Why're you asking?"

Fishing in her pocket for the card Mike had given her, Sylvia put it on the countertop. "I got to talking with Mike a bit. He's a photographer, and he's invited me to go around the Thumb with him tomorrow to take pictures."

Callie studied the card. "Mike. That's one of Ray's kids. I heard he'd gone to Ann Arbor. Pete's kids moved away, too. None of them wants to do the kind of work their folks do."

To Sylvia's surprise, Callie encouraged her to take Mike up on his offer.

"It's a chance for you to see something besides this place while you're here. By the way, I don't think you ever said how long you are planning to stay."

"My flight's at seven tomorrow night."

Callie pursed her lips, took a drag off the cigarette that she had just lit. "I don't know if you can change that, or if you even would want to, but we've got some people coming over on Monday to celebrate my parents' anniversary. Mostly just family, but, hey, I guess you are family. What I mean is, if you want to hang around, you could come to the party. Meet my people. That is, if you want."

Sylvia was stunned. Flattered and touched by Callie's invitation, she didn't have to think about her answer. "Thanks. I'd really like that," she said.

CB8O

UNDER ANY OTHER circumstances, she might have been nervous driving alone on the dark country roads, but Sylvia was too excited to even think of being fearful. Mostly, it was a sense of belonging that thrilled her. She had won Callie over! Enough to be invited to a family party. Sylvia tried to remember if she had ever actually been to a family party. There were a few Christmas Eves when her parents were in town and the three of them had gathered in a stiff and formal little ceremony in the music room to open the piles of gifts beneath a tree custom designed by whatever decorator her mother was currently favoring.

Once, when she was little, her parents had taken her to Boston to have dinner at a hotel where her grandparents were staying. It was the only time she had ever met them. She had never met her mother's sister, Julia, or any of her cousins who lived in Illinois. Her mother had always said they were so dull, and so much older than Sylvia. There would be nothing for them to talk about. Of course, in the past year, she had been to lots of cocktail parties and dinners with Pier's family, but that wasn't quite the same. Sylvia wasn't certain what to expect, but she didn't think it would be like anything she'd ever experienced before. What had Callie said her parents' names were? Peg and Jack Hanlon. That was it. And they had a restaurant near Ann Arbor. Mike was from Ann Arbor, too. Sylvia wasn't exactly sure where Ann Arbor was, but she would find out. It sounded like a nice place.

When the alarm went off at eight the next morning, Sylvia groaned. She'd only had three and a half hours of sleep. It had been nearly two in the morning before she'd gotten back to the Holiday Inn and then she'd spent another twenty minutes on her cell phone checking out Mike Kowalski's website.

His pictures were breathtaking—misty farm fields, lighthouses and shorelines backlit by satin-hued water, and macro-shots of colors, textures and forms that made the familiar new again. One particularly spectacular black and white photo was of a long, frost-covered road uncoiling beneath layers of wispy clouds. It was that image that made her decide she would, after all, meet him in the morning. Once in bed, she'd been too keyed up to sleep until well past four.

She stretched and kicked off the covers. Out of bed, she pulled open the heavy hotel draperies to see that the skies were moody, alternating between thick, roiling clouds and brilliant sun. The varying light would make an interesting day for photography. She showered and dressed quickly, pleased with herself that it was only five minutes past nine when she walked into the breakfast area.

"I was beginning to worry you weren't coming," Mike said. He stood up to hold out a chair for her, and Sylvia noticed that he didn't look worried. Quite the contrary, he looked happy. Without bothering to ask, he brought her a cup of coffee from the self-serve counter, which he carried in one hand while balancing two plates of cinnamon rolls in the other. They sat together at the small table sipping their coffee and picking at sticky-sweet cinnamon rolls, while Mike showed her a map of the area.

"We'll cut across the Thumb and start here at Harbor Beach," he said, pointing to a dot on the eastern edge of the state. "Then we'll just follow the shoreline all the way back to Cedar Beach. If you've had enough, I can bring you back here to the hotel, but if you're up for it, I'd really like to keep going all the way to Sebewaing."

Sylvia thought it was considerate of Mike to offer her choices. That was not something Pier ever did. She was more tired than she was willing to admit and the thought of spending the entire day running around snapping pictures was a bit much. The idea of putting the DO NOT DISTURB sign on her door and sleeping for ten straight hours was highly appealing. Then again, if she decided she liked Mike, maybe she'd invite him to the party at Stone's Throw on Monday. Callie wouldn't mind.

After they finished their coffee, Mike showed her some of his camera equipment. He had an impressive amount of stuff packed into a black leather bag: two digital Nikons, four lenses, a collection of filters and a couple of spare photo cards. He pulled another, smaller Canon from the side pocket of his bag.

"I thought you could use this one for today. It doesn't look like much, but it's a pretty nice little camera. Totally simple to operate, and the lens is good quality, so you should get some decent pictures. There's a new card in it," he said. "It's just a small one, but it'll hold about 175 shots."

They gathered the gear and packed everything into Mike's car, a mud-splattered SUV that he boasted had 125,000 miles on it. Heading out along the main road, it took only a minute or two before they were in the middle of the flat, vast expanses of farmland that Sylvia now recognized as typical of the area.

"So what's growing in all these fields?" she asked.

"Corn, some wheat, and lots of sugar beets," Mike answered. A minute later, he added, "Being raised around here, I learned two important driving lessons: at dawn and dusk, scan both sides of the road for deer. They come out of the cornfields in a flash, there's usually more than one, and if you hit one of those suckers, the deer won't be the only one to suffer major damage. The other lesson, which unfortunately I learned firsthand, is that you never want to follow a sugar beet truck too closely."

"What happened?" Sylvia could understand why the deer would be dangerous, but the hazards of a beet truck escaped her.

"I'd just turned sixteen, had had my license for about two weeks. My dad let me take his new Buick into town. About half the way there, I get behind this truck that's poking along. I'm just about ready to pass the guy when this huge beet bounces off his truck. Busted the hell out of the car's windshield, which my dad was none too pleased about."

Mike started to tell her about what it was like growing up in Huron County, but interrupted himself as they came upon a barn that had collapsed in on itself.

"Here's our first subject," he said, pulling the car to the side of the road. He gave Sylvia a quick lesson in how to operate the Canon before the two of them hopped out and began taking pictures. Sylvia was fascinated by both the barn's sad, dilapidated state, and by Mike, whose energy and enthusiasm were utterly contagious. She took ten pictures, and the images that she saw on the quick view screen delighted her.

"Very nice," Mike said when she showed him her first efforts. "I may be setting myself up for some tough competition."

Back in the car, he added, "Unfortunately, you'll see an awful lot of barns in that condition. It's cheaper to just let them fall down than to pay to have them pulled down. The economy in this area is pretty harsh, especially now."

While they covered the flat miles across the Thumb, he told her how getting a camera for his fourteenth birthday had been the best thing that ever happened to him.

"There wasn't a lot to do around here, as you can probably figure out. I wasn't into hunting or fishing. I had my chores to do at home, but farming was never something I wanted to do for a living. Once I got the camera, I turned into a photo maniac. I took pictures of anything and everything: old barns, people, dogs, cats, goldfish. You name it. That camera saved me from boredom, and probably a lot of trouble with drugs, alcohol, or both. That's a path I saw too many friends go down, never to return. But I was too busy taking pictures or working in the darkroom to get mixed up with that stuff."

"So, you knew right away that you wanted to be a photographer?"

"Pretty much. I sold my first print when I was sixteen to the local paper, and ever since, I've been convinced I'm the next Ansel Adams," he laughed. He explained that he never bothered with a college degree, but went to Chicago where he worked three jobs at the same time. "Yup, I was a waiter—everyone should do that sometime—and a nightshift security guard, but I also finagled a job as an apprentice in a portrait studio. Those were five tough years, but I saved enough money to move to Ann Arbor and rent a small house, which is now home, office, and studio. I tend to eat, breathe and sleep photography, but I get to do what I love."

Sylvia was impressed. Mike seemed so totally in control of his own life. She didn't think she'd ever met anyone quite so self-sufficient. Certainly, none of her friends back home supported themselves without family money, connections, or both. Even Pier did exactly what his parents expected him to do, whether he liked it or not. The funny thing, she suddenly realized, was that she didn't actually know if Pier liked what he did.

When they got to Harbor Beach, Mike turned the car north to follow the shoreline road. Spring was slow in coming to this area. The winds whipped off the lake from three directions, and the last of the accumulation of winter snow had yet to melt away completely. The morning sun was breaking through the clouds irregularly, sometimes creating such brilliant light that everything—trees, buildings, scrubby plants at the side of the road—seemed outlined in silver. They stopped the car several times for shots of the stark branches against the dramatic sky, or the textures of silvery white birch bark at the edge of deep woods.

The town of Harbor Beach, set on the western shore of Lake Huron, was a small collection of weathered buildings, most of which were shuttered until warmer breezes brought floods of summer visitors from cities and towns all over the landlocked Midwest. Mike and Sylvia took photos of the empty streets, the desolate looking storefront windows, and the sides of buildings whose paint had peeled and cracked into delicate and complex webbed patterns. Sylvia would discover that all the small towns they drove through had the same air of hibernation tinged with economic exhaustion. If only these little places could last through the winter, maybe they would once again be bustling with sunburned, tee-shirted tourists looking to spend money on food, accommodations, and kitschy souvenirs. But for now, the area had much the same hung-over atmosphere as a blue-collar bar on a Sunday morning.

"I've told you all about me," Mike said. "How about you? Where are you from? How did you wind up working at Callie's?"

Sylvia chose her words carefully, giving him only the most basic information: she was from Teabury, Connecticut, and, as she had told him the night before, she was just helping Callie out; she didn't really work there.

"Okay." Mike said the single word with the kind of thoughtful tone that made it clear he knew she was withholding information. Sylvia remained silent. Finally, he asked, "If you don't work for Callie, what do you do?"

"I work for an event planner. Organizing and managing fundraisers, corporate events, weddings."

He looked sideways at her. "Mmm. That's not a real big industry around here."

"Yeah, that's what Callie said. It is in Teabury, though. Lisa, my boss, is busy all the time. She was annoyed that I took off this weekend—there were a couple of big parties going on—but I had to come out here."

"Any special reason?"

"Just some stuff to take care of." She didn't volunteer any more information, and Mike didn't pry.

They drove along at a leisurely pace, alert to the play of light on clapboard buildings and regal stands of birch trees, whiter than the turbulent clouds. Along the coast, they stopped to capture poetic images of the glittering water. At Port Hope, they walked along the shoreline, snapping shots of the whispering grasses that grew right out to the water's edge and patterns the waves formed as they broke along the sandy beach. In Grindstone City, which Sylvia thought was the tiniest "city" she had ever seen, they walked among the giant round stones on display in a public park between the water and the town. Mike explained that the stones, some of which were over six feet in diameter, were once used to mill the county's grain. They stood like silent monoliths, a testament to better days and the agricultural history of the area.

At the very tip of the Thumb, they spent time at the Port Aux Barques lighthouse. It, too, was closed for the season, but that didn't stop Mike from climbing over the split rail fence. Sylvia followed, timidly at first, feeling as though she were trespassing, but there didn't seem to be any sign of other people, so emboldened by Mike's encouragement, she went forward. They walked around the entire structure, taking pictures of the lighthouse keeper's accommodations and the little garden at the back of the house, now forlorn and neglected. Beyond the garden, there were stone steps, overgrown with brown weeds, leading down to the rocky shoreline. From the base of the steps, the lighthouse tower gleamed white against the gray clouds above. By the time they had all the photos they wanted, it was well past noon.

"Are you hungry?" Mike asked.

"Starving. I was beginning to wonder if you literally eat, breathe and sleep photography," Sylvia said.

Mike smiled. Sylvia decided she liked him a lot. Something in his smile, in his calm manner, was very genuine. He was not the type of man she was normally attracted to. Usually, she preferred dark-haired men, and Mike's hair was the same light blond as some of the bleached out grasses they had photographed earlier in the day. He wore it cut to a traditional length, neither too short, nor too long, although his bangs tended to fall over his eyes from time to time. His face was rather long and thin, but his lips were well-shaped, and his blue eyes sparkled with humor, honesty, and steadfast determination.

"We're actually just on the edge of Port Austin," he said. "There are a couple of places we could go for lunch, as long as you are okay with something simple."

They chose the family-style restaurant over Jimmy's Pizza Parlor, the only two places open in the off-season. Inside, a few of the Formica-topped tables were already occupied. Sylvia noticed that the other diners were all older couples—the men wore bib overalls with plaid shirts and put their caps down on the table beside their coffee cups. The women had on pastel-colored outfits and wore glasses that looked two or three decades out of date. All of them were overweight. The restaurant itself was made dim by the dark paneling; the linoleum floor was scratched and grubby, the furniture, cheap to begin with, was battered. Sylvia's appreciation of Callie's clean and orderly dining room rose. She ordered a grilled cheese sandwich, figuring that it would be the safest bet. Mike was more adventurous and asked for a bowl of chili.

While they were eating, Sylvia's cell phone rang. The people at the adjoining table stared and, embarrassed by the attention it caused, she scrambled to dig it out of her purse. The caller ID showed it was Pier. Sylvia quickly set the phone to the "ignore" mode.

"Not important," she said, flipping the phone back in her bag. Mike gave her a quizzical look, but said nothing. She couldn't help but imagine how Pier would react if the roles were reversed. He wasn't really the jealous type, but he assumed it was his right to know who called her and what they wanted.

After lunch, Mike offered to return her to the Holiday Inn.

"Or you could take your chances and stay out here for the rest of the day. There're still a lot of things to see."

"I'll stay," she answered immediately.

They continued down the western edge of the Thumb. At Sebewaing, they sneaked behind a chain link fence to take photos of an old, deserted auto parts factory. Farther down the road, they continued their trespassing activities at a former sugar plant. Mike told her the place had been in operation since the 1800s, but had closed down a decade ago and been left to rust away, yet another casualty of the economy.

In Mike's company, Sylvia experienced an unfamiliar and delicious sense of freedom. She felt no pressure to impress him by behaving particularly well or particularly badly. Over the course of the morning, she watched him be serious one minute, playful the next, and always his passion for his work was undeniable. Through his eyes, Sylvia saw light and colors and everyday objects in a new way. She took dozens of pictures.

"This is so different from home," she said, knowing that the differences were about more than just the physical place. At home, she often felt as if she had been placed on a conveyor belt from the moment she'd been born. There were certain schools she'd had to attend, certain people she was expected to associate with, certain rules that had to be followed. Independence, she discovered, was a powerful state of being.

"I guess there's some sort of a party at Stone's Throw tomorrow night," she ventured. "Would you maybe want to go?"

Mike didn't answer immediately, keeping his eyes on the road. Then, when he turned to her, she could see the regret on his face. "I'd really like that, but I can't. I have to be back in Ann Arbor tomorrow afternoon for a shoot."

Sylvia swallowed her disappointment. "That's okay. I'm not sure I want to go, either."

By the time the last pink glow of the day had settled into Saginaw Bay, she was regretting that she and Mike would probably never see each other again. When this day was over, they would have to say goodbye. She would return to Teabury, with or without Callie, but Mike would remain in Michigan.

"It's after six," he said, interrupting her thoughts. "I don't know about you, but I'm hungry again."

He mentioned a restaurant that they had driven past as they'd gone along the road on the tip of the Thumb. "The dining room juts out over the water so that every table has a great view. And they serve a decent glass of wine. It's still off-season, so they might not be open, but we could take our chances, if you're up for a little more driving. What do you say?" he asked.

"Let's go!" she said, glad to extend their time together.

At first glance, the exterior of The Breakers had the same dreary, weather-beaten look as the rest of the county, but the interior was a different story. The tables were topped with crisp white linens, the crystal wine goblets sparkled in the last rays of the setting sun, and the view of Saginaw Bay was spectacular. They ordered a bottle of merlot, salads, and beef tenderloin. The meal, to Sylvia's surprise, was wonderful, surpassing dinners she had had in far more cosmo-politan surroundings. Her enjoyment was heightened by sitting at the table in the comfort of her jeans and a sweatshirt, a breach of protocol that her parents and Pier would never excuse.

It was almost ten when she and Mike returned to the Holiday Inn. He parked the car and walked her to the lobby.

"I won't come in, but would you email me sometime, just to say hello?" he asked, providing a small glimmer of hope that maybe she would see him again someday.

He kissed her goodnight, just a gentle brush of his lips against her cheek, before turning away with only a momentary backward glance. She took a breath, ready to call out to him, but she didn't know what to say.

In spite of being dog-tired from too little rest the previous night and spending a very long day trekking around in the fresh air, Sylvia was too wired to sleep. Retrieving the business card he had given her, she looked up his website once again. For the better part of an hour, she scrolled through his gallery of pictures before exhaustion took over and she crawled into bed. Half-formed thoughts danced just at the edge of her conscious mind, but they wouldn't quite come out in the open, even under the cover of darkness. The dark had never bothered her; instead, she thought of it as a soft, protective cover, and night was a good time for thinking. In her mind's eye, she could still see Mike's photos. After watching him today, she knew he put his entire being into his work, crouching and crawling, climbing on things and balancing himself precariously to capture images that, through his vision, became art. He cared about things. It showed in the way he honored the dilapidated barns and disused factories, by the way he recorded the remnants of their glory days and the poignancy of their neglect.

He had been careful with her, too, going out of his way for her comfort, never insisting he was right, or pushing her with questions that she didn't want to answer. Except she knew now that she wanted to answer his questions. She wanted to tell him everything: the truth about Callie, about her mother, and about Pier. But first, she needed to figure out exactly what the truth meant.

6
CALLIE

AFTER SATURDAY NIGHT, Sunday was quiet in comparison. The Walleye Festival turnout was less than they had anticipated, barely enough to keep them busy. Alyssa came in at noon, as scheduled, apologizing profusely for her absence the previous day.

"I am *so* sorry. I had this terrible migraine. I swear I couldn't even pick up the phone," she explained.

"Yeah, well, it was kind of crazy around here," was all Callie said, even though she was tempted to toss off a disparaging comment or two. Noting the dark circles under Alyssa's eyes, Callie figured she was telling the truth.

Alyssa redeemed herself by cheerfully taking all the tables, charming customers into ordering another round of drinks and extra orders of fries, running around like a woman possessed so that Brad could stay behind the bar and Callie only had to do the cooking. As a peace offering, it worked.

But if Sunday had been quiet almost to the point of dullness, Monday was proving to be just the opposite. Callie was having second thoughts about inviting Sylvia to the anniversary party for Peg and Jack. That morning, she'd realized that she'd had to call them ahead of time to tell them about Sylvia; it wouldn't be fair to just spring the surprise on them at the party. They'd both reacted with their usual good-natured calm, saying they would look forward to meeting her. Callie sometimes wondered how her parents got through life with such rosy, accepting attitudes; she had been more cynical at fifteen than Peg and Jack would ever be. Maybe it was because of their positive outlook that very little seemed to trouble them. And maybe it was nature rather than nurture that had given Callie her more cynical, distrustful outlook.

Throwing a party on her only day to relax had been a dumb idea. Giving Alyssa the day off had been even dumber, but Brad would have balked at paying her, and Callie didn't like the idea that she'd be the hired help at a family party. Alyssa had been with them long enough that she almost seemed like family, too. Callie could count on everyone to pitch in, but until they arrived, there was still cleaning to be done and food to prepare. Tables needed to be set up to accommodate fourteen. No, make it fifteen. Sylvia would be here, too. At least she assumed that Sylvia would be coming, since she had neither seen nor heard from her half-sister since Saturday night. For a half-second, she wondered if Sylvia had given up and gone back to Connecticut, but then she remembered that Mike Kowalski had asked her to go on that photo shoot. They'd probably both show up looking for dinner. Callie wondered idly how the fiancé would feel about that, but decided she really didn't care. She had enough problems of her own.

The only bright spot in this crazy day was that Ethan was certainly feeling better. Two breakfasts. Jeez. This morning, he'd wolfed down two eggs, toast, and a banana.

"Mom, I'm bored," he said half an hour later. "And I'm hungry again."

"You just ate."

"I want something to do."

"Sweep the floor for me."

"Noooo. I want something good to do."

Finally, Brad took him outside to play so Callie could get her work done. Now, three hours later, she was still playing beat the clock; it was already almost noon.

Sylvia showed up just after one o'clock looking like she should be lounging at some hoity-toity resort instead of grubbing around at Stone's Throw. The sky-blue linen jacket she wore over a matching knit top and white slacks looked like it cost more than Callie spent on clothes in a year. When she offered to help, Callie said the only thing she needed was someone to keep an eye on Ethan.

"You might want to grab an apron," Callie said, nodding at the white slacks.

"Okay, no problem," Sylvia said, casually tossing her jacket on a chair.

"It's only fair to warn you the kid is back to normal. He'll probably exhaust you before the party starts."

Sylvia took the little boy by the hand and asked him to show her his favorite toys. Ethan responded enthusiastically, launching into a detailed inventory of his Match Box cars and Toy Story action figures. The two of them disappeared upstairs to the apartment while Callie and Brad worked together cooking. An hour later, Ethan and Sylvia returned, and Ethan had obviously made a new best friend. He chattered away to Sylvia like he had known her all his life.

"Hey, buddy, you still feeling okay?" Callie asked her son.

"I'm hungry!" he answered.

"Again?"

"Gosh, he's not the only one," Sylvia said. "What are you making? It smells divine in here."

"Nothing fancy," Callie replied. She had just chopped half a dozen onions, which she added to a mountain of beef simmering in a giant saucepan.

"Brad and I have a recipe for a fairly amazing Irish stew, if I do say so myself. The secret is that it's heavy on the stout. And we've got some garlic bread that will keep the vampires away for months."

She had just asked Sylvia to make Ethan a peanut butter sandwich when the ring tone of a cell phone went off.

"Sorry," Sylvia said, pulling the phone from her pocket. Callie didn't think she was all that sorry because she answered the call and walked out of the room to carry on her conversation. Brad had disappeared somewhere, so Callie turned down the flame on the stove, quickly slapped together a sandwich for Ethan and got him settled at his table, then went back to cooking. She wondered if Sylvia's phone call was from the Kowalski boy.

Ethan ate all but the crusts of his sandwich before he started pestering his mother for a Popsicle. "Not now, honey, I'm busy," Callie said, pouring more stout on the browning beef and onions. Without taking her eyes from her work, she added, "Finish your sandwich."

Out of the corner of her eye, she watched him pick up his plate, sidle over to the trash, toss in the scorned crusts and put the plate in the sink.

"You're not fooling me," she said.

"Can I still have the Popsicle?"

For two seconds, Callie forced a scowl, but then relented. "Yeah, go ahead."

"Honestly, this child would live on nothing but junk food if I gave him the chance," Callie said when Sylvia returned. "By the way, tell me about yesterday. You obviously made it back safe and sound. Did you have a good time?"

Sylvia began talking about the places where she and Mike had taken photos, and it was obvious to Callie from the way she described familiar locations that she was seeing everything through the rosy light of romance.

"Was that him on the phone just now?" Callie asked.

"No."

Callie hesitated a second, then asked, "Do you want to call him and see if he's up for joining us tonight?"

A wistful looked crossed Sylvia's face. "Thanks, that's really nice of you to offer, but he left this morning. He had to get back to Ann Arbor."

"I guess that means you're on your own with us, then. There should be about fifteen of us: my parents, some friends of theirs from church, my brother Bill, his wife and kids, and my sister, Molly."

"No wonder you're making so much stew."

"Hey, that's on the small side for our family gatherings." Callie put a lid on the stew pot. "Okay, now for the garlic bread. While I'm doing that, why don't you and Ethan get started setting the tables for us? Ethan, you can show Sylvia where to find everything."

Peg and Jack Hanlon, along with their youngest daughter, Molly, were the first to arrive. Molly went straight to Ethan, scooping him into a big hug and cooing to him about how tall he had grown since she last saw him while he wiggled to get free. Jack was carrying an enormous bowl of salad, which Callie told him to put straight into the refrigerator. "Mom always has to bring something," Callie explained to Sylvia. "I think it's hard for her to let me do all the food when she's so used to cooking for the whole world."

"Now, don't be talking about me like I'm not even here," Peg teased. "And you know I make a better salad than you do anyway. You don't chop the vegetables small enough."

"That's because I like to see what I'm eating." Callie shot back. It was all good-natured kidding. The same banter had gone back and forth time and again whenever the group got together. It was just part of the standard playfulness of a close-knit family, but Callie could see Sylvia watching the exchanges carefully. She couldn't decide if that was flattering or a little creepy.

Peg walked over to Sylvia. "So, you are our Callie's half-sister," she said, emphasizing the words 'our Callie.' "I'm so pleased to meet you."

For a brief moment, Callie wondered if it had been a mistake to include Sylvia, since this was party was for her parents. She realized quickly, though, that there was no need to worry when she saw Peg pull Sylvia over to introduce her to Jack. "Welcome to the family," he said, enclosing her in a bear hug.

The next to arrive were two older couples, long-time friends of the family, followed by Bill Hanlon. As Callie surveyed the gathering, she glanced at Sylvia, and realized that for the first time in her life there was someone at a family party with whom she shared physical features.

"Where are Susie and the kids?" Callie asked her brother.

"The kids have had the flu all week, so Susie thought they had better stay home," he answered.

"There must be something going around. Ethan hasn't been one hundred percent either, though he's looking better now."

Callie introduced her brother to Sylvia. "This is Bill, otherwise known as Big Bro." The two shook hands, and Sylvia's slim hand disappeared in Bill's enormous paw. Her eye level was about mid-chest for him and she had to crane her neck to look up at his face.

Busy trying to get everyone settled and make sure food was organized, Callie left Sylvia to manage on her own. At one point, she saw Sylvia and Molly, their heads together, in what looked like a pretty intense conversation. My two little sisters, Callie thought. She figured they were talking about Mike, or clothes, or whatever twenty-somethings found interesting.

The Irish stew was a big hit, as usual, and everyone seemed to be having a good time. Callie began to relax, optimistic that the recent string of troubles had run its course. It was good to see Marge and Dan Truby again. They were Peg and Jack's oldest friends from church and had known the whole family for decades. Once or twice, Callie saw Marge staring at Sylvia, but otherwise everyone seemed to accept her as just another addition to the large Hanlon clan. At dinner, when toasts were offered, Jack thanked everyone for being there to help them celebrate forty years of marriage. It didn't escape Callie's eye that he made a special point of looking directly at Sylvia as he spoke. She understood it was his way of saying, "she's one of us."

And it was typical, Callie thought, of her father's generous nature that he would accept Sylvia more readily than she herself had done. She marveled again how fortunate she was to have been raised by such good people. For the first time, it occurred to her that it must have taken quite a lot of courage on Sylvia's part not just to come to Michigan, but to walk in here tonight all alone. Callie chided herself, feeling that the least she could do was be as gracious and welcoming as her father.

After the meal, when everyone had been quiet for a few minutes and Callie wondered if the party might be winding down, Bill said, "Hey, Brad, I just happen to have my guitar in the car. How about a few tunes?"

"I don't know…I'm kind of out of practice."

"Hey, when has that ever stopped you?" Bill fired back. Everyone laughed. "Go on upstairs and get that Gibson."

"Yeah, come on, Brad. You guys haven't played together since Christmas," Molly added. She turned to Sylvia. "They're amazing. Especially Brad. I mean, seriously, he could be on American Idol and blow everyone away. He's that good."

"Yeah, come on, Brad," Bill pushed.

"Well, if you insist," Brad answered, clearly pleased by the compliments. He pushed his chair away from the table and cleared away empty dessert plates on his way through the kitchen.

"Okay, you lot, you're in for it now," Jack said, looking at the group. "Once those two get going, it can be a long night."

"Oh, hush. You're just jealous that you're too old to play with them," Peg said, slapping playfully at her husband's arm. She spoke across the table to Sylvia. "Those boys really are terrific. Wait till you hear them. They've been offered money to play for parties around here, but they're both just too busy with their businesses to take any time off for music."

A few minutes later, Bill and Brad stood in front of the party, guitars strapped across their shoulders. They fiddled with tuning, made sure they had glasses of beer within easy reach, then launched into a Dave Matthews tune. Half way through the next song, Molly joined in with a clear alto that harmonized beautifully with Bill's baritone and Brad's tenor. After half a dozen songs, when the musicians set down their instruments to get more beer, Callie moved her chair so she could sit next to Sylvia.

"Guess I should have warned you that this usually happens," she said.

"They're really good," Sylvia answered. She sounded sincere enough, but distracted.

"This is where genetics shows up in our family," Callie continued. "Molly and Bill could make careers with their singing; Kevin, Bobby and I can't carry a tune in a basket."

Sylvia toyed with the bottle of beer in front of her and replied, "I can't carry a tune, either." Again, there was something in her tone that put Callie on alert, a sharpness in her voice that had not been there before.

"Are you okay?"

Sylvia kept her eyes on her empty beer bottle, saying nothing.

"Okay, what's going on?" Callie asked.

"Why didn't you tell me you'd been in contact with our mother?" Sylvia said.

"Uh-oh. Sounds like someone spilled the beans. I figured this might come up sooner or later. Who told you?"

"Molly."

"Look, let's go into the kitchen. You need to hear my side of the story."

They slipped out to the kitchen. Callie dragged a bar stool with a broken runner from the back storage area to the counter and indicated that Sylvia should sit while she leaned against the stainless steel, propping herself up with one elbow. She had a bottle of beer in her left hand.

"You want something? Shot of whiskey might go down pretty good about now," Callie suggested.

"No, thanks." Sylvia watched her with steady eyes.

"Suit yourself." Callie took a pack of cigarettes from her shirt pocket, tapped one out, flicked on a lighter and sucked in a lung full of smoke. "So, what exactly did Miss Molly tell you?"

"She said you tried to see my mother—our mother—but she wouldn't talk to you. She just gave you money and told you to go away."

"That's pretty much the story, but if you want the whole truth, it's a little more brutal than that."

"I'm not surprised." Sylvia's voice was flat, and it dawned on Callie that however unpleasant her experience had been, Sylvia had grown up living with that unpleasantness.

"Okay," Callie said, crossing her arms protectively across her chest. The cigarette smoke curled like a screen in front of her face, and she watched it rise toward the ceiling lights before she began to talk.

"I told you Kevin, my brother, messed around on his computer until he got names and addresses for birth parents for both of us. I didn't really care that much, but he was pretty revved up. He'd kind of built up in his mind that we'd both find we were the children of someone famous or something. Turned out his mom was a major druggie and died of an overdose, and his dad was in jail. Then he started pestering me to write to Anne. It was like he needed one of us to find out something good. But things just don't work out that tidy, you know.

"Anyway, a few years ago, I wrote her a letter saying who I was and that I'd like to meet her. No big deal. I wasn't going to ask for anything; I just wanted to see what she was like. About three weeks later, I'm working at Mom and Dad's, just about to close the place up for the day, and this guy in a fancy suit walks in. He comes right up to me, asks if my name is Callie Hanlon. I say, 'Yeah, what about it?' And he gets all mysterious like, and he wants to go talk some place private. I tell him anything he's got to say, he can damn well say right there. So, we sit down in a booth and he pulls my letter out of his pocket. Long story short, it turns out he's a lawyer she hired. He tells me that she wants nothing to do with me. Ever. 'And by the way, here's a check for fifty grand,' he says. My eyes just about fell out on the table, because sure enough, he has a cashier's check made out to me for $50,000. The money is mine, he says, as long as I agree to sign some papers and never try to contact Mrs. Bennett again."

Callie pulled on the cigarette, then ground it out in the ashtray before continuing. "Do you see now why I'm not too interested in being in your wedding?"

"Actually, no I don't. What was in the papers you signed?"

"I told you, the guy said the money was mine as long as I stayed away from Mrs. Bennett. I was so pissed off that she'd treat me like that, I took her damn money. It's how I bought this place. I'll keep my part of the bargain, which really isn't too tough, since…well, since I don't want to see her any more than she wants to see me."

"Okay. I get that, but there was nothing in those papers about having contact with me, right? And I don't give a crap what the lawyer said."

Callie studied her half-sister. "Look, honey, you need to look at this from my point of view. I have my life here. I have a family, and I don't want to go upsetting anyone, including myself. Besides, I don't think you're so much interested in me being in this wedding of yours as you are in pissing off your mother by having me show up in town for all her friends to see."

The two women regarded each other for a minute before Sylvia slid off the bar stool, saying, "Thanks for dinner. I'll be leaving now."

Callie watched her push through the swinging doors and head back to the dining room. She heard her saying good night to everyone. She heard Peg and Jack fussing over her, telling her to drive carefully. She heard Brad call out, "Come back any time!" and Sylvia's falsely cheery reply. There was a brief silence once Sylvia was gone, which Callie wasn't certain came from the other room or from somewhere inside her. Then the gradual rise of familiar family voices filled the quiet. Callie felt, rather than heard, an echoing sense that in spite of her best efforts to avoid her own history, something fundamental had shifted in the balance of her life, and it would be a long time until all would be right with the world again.

7
ANNE

ANNE BENNETT STIFLED a yawn and thought that, at this rate, the ghastly meeting was going to go on forever. Bunny and Tricia were actually arguing over which florist supplied better orange blossoms, for God's sake. Anne shifted in the uncomfortable chair. With her right hand, she slid the collection of bracelets over the watchband on her left wrist, twisting the band so that she could glance surreptitiously at the time. Eleven-fifteen. An hour before she was to meet Sylvia for lunch at Oceanaire. She tried to refocus her attention on the meeting, but it really was too tedious. They had gone over the same points a million times already.

The Women's Board was sponsoring a benefit for the Institute of Contemporary Art, which would be held, as usual, at the Yarmouth Club. Two hundred fifty engraved invitations would be sent out to an elite roster of guests, and Sir Randolph Ward, art historian and guest lecturer at Harvard this semester, had been booked to give the keynote address. All this had been decided months ago, but the devil certainly was in the details at this morning's meeting. The last half-hour had been taken up with discussion about tablecloths. Jane Compton felt strongly that pink would be far better with the floral arrangements than the dove gray Bunny had chosen, but Tricia preferred gray. A model of Bunny's arrangement sat on the table in front of them: a profusion of orange blossoms, cream roses, and smoke bush. It was rather nice, and Anne agreed with Tricia about the gray cloths. Jane could be such a twit.

They began discussing the menus. Fortunately, everyone agreed on wild-caught salmon served with *haricot verts* and fingerling potatoes. Anne mentioned that if they served a high quality Spanish *cava* instead of the usual Moët & Chandon, the evening might bring in as much as $500,000 in donations. Tricia agreed, but Jane countered with a snide glance at Anne and declared that there were no high quality *cavas*.

Anne tuned out again. She and Henry had just returned two days earlier from an interesting but exhausting trip to China. Jet lag was always so much worse flying west to east. She had spent yesterday trying to rest, but there had been phone calls to make and eight weeks' worth of mail to sort through. To make matters worse, Sylvia had been exceptionally annoying. She kept insisting that they had to talk. Ridiculous girl. Why didn't she just say what was on her mind? Whatever it was, Anne didn't have time to sit chatting, but neither did she have the energy to put up an argument. She knew she had to drive up to Boston today for this wretched meeting, so since the day was ruined anyway, she told Sylvia she would meet her for lunch.

"Anne, what do you think?"

"What? Oh, sorry," Anne shook herself mentally, realizing that Camille Osbourne, the committee chairwoman, had just asked her a question. "I guess I'm still a little jet lagged."

Camille offered a dry smile. "Oh, that's right. China this time, wasn't it? Sounds terrifically adventurous, but right now we could certainly use your expert opinion on the seating arrangements—should the tables have eight or ten place settings?"

For an instant, Anne was tempted to shout, "Oh, for Christ's sake, what difference does it make?" But instead, she tapped her perfectly manicured index finger against her lips as though contemplating this important decision. "Tables of eight, I think. It's so much easier to carry on a conversation when the table is smaller."

Anne surveyed the women around her. After spending two months in the Far East, the group seemed oddly foreign to her. Of the eight women on the committee, six were slender, blue-eyed blondes who wore their hair in nearly identical chin-length bobs. Anne herself was the thinnest, and though not the youngest, she was also arguably the wealthiest in a room where the average net worth was in the eight-figure range. But it was not her own attributes that Anne dwelt on. In fact, she had spent a great deal of her energy trying not to think about her circumstances. Her life, like anyone's, had its ups and downs, but keeping calm in troublesome times was something on which she prided herself, and long ago she had perfected the art of suppressing her emotions. With this rigidity of spirit, she considered Sylvia's phone call. Though mildly curious, she refused to be particularly concerned, much less alarmed.

When the board meeting finally wore itself out, Anne decided to walk to the restaurant. It was a pleasant mid-summer day, the kind of day when Boston shows itself best: the historic buildings looked charming instead of old and seedy, the sky sparkled deep blue, and the freshening scent of the ocean floated in to mask over the constant stench of exhaust fumes. The walk proved to be longer than she had planned, but it afforded her time to ponder the possible reasons for Sylvia's insistence on some mysterious meeting. What puzzled Anne most was that it was rather out of character. Sylvia had, from an early age, been quite independent. To Anne's knowledge, her daughter had never before requested advice of any sort. For a brief moment, she wondered if Sylvia might be thinking of calling off the wedding. That would be inconvenient. Anne dismissed the idea almost as quickly as it had occurred to her. Sylvia rarely missed an opportunity to point out qualities she admired in the Kent family. Several times, she had made specific comments about what a good mother Moira Kent was, and how nice it was that the Kent family spent so much time together.

Anne had not been a good mother. With calculated and steely resolve, she'd refused to be drawn into a miasma of maternal fussing and cooing, eschewing even the least interest in her child. Henry had been a bit intrigued with his daughter at first, but when the novelty wore off, he was quite happy to follow Anne's lead and leave Sylvia to the care of hired help. Later, boarding school took over the majority of parental responsibility, an arrangement that suited Anne and Henry quite well. Sylvia had survived adolescence with only one or two awkward incidents, and now, at twenty-two, should certainly be past all her fussy little demands for attention. Still, Anne wondered what on earth her daughter might find so pressing that she had knocked on Anne's bedroom door yesterday, waking her from the first decent sleep she'd had in weeks.

"Mother," Sylvia had said through the closed bedroom door, "I need to talk with you right away."

"Not now, Sylvia. I'm trying to get some rest."

"Then when? Pick a time and pencil me into your little date book. Your choice, any time, any place, but just you and me. Not Daddy."

Later, Anne left a text message for her daughter about meeting for lunch in Boston. It seemed silly when they lived in the same house, but their schedules were so different, and Sylvia had been clear that Henry was not to be present. *Good grief,* Anne thought. Such drama. It was unbecoming.

She arrived at Oceanaire at twelve-thirty exactly. The *maitre d'* showed her to a table where she was slightly dismayed to find Sylvia already occupying the chair facing outward. Anne disliked having her back to the room, not knowing who might be coming in behind her.

"Hello, dear," Anne said, sliding gracefully into a chair the *maitre d'* held for her. She had not bothered to offer her daughter an air kiss, that standard greeting amongst her acquaintances.

"Mother," Sylvia said, raising an already half-empty wine glass in salute. There was an unusually obdurate look in her eyes.

Feeling suddenly apprehensive, Anne decided that a glass of wine might be a good idea indeed. Perhaps it would take the edge off of whatever was about to happen in this increasingly uncomfortable situation.

"How was China?" Sylvia asked when their server left to get Anne's wine. Still thinking that her daughter had the look of some creature waiting for its prey to make a wrong move, Anne answered as casually as she could, "Oh, you know, the usual. Two weeks here, three weeks there. Packing, unpacking. We did see some lovely scenery, though. In places out in the country, it really does look like those paintings one sees everywhere—mist covered mountains and scrubby little fir trees. Quite remarkable."

The glass of wine arrived, and both women ordered the small crabmeat salad, after which there was a prolonged and awkward silence.

"So, tell me, what have you been doing, dear?" Anne finally asked. "Is your job going well?"

"The job is fine," Sylvia replied, taking another sip of wine.

"You are very fortunate to be working for Lisa. She's absolutely marvelous."

"Yeah, lucky me. Party planning is a dream job."

"Don't be flippant." Anne sipped her wine, letting its crispness linger on her tongue. She surveyed the young woman across the table. Sylvia was wearing a fuchsia and black print silk dress, quite possibly Marc Jacobs, with a black leather biker style jacket. The edginess of the look suited her. Anne was impressed, but didn't understand why it was that Sylvia must always be so unpleasant.

The waiter returned, putting the plates of salad before them, then fled when Anne dismissed him with a curt, "Thank you, that will be all for now."

She pushed some of the food around on her plate but, having no appetite, put nothing in her mouth. She watched Sylvia efficiently pick out the choicest morsels of crab.

Another long silence stretched out during which Anne resisted an urge to rub her tension-weary eyes. Instead, she pursed her lips tightly to divert the stress.

"Well, then," she said, forcing a smile and trying to keep her tone bright, "how are plans for the wedding coming along?"

"Fine," Sylvia answered without bothering to look up from her plate.

Anne detested monosyllabic answers to questions that were obviously meant to start conversation. It was rude and completely uncalled for, especially when Sylvia herself had been the one to insist on this rendezvous. Anne put down her fork, all pretense of amiability dissolving. "Why don't you tell me what this is all about?" she asked.

Sylvia's expression of bored insolence took on a more defiant aspect. She took another sip of her wine, then put the glass down carefully, pinning the base between her salad and bread plates with the tips of her fingers. "You've never told me how you met my father."

"That's what you wanted to ask me about?" Anne let out the breath she had been holding. Maybe this little *tête-a-tête* was about nothing more than Sylvia's pre-wedding nerves.

"I met him," Anne began, "at the golf club. Your father and grandfather were paired together for a tournament. After the tournament was over, there was a dinner dance. Standard sort of thing. Henry and I were introduced, and that was that. Why do you ask?"

"Did you love him? Do you love him now?" Sylvia snapped out the questions, her tone alarmingly aggressive.

Anne felt her upper lip begin to perspire. "What ridiculous things to ask."

They were, in fact, questions that Anne had always avoided answering. She was well aware that love had little to do with her marital relationship. Henry was a convenience. He behaved himself, they traveled well together, and he had inherited a vast sum of money from his family. If golf was the only thing for which he had passion and talent, she could live with that.

"Mother, " Sylvia said, "I know about Callie. I met her. I spent a whole weekend with her as a matter of fact."

Anne felt the blood drain from her face. "What? What are you talking about? Who is Callie?"

Sylvia leaned across the table, and Anne had to force herself to meet the intensity of her daughter's glare. "Don't give me that crap. You know perfectly well who I am talking about. She's your child, for God's sake. My sister."

Anne said nothing. Her face froze over, sphinx-like. She did not want to be hearing this.

Sylvia glared at her. "Why haven't you ever told me about Callie? Does Daddy know about her? I assume he isn't her father, so maybe you've never bothered to tell him, either."

Anne said nothing.

"How can you be so horrible?" Sylvia's voice was rising.

"That's enough. Stop."

"No, I won't stop. What is wrong with you that you would give away your own child, and then when she comes to you, you reject her like some…some servant you think you can fire?"

"This is not a conversation I want to have now, or at any time in the future."

"Well, guess what? That's no longer your choice." The two women glowered at each other, two genetically matching pairs of eyes, vying for control.

"What do you mean?"

"I mean you need to stop playing games. By the way, do you

have any idea how long I've known about Callie? Ten years. Ten fucking years. Not once in all that time did you ever mention her to me. Was that because you didn't remember her, or because you never talked to me anyway?"

Anne was shaking. She hated confrontation of any sort, but most especially in a public place. "This is none of your business." She kept her eyes lowered, terrified that Sylvia's coarse language might draw attention.

"Of course it's my business. She's my sister. Part of my family. I have a right to know. And, she's your daughter, for God's sake. I don't know what happened in your past, and maybe it isn't any of my business to know *why* Callie exists, but she does exist. I like her. She's a decent person—no thanks to you—and I don't understand why you don't care enough to at least admit she's your child. But then again, you barely admit that I'm your child. And what about your grandson? You didn't even know you had a grandchild, did you?"

Anne's eyes betrayed her for just a fraction of a second. Keeping her voice just above a whisper, she said, "Sylvia, I don't know how you came about this information, but since you have, I will tell you that your father is aware of my…past. He has always known and, no, he is not the father. We both felt it was very much for the best just to let…her…carry on without any interference from us." Anne paused to toss back a generous swallow of her wine. "It is a chapter in my life that has been closed for many years, and I'm not about to delve into any of it with you or anyone else. Not now, or ever. That is the end of this ridiculous conversation."

She would not let Sylvia have the upper hand. Long ago, she had learned that the best way to disarm an unpleasant situation was with distraction. Demurely, Anne dabbed at her lips with the starched white napkin. "Will you and Pier be joining us on Amelia Island for your father's sixtieth birthday next January? I need to book the rooms well in advance."

Sylvia held her gaze for a full minute before rising from her chair. "You're pathetic," she said, leaving Anne alone among the curious stares of the other restaurant patrons.

CRISO

THE GARDENS AT Wheatley House, the house in Teabury where Anne and Henry Bennett had lived for twenty-four years, were impressive enough to be worth a charge for admission. Once or twice a year, two or three carefully selected charitable groups were permitted to raise money by offering tours of the house and grounds.

Magnificent herbaceous borders running the length and breadth of the property behind the house stood against massive fifteen-foot privet hedges, each neatly squared off at the top. The gardens displayed all the colors of Monet's palette: vivid blues, rich purples, electric reds and pinks, soft oranges, crisp yellows, and every imaginable shade of green. The knot garden, a simple Celtic design entwining boxwoods with rosemary, germanders, and barberry, filled five thousand square feet at the base of the blue stone terrace that ran along the back of the house. Along the exterior wall of the kitchen, there was a prolific herb garden, and to the south of it lay a generous cutting garden so that the house, too, could be filled with fresh flowers all summer. To the west was the white garden, so named because majestic white pines, white roses, lilies and hydrangea blossoms enclosed a small, rectangular reflecting pool. The water in the pool was mixed with India ink to create more vivid reflections. A vegetable garden took up a portion of the south lawn, and beyond that lay a small wood where wildflowers and native plants flourished.

Anne adored the gardens. Henry was benignly indifferent, as he was to most things except golf, but Anne had a talent for visualizing the most attractive combinations of plant materials, obtaining them from garden centers or botanic suppliers, and then seeing to it that Mr. Tandy carried out her instructions. Tandy was ancient now, well into his eighties. He had worked many years for her parents, and when they moved to Florida, shortly after she and Henry were married, Tandy had come to work for her. In addition to living quarters and a fair salary, Anne provided him with money to hire additional temporary workers whenever he felt it necessary, which she left completely to his discretion. She trusted him implicitly.

Occasionally, Anne liked to work the soil herself. The morning after her meeting in Boston with Sylvia, she woke thinking of lavender. The lavender that had been planted on the southeast side of the border was looking poorly. It had not fared well through the brutal winter weather of last year and needed to be replaced. She rose, donned an old shirt of Henry's and a pair of khakis that had seen better days, and after a quick cup of coffee but no real breakfast, she headed to the local garden supply store where she purchased a dozen small but sturdy lavender plants, a new pair of gardening gloves, and a shovel. (She didn't know where Mr. Tandy might have put the shovel, but she didn't want to bother him by asking. It was easier to get a new one, which she assumed he could always use.)

In the car on the way home, she rolled down her window. This day, like the previous day, was sunny, with a soft, sweet breeze. Anne deliberately turned on the radio, something she rarely did. So-called popular music struck her as ridiculously crass, juvenile, or both, and the works of the great masters elicited emotions that she preferred to deny. Today, however, she sought distraction. WCRB was broadcasting Vivaldi. Anne listened for a short time, but when the haunting melodies evoked memories of her youth, she snapped the radio off.

Back at the house, she carried her purchases in four trips to the border where the scraggly leftovers of the old lavender stood. She pulled on the gloves and began to rip out the old, twisted strands of the spent plants. She had forgotten to get gardening shears, so she was forced to hack at the tougher stalks with the blade of the shovel. The sun was growing warmer, and Anne perspired as she worked. Her hair escaped its usually tidy ways, and bits of dirt streaked her face. She hoped Mr. Tandy would stay away. Years ago, if he saw her working in the garden, he would rush over to offer help, or worse yet, try to take over the task. But he had learned. When Anne was gardening, she did not want to be disturbed.

When she had cleared and prepared a patch of ground sufficient for the new plants, she placed them, still in their containers, on top of the soil positioned as she thought they should be in the ground. Then she stood back, studying, thinking, scrutinizing. She would shift one plant a few inches to the right or left, move another plant forward or back. This fiddling around, playing with the placement, was rather silly, she thought, but somehow it was terribly important to her to determine the exact spot where she would set these living things in the ground. Their place in the world was entirely up to her and she wanted it to be right. An inch this way or that might not—would not—make a bit of difference in the grand scheme of things, but Anne would always know that she hadn't done her best, that she hadn't looked at every possible angle to be absolutely certain what she was doing was correct. When, finally, she was satisfied, she moved the containers back out to the edge of the lush green lawn, picked up the shovel and began to dig. The ground, still soft from the rains of a few days earlier, came up in loamy, cambered portions. The scent of the earth, of the primordial essence of life, rose around her. She dug deeper, her thin arms straining to lift each heavy load, pushing herself to relish the aching soreness radiating through her body. Only out here, alone in this garden, could she allow the memories and the passion to take over, to overwhelm her.

8
ANNIE

I T IS THE summer of 1978. Annie Charles is at home in Bay River, New Jersey, a mid-sized town tucked between the river and the shoreline. She has just graduated from Miss Porter's School, and will be going to Tufts University in the fall, but the fall seems a long time away right now. It's the third week in June. Boarding school had been okay, but it's a pain in the ass to be the only person she knows who is stuck at home for the entire summer. There is absolutely nothing to do, no one to hang around with, and she refuses to follow her father's hideous suggestion that she learn to play golf. When she was younger, she spent the whole summer at camp year after year. Then, for the past three years, she traveled in Europe with her parents, which had certainly been boring some of the time, but definitely better than this. Now, when all her friends are scattered and she has absolutely nothing to do, even her parents aren't paying attention to her. This summer, her fat, boring, stupid older sister is the center of everyone's attention. Two years ago, Julia, who is six years older than Annie, found herself an equally fat, boring, stupid husband, and now—ick, ick, and double ick—the two of them have produced a child.

Annie's mother is away. She's gone to Chicago to help Julia, who can't seem to cope with motherhood, even though she has a full-time nanny and a live-in housekeeper. How much additional help Mrs. Charles could supply is extremely questionable, but Annie knows better than to go down that particular road. She'll keep her mouth shut, stay here in Bay River, and occasionally have dinner with her father, who, more often than not, is working. Dr. Charles is head of Bay River General Hospital and has always spent a great deal more time with other people than with his own family.

In comparison to many of her schoolmates' homes, the Charles' house is rather modest: a traditional white clapboard containing an assortment of well-appointed rooms on the ground floor and five bedrooms upstairs. There is an impressively large expanse of lawn with extensive and elaborate flower gardens at the back of the house. The lawn is dominated by a magnificent old oak tree in whose shade has been set a pair of wood-slatted Adirondack chairs. It is to these chairs that Annie makes her way on this summer day when the late morning air is still heavy with the scents of new blossoms and young, green things are finding their way through the rich, dark earth. She has a book, Gottfried Von Strassburg's *Tristan*, which she hopes will lift her from the tedium of day after warm, heavy day with not enough to occupy her. Annie has a secret appreciation of classic literature, which she would never admit to in front of her peers. At school, she hides her intellect by spending most of her energies on art class, which no one takes seriously. It's not cool to be bookish, and she pretends that she doesn't work at all to earn her excellent grades. On her own, without the burden of an image to maintain, she is reading this classic story with a depth of understanding that would be foreign to most of her friends. It is the pleasure of the language, the tale of enduring love, the history and romance of ancient days, which captivate her. She settles herself in one of the chairs and immerses herself in the tragic story of lovers and the idealism of youth.

Some moments later, voices rise to her from the edge of the garden. Two men, one of whom she recognizes as Mr. Tandy, the gardener, tromp through from the small greenhouse at the far end of the property line. Tandy is pushing a wheelbarrow full of new plants, and the other man, young enough to be Tandy's son, is carrying several long-handled gardening tools over his shoulders. When they stop at the edge of the largest flowerbed, the younger man drops the tools in a clattering heap. Distracted, Annie watches them. Tandy points to various things in the ground, his instructions an indecipherable murmur, and the younger man nods his head. Tandy leaves the wheelbarrow and returns to the greenhouse. The other man picks up a rake and begins work, and Annie returns to her book, hoping he will be quiet while he works. She is just starting the story; Blancheflor is in love. *Love, the Tyrant, had entered her soul somewhat too tempestuously, and robbed her of her composure for the greater part. Contrary to her custom, she was, in her demeanor, out of step with both herself and the world.*

Annie looks up from the book. The young gardener is clearing twisted roots, raking at the weeds, bending to pull tangled strands from the ground. He kneels on one knee, and under the coarse fabric of his tee shirt, Annie can see the muscles of his shoulders. Her eyes travel the curve of his spine, a curve that holds tension like a piece of wrought iron. That is the kind of tension she was supposed to get in her lines in life drawing class, she thinks, and suddenly she has a desire to draw this man-boy working the earth, kneeling in supplication to the power and the grace of nature. He stands, altering the balance of the moment, and turns. When he catches her staring at him, he cocks his head to one side and lifts his gloved hand with just the slightest of movements. Embarrassed, Annie looks back at the words in the book on her lap. She does not wave back. Neither does she read. She won't look up, but his face is already there in her mind's eye. His hair, hanging almost to his shoulders, is a dark chocolate brown. It's kind of messy, but not unattractive, falling in tangles across his forehead, much like the weeds he clears. She thinks his eyes must be the same rich brown though she really can't see them from this distance. Looking up, she is oddly disappointed that he has gone back to clearing the weeds. With an imperceptible shrug of her shoulders, she returns once more to the story. He is just a gardener; he isn't interested in her. She reads on, slowly, savoring the antiquated, convoluted structure of the sentences.

Now that the noble young lady perceived within her heart with her whole being (as lovers do) that her companion Rivalin was destined to be her heart's joy, her high hope, her best life, she gave him look on look and saw him whenever she could.

Drawn deeply into the story, Annie is only peripherally aware of the sun's increasing heat as it rises to its noon zenith.

A shadow crosses over the pages, and she hears, "You'd better be careful. You might get burned." Annie looks up, squinting into the sun, into his face. It takes her a moment to return to the present century, a moment of silence.

"I was wondering if maybe you could get me a glass of water," he asks.

"Water? Um…yeah. Sure," she replies, brushing a strand of her light blond hair away from her face. She wants suddenly to say something more, something clever, but for God's sake, what can you say about a glass of water? She swings her long legs to one side and tries not to look ridiculous as she clambers awkwardly out of the deep-seated chair. She bangs her right elbow hard against the wooden frame.

"Ouch," he says for her.

She blushes, makes a little face, and rubs her elbow. *Very graceful, you birdbrain,* she tells herself, but she smiles at him. She puts the book down, splayed open, on the chair seat.

"I'll be right back," she says. Annie can feel him watching her as she walks toward the house, and she hopes she looks more graceful than she feels. She's wearing a particularly hideous pair of shorts that her mother gave her. *Great.* She refuses to allow herself to turn around, but instead slips across the terrace to the side door near the kitchen.

The cool inside the house suddenly chills her. He was right; she's been out there for well over two hours, so she probably has a nasty sunburn. She pushes her left index finger onto the skin of her right forearm and, when she pulls it away, the little fingerprint mark glows hot pink. She goes to the sink and turns on the water, letting it run cold while she fetches a glass from the cabinet. By the time she carries it out to him, the outside of the glass is wet with condensation, and she cautions him it might be slippery. He thanks her. When he takes off his gloves, she sees his hands are strong, long-fingered, with graceful wrists. Her own hands are rather ordinary. She puts them behind her back.

He tips his head back, raising the glass to the blue, blue sky and drinks quickly while Annie stands watching him. When the water is gone, he wipes his mouth with the back of his left hand and gives her the glass. "Thanks," he says again.

"Do you want some more?"

"No. That's good."

Now she studies his face. Up close, he is maybe not quite as good looking as she had thought when she first saw him across the lawn. His nose is a little too big for the rest of his face. She had been right, however, about his eyes. They are a deep, lustrous brown, so dark the pupils are impossible to discern. His lashes are long and heavy, his brows neatly defined arches. His mouth is…well, she thinks his mouth is perfect. Like something Michelangelo might have carved: proportionately correct for the rest of his face. His lips are finely shaped and thick enough to be sensual without being vulgar. She wants to touch them.

"Ah, here's your glass," he says, and mortified, Annie realizes that she has been staring while he patiently waited for her to take the empty glass.

"Oh. Are you sure you don't want any more?"

"Not right now, thanks." He smiles at her. "Maybe tomorrow. I'll be here all week."

"Really?" Annie fears that the word might have come out almost as a squeak.

"Yeah. Your gardener, Tandy, he's a friend of my boss. Mostly, I work for Gus Moretti, but I guess the two guys help each other out from time to time, so I'm sort of on loan to clear out weeds, put in a truckload of new plants, and reset most of that stone wall over there."

He points to the low stone wall crumbling along the border between two of the flowerbeds at the other end of the lawn. "Everything is supposed to be done by the end of the week."

"Okay. Well, let me know if you need anything, um..." Annie didn't know his name.

"Chris," he answers, "Chris Garnet. And you are?"

"Annie Charles. I live here." *Oh, how stupid was that comment?*

'Yeah, I kind of gathered that," he chuckles. He holds the empty glass out to her again, and when she takes it, he says, "Nice to meet you, Annie Charles." He turns and heads back to his work. Annie retrieves her book and goes inside the house.

CCloseSO

THE NEXT MORNING, Tuesday, Annie is standing at the kitchen counter, still in the tee-shirt she slept in, eating a piece of toast. Classical music drifts through the entire house via the new intercom speaker system her father has had installed. He thinks playing music is a deterrent to burglars, so he's taken to leaving the system on when he's at work.

Through the kitchen window, Annie sees a turquoise-blue Dodge pickup truck turn in the driveway. Chris is behind the wheel. The toast in her mouth turns dry all of a sudden, so she spits it in the garbage and throws the uneaten portion in after it. She runs upstairs to shower and change, leaving toast crumbs and the butter knife on the counter. Her father has been at the hospital since early in the morning and she hopes he won't come in unexpectedly. He goes crazy if she leaves the kitchen in a mess. She'll clean it up, but first things first. If Chris comes to the door for anything, she doesn't want to be looking like a slob. She grabs a pink polo shirt and cutoffs and heads for the shower. Taking off her clothes, knowing that Chris is on the property, only yards away, excites her. It feels dangerous but delicious. Her figure is good; she thinks that she wouldn't really be embarrassed if he saw her naked.

In the shower, she turns the water a little cooler than normal and lathers the soap on thickly. This is crazy, she tells herself. Here she is, fantasizing about some guy she only met yesterday. And she didn't really *meet* him; he's just some guy hired to do the gardening. Hah, she could just imagine what her friends from Miss Porter's would have to say about that. Sally, Betsy, Muffy, and Cathy. They'd say she had gone berserk. Especially since she is the least flirty of them all. She has plenty of friends, and has gone out with a few different guys, but none of them were very interesting. Certainly, none of them sent her into a cold shower. Most of the boys she knows are so…boyish. They're like puppies. Amusing, even fun from time to time, but not…sexy. Annie gets out of the shower and rubs herself gently with the towel. Her arms and legs are sensitive from the sun yesterday. She smoothes lotion over her skin, then pulls on the polo shirt and cutoffs. It takes her an hour to put on her makeup because she keeps redoing it. Too much blush, not enough mascara. Eye shadow in the middle of the day? She tries it; it looks horrible. She takes it off, then has to re-apply the mascara. At least her hair behaves. She's always worn it the same way: cut evenly at a line between shoulder and chin, parted just off-center on the right side, and held back with a narrow headband. It suits her.

When she is finally ready, she goes back to the kitchen. She clears the toast crumbs, wipes down the counter and puts the butter knife in the dishwasher. She goes into the dining room and peeks out the window. Chris is working on the nearest of the four flowerbeds. He's on his hands and knees, piling up discarded vegetation. The places where he has already finished clearing the undergrowth show neat, rich black earth between the individual plants, and the plants themselves stand proudly, free of the distracting weight of weeds and withered stems.

Annie returns to the kitchen. She pulls a tray from one cabinet, a glass and small plate from another. From the pantry, she selects an assortment of Pepperidge Farm cookies: Chocolate Milano. Chessboard. Molasses Crisp. They are her father's one dietary indulgence, and she knows she'll have to replace them before he discovers they've been pilfered. There is lemonade in the refrigerator because she made it early this morning. She puts ice in the glass and pours in the lemonade. She thinks about bringing him the whole pitcher, but then, if he wants more, he won't have to ask. She wants him to ask her for more.

Her heart is pounding unreasonably as she carries the tray to the garden. She smiles and watches while he drinks one glass of the lemonade and eats two cookies, but he doesn't ask for a refill. Annie returns to the house annoyed with herself for her ridiculous expectations. She eats the leftover cookies and thinks about drinking the melted ice from his glass, but changes her mind and simply washes everything and puts it all away. She picks up her book and goes into the sunroom to read, but sitting in the glass room feels too exposed and she can't concentrate on the words anyway. She wanders into the house, pacing from room to room, finally moving upstairs.

From the big window on the stairway landing, she has a good view of the back yard. She stands, watching Chris work, then remembers her father has a pair of binoculars in his study, and though she feels guilty, she can't help herself. She fetches the binoculars and returns to the landing, careful to keep far enough away from the window that he won't be able to see her if, for some reason, he should turn and look up at the house.

When her arms ache from holding the binoculars, and Chris hasn't done anything but dig away at the stupid plants, she gives up. She's bored. Bored to tears. In fact, she begins to cry a little, frustrated with herself and her life. She lies on her bed, pulls the summer-weight cover up to her chin, and goes back to reading about Tristan and Isolde, feeling that the world can be an extremely unfair place.

In the evening, when she and her father sit at the kitchen table for dinner, her father asks what she did all day. It takes her some time to convince him that "nothing" really means nothing and, no, it is not just childish sarcasm. She is not trying to be difficult. He suggests she spend some time volunteering at the hospital. They always need someone to deliver flowers or read stories to the children. Annie surprises herself and her father by agreeing to try it. For the next three days, she rises early enough to leave the house with him at six in the morning. They don't return until late afternoon when the gardening has been finished for the day.

♋♌

SATURDAY, NO ONE is working in the garden. Dr. Charles spends most of the day at the club playing golf, and Annie has errands to run. This evening, her mother will be returning home from Chicago. At her father's request, Annie has agreed to help him cook dinner, which means she has to do the grocery shopping. She's almost to the store when she feels the familiar cramping sensation that always signals the start of her period. Damn. She has no Tampax in her purse and she's wearing white shorts. She pulls into a parking space across the street from Walgreen's and dashes into the store. She's at the checkout counter, right next to the door, paying for two boxes of Tampax, when Chris and another guy walk in, laughing about something. He sees her.

"Hi, there, Annie Charles," he says. "How's it going?" He looks right at the Tampax boxes, and Annie wants to fall through the floor.

"Umm. Fine. Thanks." She is tight-lipped, curt with shame.

"Annie, this is Pete. Pete, meet Annie," Chris introduces them. Pete looks like a blonde version of John Lennon. Annie mumbles something at Pete that she hopes sounds more like "hello" than what she is thinking, which is more along the lines of "go away." The store clerk waits impatiently, but Annie ignores him.

"I haven't seen you the last couple of days," Chris says.

"No, I've been working. For my dad. At the hospital. Just volunteer stuff, you know, like delivering flowers to patients' rooms and stuff like that." Now she's prattling.

"Cool." Chris nods his head. The three of them stand awkwardly for a moment before Pete prods Chris.

"Well, maybe I'll see you on Monday."

"I thought you were finished with everything."

"Yeah, we were, but Tandy wants me back for a couple of days. Guess there's some more stuff he needs help with."

"Sure. Okay."

Chris and Pete head into the depths of the store. Annie hands over her money, takes her package and leaves as fast as she can.

That evening, she sits with her parents on the terrace looking over the back garden while they have a pre-dinner cocktail. From the new speaker system, soft strains of classical music accompany dust motes that dance in the last of the day's light. Annie is offered and accepts a small cordial glass of sherry. Her mother has endless pictures of Simon, Annie's six-week old nephew. Simon. Who in their right mind would name a child Simon? It confirms Annie's notion that her sister, Julia, and her flabby husband are hopelessly idiotic and should be forbidden from breeding. However, she looks dutifully at all the pictures and makes non-committal utterances when her mother says things like, "Julia would love to have you come out and stay with her for a while. You really ought to see her house. It's quite beautiful, and Simon is just precious. I'm so proud of your sister."

Annie says nothing, focusing instead on the barely audible Vivaldi concerto.

"They belong to a very nice country club," her mother continues. "You could swim every day, and I'm sure you would meet some people your own age."

Ick. Annie is saved from having to make any reply by her father, who has been bashing around with the charcoal grill while she endured the photo show. "I think these coals are about ready," he says. "Helen, do you want another gin and tonic before I start cooking?"

"No, thank you, dear," Annie's mother answers. "Are you sure there isn't anything you need me to do?"

"No, no. We've got it all under control, right, Annie? Where are those steaks you bought today?"

"They're in the refrigerator. I'll get them. I need to cut up the tomatoes, too," Annie says. She also has to put the potato salad that she bought at Meyer's Deli in a bowl and hope that her father will think she made it from scratch. He thinks deli food is rife with bacteria and refuses to eat it, but Annie doesn't agree and didn't want to spend half the day boiling potatoes.

In the kitchen, she quickly puts the potato salad in a serving dish, and sprinkles it with fresh chives. She rinses out the container, and quickly buries it deep in the garbage under various disgusting things so there's no chance her father will catch on to the trick. She puts the raw meat on one clean platter and covers it with Glad Wrap, then gets out another platter for the cooked version. She carries everything out to the terrace, where she has already placed a clean, white cloth on a table beside the grill and organized the long-handled tongs, spatula, and carving tools her father will need. While her parents are deep in a discussion of the sorry state of the airline industry, Annie makes several trips back and forth to the kitchen as she puts place settings before each of them. Finally, Dr. Charles moves to the grill and nods with curt approval at the covered meat and the sterile-looking utensils on the worktable beside the grill.

Back in the kitchen, Annie finds a pretty French dish for the tomatoes. She takes out a plastic cutting board (wooden boards hold too many germs, her father insists) and begins to slice the tomatoes she bought from the farmers' market that morning. They smell of summer sunshine and, as she twists off the stems, she holds them beneath her nose, inhaling their earthy, warm scent.

She is slicing through the second tomato when the phone rings. Six o'clock on a Saturday? It must be stupid Julia.

"Hello?"

"Ah…Annie?" It's a male voice, but it doesn't sound like her brother in law.

"Yes."

"Ah…this is Chris."

Annie almost drops the phone, but manages to reply in a normal voice, "Oh, hi, Chris." She wonders how he got her phone number since it isn't listed in the phone book; then, as if reading her mind, he answers, "Mr. Tandy gave me this number. I hope you don't mind."

"Um, no." There's a pause while each expects the other to say something.

"Well, there's a bunch of us that are going to Buffo's tonight," Chris says, "and I was wondering if maybe you'd like to meet us there."

"Buffo's? What's Buffo's?"

"You don't know Buffo's? How can you not know Buffo's?" he asks. "It's the pizza place down on Waterfront Street. You know, the one with the pool table and pinball machines."

"I guess I've never been there," she answers. Waterfront Street is in a part of town where she and her friends never venture, but after the boredom of the past few days, she doesn't hesitate. "It sounds like fun."

"Can you meet us there in, say, an hour?"

She says she'll be there by seven. She hangs up the phone just as her mother comes into the kitchen.

"Your father is getting antsy, dear. Do you need some help?"

"No. Sorry it's taking so long. I got...distracted."

"Were you on the telephone?"

"Um...yes. That was Nina Bent. She called to say she's back in town just for tonight and wants to know if I can meet her for dinner in town. Would you mind?"

"I suppose that would be all right. You certainly haven't had much of a social life this summer. Let's see what your father has to say about it."

Annie puts the last of the tomato slices on the dish and follows her mother back to the terrace.

"Steaks are done," her father announces. "What took so long with those tomatoes, Anne?"

"Annie had a phone call from one of her school friends," Mrs. Charles answers for her daughter. "She's been invited to dinner this evening. I think she should go."

"What, now?"

"It is rather last minute, but you know how these young people are."

Annie watches her parents debate her social options until finally her mother wins, and her father hands over car keys and some cash.

"Which restaurant did you say you were going to?"

Thinking fast, Annie answers, "Prindle's." It is the nicest restaurant in town, and a far cry from Waterfront Street.

"Prindle's? I hope you have a reservation. Otherwise, it's impossible to get in there on Saturday night. I'd better give you a bit more cash, too." He peels another ten off the wad of bills he carries.

"Thanks, Dad." Annie can't help grinning from ear to ear.

"Be home by eleven," her father adds. She knows he will wait up for her.

Bay River's downtown area is split by railroad tracks that very well might have been the place where the phrase "wrong side of the tracks" originated. To the east of the railroad line are the spacious, well-kept homes of doctors, lawyers, stockbrokers and their like. The shops and restaurants to the east of the town's midline cater to the more affluent. Mannequins in the clothing stores sport tuxedoes and elegant evening gowns, the toy store sells miniature castles and children's cars with working motors, and the Eastside Bakery does a brisk business in croissants and brioche. Prindle's is on the east side; Buffo's is on the far western edge of town.

Annie drives west and, across from the pizza place, finds a parking place in front of an empty storefront with rusted metal grating pulled over its darkened windows. She checks her image in the rear view mirror, and gets out of the car at five minutes to seven. As she crosses the street, she sees Chris standing at the door waiting for her.

"Hey, glad you could make it," he says. She follows him to a table near the back of the restaurant, which is much larger than it appears from the outside. Along the way, he introduces her to several people. She recognizes Pete from earlier in the day, and a flush rises to her face as she recalls the circumstances of meeting him. Buffo's is noisy and smells of spilled beer and pepperoni pizza. It's crowded with teenagers and college-age kids, most of whom are drinking beer, and all of whom seem to be shouting. A jukebox is blasting Janis Joplin and pinball machines ding furiously. It takes Annie a few minutes to acclimate to the racket. Chris hands her a beer and a slice of pizza large enough to feed a family of four. Annie juggles the beer glass and pizza slice awkwardly, slightly grossed out by the greasy pizza, which smells as bad as it looks. She feels shy and says very little. When Chris insists that she play pool with him and Pete and another girl whose name Annie never quite hears, she wishes she hadn't come. She's never played pool before. The other couple waits impatiently while Chris shows her how to hold the cue stick and how to look for a shot. He touches her hands as he helps her chalk the tip of the stick. When she looks at him, he smiles, his brown eyes dancing, and then she's very glad she did come.

"Okay, Annie, try the three-ball in this pocket," Chris says. When Annie leans over the table, she can see an imaginary line from the ball to the pocket. She pushes the stick at the white cue ball, which hits the three-ball with a satisfying smack, sending it straight into the side pocket.

"Hey, not bad!" Chris says. He's looking at her like there is no one else in the room.

"Yeah, yeah. Beginner's luck," Pete teases.

"Okay, you get another turn," Chris tells her. And while he's scoping the table, trying to figure her next shot, Annie sees another one of those imaginary lines from the six-ball to the corner pocket. She starts to position herself for the shot. Chris says, "No, wait…" but before he can finish his sentence, she's sunk the six without scratching.

"Whoa, I think we've got a hustler on our hands," says Pete.

"Or a natural," says Chris.

"Are you sure you've never played before?" Pete asks.

And from there the evening is nearly perfect. Annie doesn't run the table, but she does well, playing almost as deftly as Chris and Pete, which gives her the confidence to be herself. It's almost eleven when she remembers to look at her watch, and feeling much like Cinderella, she knows she has to leave. Chris offers to walk her to her car.

"I'll see you Monday," he says as she opens her car door. She gives him a quizzical look. "In your back yard. Remember? I'll be working there?"

"Oh, yeah. Of course."

"Hey, thanks for coming out tonight. Can I call you again?"

"I'd like that."

She drives away tingling with excitement and more than a little disappointed that he didn't kiss her good night.

CS&O

ON MONDAY MORNING, he comes to her house about ten. She has been watching for his turquoise truck since eight, and when it finally pulls in the driveway, her stomach does the fluttery thing that she's come to associate with his presence. But Annie's mother is home now, so she can't exactly go running out to greet him. Not that she would anyway, but it's nice to think about it. In fact, since Saturday night, she has thought about little else. By noon, when the sun is scorching hot, she can no longer contain herself. She goes to the kitchen and prepares another tray of cookies and lemonade, which she carries out to him without knowing or caring if her mother is watching.

There are four large rose bushes and half a dozen lavender plants sitting in two wheelbarrows by the side of the flowerbed, and Chris has just finished digging four deep holes. He is sweating, and his face is streaked with dirt. Annie wants to touch his face, wipe the dirt away, but instead, she holds out the tray.

"I thought maybe you could use a cold drink," she says. She can smell the lavender.

"You are an angel," he replies, taking the glass from the tray. He drains it in seconds.

"Don't drink too fast, you'll get a stomach ache."

"Can't help it. This is great. Did you make it?"

"It's just a mix. No big deal. Do you want some more?"

"I'd love more," he says. Suddenly, Annie realizes there's an undercurrent in that answer and Chris is looking at her with a devilish grin. She blushes.

"I'll leave the cookies here." She puts the tray on the ground. She takes the glass from his hand and their fingers brush together. Electric shocks run up her arm. "I'll be right back." She has to force herself to walk normally to the house. She would rather run and thinks perhaps she could actually fly. In the house, her mother gives her a startled look as she dashes into the kitchen, whips the lemonade pitcher from the fridge and dashes back to the garden.

"So, you're not working today?" he asks when he's half-way through the second glass of lemonade.

"What? Oh, you mean the hospital volunteer stuff. No, I'm only there three days a week."

He finishes the lemonade, spinning the ice around in the glass. "Yeah, this is probably the last day I'm here. The boss has me over at another place the rest of this week." He pauses, turning his luminous brown eyes to her. "I have Saturday off. I thought I'd go on a hike through Beecham Woods. Would you want to go with me?"

"Yeah. That would be great." She tries to sound casual.

"Good, then. Pick you up about eleven?"

"Sounds good." Annie is thinking: Saturday morning her father will be playing tennis. She hopes her mother will be out, too.

"Okay. Well, I guess I'd better get back to this," he says, nodding at the holes in the ground. "Hey, wait," he says after she's turned away. He bends down, snaps off a sprig of the lavender, and hands it to her.

"Thanks." The delicate perfume of the flower imprints this moment on her memory. She takes the lemonade and cookies back to the house, where her mother looks up from the grocery list she is writing and asks, "What on earth are you doing?"

"Nothing."

"Annie?"

"I was just reading. On the terrace. I thought I wanted some lemonade, but then I changed my mind." She picks up Chris' glass, putting the rim to her lips, hoping she can taste him.

"Hmm." Her mother watches her put the glass in the dishwasher and the pitcher, now half empty, back in the refrigerator, but she says nothing else.

Saturday morning, luck is with Annie. Her father leaves for his usual game of tennis at nine, and her mother announces she has an appointment with her hairdresser and then plans to have lunch at the club. "We'll be out tonight, too, dear," she says. "It's the Birmingham's fortieth anniversary. I don't expect we'll be late, but we do have to make an appearance."

The minute her mother is out the door, Annie changes out of shorts and tennis shoes to jeans and work boots. All those summers at camp taught her better than to go hiking in tennis shoes.

Chris' turquoise truck swings into her driveway at exactly eleven o'clock. When he rings the doorbell, she forces herself to count to twenty before rushing down the stairs to open the door.

He nods with approval at her hiking boots. "You'll need those. There are some rocky parts on the trail that can be tough going."

She follows him to the truck, trying to climb in gracefully as he holds the door open for her. She doesn't want him to know she's never ridden in a truck before. The bench seat is surprisingly uncomfortable and the dashboard is littered with scraps of paper, a screwdriver, sunglasses, and a cassette tape.

It takes twenty minutes to drive out of town to the parking lot at Beecham Woods. When they get out of the truck, Chris pulls a daypack from behind the driver's seat, which he slings over his shoulder. "I brought some stuff to snack on. Nothing fancy, just some cheese and crackers, peanuts, and a couple cans of Coke." They head to the start of the trail.

"Ever been here before?" he asks.

"Once. When I was a kid. It was a school field trip. I think it must have been fifth grade."

"Did you go to McCrady?"

Annie knows McCrady is the public elementary school in Bay River, but she's never set foot in the place. "No, I went to Bay River Day School, then Miss Porter's." He gives her a puzzled look, so she adds, "It's a boarding school in Farmington." There's a moment of silence between them until she asks, "How about you? Did you go to McCrady?"

"No. My dad was in the Navy, so we bounced all over the country. I was always the new kid in school. I don't think we ever stayed more than two years in any one place."

"How did you wind up in Bay River?" Annie asks as they pick up the trail. The path is worn, the earth packed solid and dry, and the branches of the trees arch overhead, creating a cool green tunnel protected from the sun's heat.

"Dad was transferred to Newport when I was a junior in high school. He was high enough in rank that we could live off-base, so Bay River it was. I remember we rented this crazy old house with three floors. There was a widow's walk that ran around the roofline. You could get to it from a trap door in one of the third floor bedrooms, but my brothers and I had to sneak up there because all the floor boards were rotten and my mom was sure we'd fall through and kill ourselves."

Annie is watching where she is going. There are thick, twisting roots and large rocks jutting out of the path. She's not generally clumsy, but it would be so embarrassing to fall on her face.

Chris keeps up a good pace as he goes on to explain that by the time he was in high school, he was fed up with moving, so when his father was transferred again, Chris opted to stay in Bay River. "It was six weeks before graduation, and I had just turned eighteen, so there wasn't much the old man could do about it. That was three years ago and I've been on my own ever since."

The two of them walk in silence for a while, and Annie is aware of an undercurrent of tension. She senses some unmentioned but tangible shadow between Chris and his family. She is also aware of the increasing struggle she is having trying to match his pace as they climb a steep, meandering path to the crest of the ridge. When they reach the top, they sit side by side on an outcropping of rock that looks over a patchwork of farms. Annie feels the sweat trickle down between her breasts. Chris pulls out the Cokes and hands her one. They are still icy cold, and the sweetness is exhilarating. He offers her peanuts from the cardboard can, which she takes, and chocolate, which she declines, but he does not hold her hand or kiss her, which is what she really wants.

"Tell me more about your family," she asks, mostly to distract herself from sensual thoughts.

"There's not much more to tell. My mom died two years ago, my two brothers both joined the Navy. I don't even know where they are now."

"What about your father?"

"The less said about him, the better."

"Oh." She sees a bit of salt from the peanuts on his upper lip and it is almost more than she can stand to keep herself from leaning into him and licking it off. "I don't get along so well with my parents, either."

"Why's that?"

"They're always telling me what to do. Mostly, I think they want me to be like my older sister. She and her husband live in Chicago. My mom just came back from visiting them and all she can talk about is how beautiful their house is, how cute the baby is, blah, blah, blah."

Chris gives her a funny look, a little half-smile that she can't interpret. She doesn't know what to think about him; he's so different from anyone she knows. There's electricity between them, but it's more than just the typical boy-girl attraction. Chris makes her feel grown up. Free.

They sit in silence for another few minutes before he says, "What d'ya say we head back now?"

On the way back down the trail, she puts her hands out as if to keep her balance, really hoping that he will take her one of her hands to hold her steady, but he doesn't. It is only when the car is once again visible down a short, straight, narrow track through the clearing that Chris finally reaches out, twining his long fingers through hers. She smiles at him, and he smiles back, his brown eyes communicating an unspoken message that makes her catch her breath. They walk arm in arm the short way back to the car. Annie thinks of Sleeping Beauty, her favorite childhood fairy tale, because the minute Chris took her hand, she felt an electric current run from her fingers up her arm until it surged over her entire body. She feels as if she has been awakened from a deep sleep and now all around her the colors are brighter and the air is sweeter and sharper and the sounds of the forest are clear, and it seems corny as hell, but she understands the reason for all those sappy songs about love.

They get back to the car and she thinks, *Now. Now he will kiss me,* but he goes about the business of stowing the daypack and throwing the empty Coke cans in the trash. They drive back to her house with only the sound of the radio, each of them absorbed in their own thoughts. He steers the pickup into the driveway and turns to her. "Would you want to go see a movie sometime?" he asks.

It's not quite four in the afternoon. Plenty of time to go to a movie tonight, she thinks, but she doesn't want to sound pushy or rude.

"A movie would be great." Annie's worried that maybe her parents have come home early. She hasn't figured out what she will say if they see her with Chris.

"Um, I guess I'll call you?" He says the words like they are a question instead of a statement. She gives him her phone number—not the main number for the house that he called last Saturday, but another number for her private line, the number to the white Princess-style phone that sits on the table beside her bed. He pulls a pen and a scrap of paper off the dashboard, scribbles down the number, and tucks it in his shirt pocket.

"Okay, then," he says. Annie hears the words as a dismissal, and she wonders why he doesn't at least get out of the car to see her to the door, but all she says is, "Thanks. I had a great time." She scurries out of the car and into the house.

∞

SHE DOESN'T HEAR a word from him all the following week. The phone doesn't ring and Tandy is working alone in the garden. The following Friday is the Fourth of July, and she thinks surely he will call, ask her to go to the fireworks, but the Princess phone sits silently beside her bed. In the days leading up to the holiday, she fantasizes about his phone call. She imagines they will talk for a while, then he will ask if she has any plans for the Fourth, or if she'd like to spend it with him. Annie works out the details of their date. First, they can meet early and go to the American Legion pancake breakfast (she'll be too nervous to actually eat anything). Next, they'll watch the parade go through town and follow it to the park where there is a carnival with rides for little kids and booths selling cotton candy, funnel cakes and hotdogs. There are games where you can try your luck winning live goldfish, troll dolls or toys. Chris will step up to one of those—maybe the one where guys throw baseballs at wooden milk bottles—and he'll win a giant stuffed panda bear for her. After that, they'll share a pizza while they wait for evening to fall and the fireworks to begin.

Annie knows her parents are bemused by the way she answers the main line phone as quickly as possible, sometimes before the first ring tone is finished. Maybe he lost the scrap of paper with her number, she thinks. Each time the main line rings, it's only the dry cleaner, or workmen trying to schedule a time to install the new air conditioner, or some woman from her mother's bridge club. By parade time on the Fourth, Annie is in a foul temper wondering where Chris is, and trying not to think about who he is with. He never said anything about another girlfriend, so she doesn't know what to think. Maybe there's someone else. But if he had a girlfriend, why would he ask Annie to come to Buffo's or go on that walk? Why did he hold her hand, and why did he ask if he could call again? Then again, why didn't he kiss her? Maybe he doesn't like her. Maybe he met someone else since their hike in Beecham Woods. And then she wonders if something bad happened to him. What if he fell off a ladder? Or got hit by a car? There are suddenly so many possibilities for injury that she is overwhelmed with fear and wishes she knew his phone number, or how to contact Pete. She realizes that she doesn't even know Pete's last name, so she can't look for his number in the phone book. She would ask Tandy, except he's nowhere to be seen. While the rest of the world is enjoying parades and picnics and fireworks, Annie sits cross-legged on her bed, playing endless games of solitaire, listening to FM radio, and occasionally tossing evil glances at the uncooperative Princess phone.

 C3&O

ON JULY 9TH, at nine o'clock in the evening, the Princess phone finally rings. Belligerently, she stands looking at the damn thing, refusing to answer until at least the third ring tone.

"Hello?"

"Hey, Annie Charles. It's Chris here. How's it going?"

"Fine." She sounds cold.

"Yeah? You don't sound so good. Am I catching you at a bad time?"

"No," she pauses. She wants to ask where the hell he's been, but instead she hopes he'll just tell her. She asks, "How have you been?"

"Crazy busy. My boss is a maniac. He's got too many customers and not enough workers, but he never says no to anyone. I've been putting in ten-hour days every day for the last week, including the Fourth. But, hey, at least the money's been pretty good, so I'm not complaining too much. It could be a lot worse."

He was working over the holiday? This is something that never occurred to Annie. She likes to think of herself as an intelligent, aware person, and on an intellectual level she knows very well that a lot of people have to work on holidays. Just not anyone she knows in person.

"I have Wednesday off," he says. "Do you want to do something? Maybe we could grab some lunch, take in a movie."

Wednesday. Day after tomorrow. She's supposed to be at the hospital, but she can work a couple of hours in the morning, then make up some excuse to leave early. That will also nicely avoid any problem with her parents; they'll simply assume she's at work all day.

"Sure, Wednesday would be fine."

"You want me to pick you up around noon?"

"Umm, how about meeting me in the hospital parking lot? I'm supposed to work that morning, but I'll be done by noon."

CB&SO

WEDNESDAY DAWNS WARM but rainy. By noon, there's a steady downpour and the streets are gullies of water. Annie is wearing her standard outfit of jeans, a polo shirt (today's is navy blue), and Dr. Scholl's sandals. She watches out the window of the hospital lobby until she sees his turquoise pickup truck pull in the visitor parking lot before she dashes out the door. The wooden soles of the sandals slap through rivulets of water on the asphalt as she jogs through the rainfall toward the truck. By the time she climbs in, the bottoms of her jeans are soaked through and her hair is wet. Safely inside the vehicle, she tosses her hair band on the dashboard and runs splayed fingers through her hair. She looks over at him as he drives the truck out of the parking area, and her breath catches as she feels that rush of excitement all over again. She tries to fight down the sensation, telling herself that even if he's incredibly cute, he's just a guy. No one special. She doesn't want him to be special; he's not even someone she can bring home to her parents. Seeing him is an adventure in a dull summer when her friends aren't around and there is nothing better to do. It's all just a lark.

They drive through town, heading west on Milburne Road, out to the edges of the clustered neighborhoods to where the landscape rolls into the rural quilt beyond the towns, the windshield wipers swiping bravely at the constant rain. He points out the things along the way that matter to him: a magnificent black walnut tree, a two hundred-year-old stone bridge, the section of woods where the Red Coats mistakenly thought a stash of ammunition would be safe from the American rebels. Annie is a little embarrassed and more than a little surprised that his knowledge of history, of the area's natural surroundings, is so much greater than her own. When they reach a decrepit brick building with a signpost that reads "Stage Coach Inn," Chris pulls the truck onto the adjacent gravel apron and parks.

"For an old place, they do pretty decent burgers," he says, "and they don't ask for an I.D. when you order beer."

The two of them jump out of the truck, skitter through the rain, and tumble inside the building. Although it's lunchtime in the middle of the week, the place is almost empty. Chris and Annie sit at a well-worn wooden table against a window. The panes of glass are rippled unevenly and distort the storm clouds shifting and roiling above the woodlands across the road. The waitress brings them thick mugs of beer, which Annie has never had in the middle of the day. It tastes wonderful. They order cheeseburgers and fries and sit talking about everything and nothing for two hours, until Chris points out that if they want to catch a show, they'd better get a move on. He doesn't explain why there is a time limit on the day. Annie doesn't ask. The rain hasn't let up, so they have to run back to the truck. He opens her door, tucks her safely inside, then goes around to the driver's side. After he clambers in, brushing the rain from his hair, he turns to her. She studies his face, mesmerized by the texture of his skin, the shadow of his beard. His teeth are white and even, and his eyes have that magic dancing quality that she loves.

"C'mere," he says, drawing her close. On his lips, Annie tastes the salt from the fries, and the headier flavor of the beer, along with a sort of musky cinnamon that she will later learn to recognize as the taste of Chris. They are late getting to the movie, but Annie doesn't care and can't focus on the story in any case. There are too many other stories playing out in her head. By six o'clock, he returns her to the hospital parking lot, to her car. She hopes her father hasn't noticed that, even though she left work at noon, the car has been sitting in the same place since early morning.

CR80

CHRIS CALLS HER two days later, again late in the evening. He tells her about his day working in the garden of some enormous house where all the flowerbeds had to be dug up and replanted because there was going to be a wedding and the bride wanted all the flowers in the garden to match the colors of her bouquet. Annie doesn't have any interesting stories, so he does most all the talking. He tells her his plan to eventually take over the landscaping firm from Moretti, that the business is worth a fortune, and he will do whatever it takes to own the company one day. She is only vaguely interested in his plans; mostly she is disappointed when they hang up and he hasn't asked her out again. But he has promised to call when work is less demanding. Still, the days tick by with no word, and once again Annie spends too much time sitting in her room playing solitaire. July slides toward the dog days of August, and Mrs. Charles begins making plans to take Annie shopping for school things.

"And then, there's your birthday," Mrs. Charles says one night at dinner when the discussion of school supply purchases has worn itself thin. "I can't believe you will be eighteen in two weeks' time. Is there something special you would like, dear?"

Her parents are both regarding her over the remains of their lobster salad dinner, and the only thing Annie can think of wanting is freedom. She smiles politely and says, "Oh, gosh, I haven't thought about it. How about a trip to Paris?"

Her parents laugh as though that's the most amusing thing they've heard in ages. In theory, they could provide her with that gift, but they are not flamboyant spenders like so many of her school friends' parents. Dr. Charles' income is substantial, but they prefer to spend the money wisely on things they believe are in Annie's best interests. Annie often disagrees with their choices.

The Princess phone rings the following day at three in the afternoon. Annie has just returned from her shift volunteering and she is about to step into a long, cleansing shower. She hates the smell of the hospital and rushes home every afternoon to wash it from her skin, so she is standing in her room, stark naked, when the phone rings. She holds the handset in her left hand while she talks. Again, Chris starts by telling her about his work, the elaborate houses and gardens, the names of plants she cannot visualize. His world is an exotic place in her mind, and he reminds her of a wild creature. If she approaches too boldly, he will run away. She forces herself to hold back, waiting for him to make the first move.

By the time he gets around to asking her if she will meet him and his friends at the beach on Saturday night for a cookout, she is caressing her naked breasts with her right hand, quivering with delicious anticipation. She falls asleep that night thinking of their last kiss, remembering as much detail as she can of every sensory element: the taste, smell, touch, the imagined sight behind her closed eyes of the two of them blended together, entwined like something wonderful in the proverbial garden of delights. Though it is less than forty-eight hours, Saturday seems too far away.

CB&O

HER PARENTS ARE out for the evening when he comes for her, and though she has been watching for his truck from the upstairs landing, and her adrenalin surges when he turns in the driveway, she makes herself wait for him to get out of the truck and ring the doorbell. Once again, she counts to twenty before running down the stairs to open the door.

At the beach, just as the sun has set behind the scrubby grasses and B&Bs that line the coast, Chris leads her to a small group gathered around a fire. A few feet away is a picnic bench on which sits a cooler and some paper grocery sacks. For the last night in July, the air is cool at the shore. There is a good breeze blowing straight off the water, occasionally sending showers of sparks from the flames toward the darkening sky. Chris doesn't bother to introduce her to the others, but she recognizes Pete, who hands her a beer from the cooler.

She and Chris settle on the blanket he has brought from his truck. One of the girls is telling a story about a family camping trip: a bear had come within a few feet of their tent because her little brother had tossed the crusts of his peanut butter sandwich in the woods. The others chime in with their own camping stories. Annie can't imagine camping, especially with her parents. Thinking about her mother sleeping on the ground or peeing in the woods makes her giggle.

"Speaking of food," Pete says, pulling a package of hot dogs from the cooler, "I'm starved."

The girl with the camping story begins rummaging through the paper grocery sacks from which she produces paper plates, packages of chips and hot dog buns, mustard and ketchup. Dinner will be roast-your-own hot dogs over the fire.

"How the hell are we going to cook those things?" someone asks. "Don't we need some sticks or something?"

"Coming right up," Chris volunteers. He and Pete go off to gather roasting sticks.

Left alone with the others, Annie feels out of place. They don't make any effort to include her in their conversation, until one of the girls asks, "How did you manage to bewitch the lone-wolf boy? I don't think I've ever seen Chris bring a date anywhere."

Chris and Pete return before Annie can reply, but she doesn't forget the comment. It is tucked in the back of her mind while the more immediate concern of keeping a hot dog on the stick without dropping it in the fire or burning it to a crisp takes over. It's harder than she imagined to keep the sand off her potato chips and out of the mustard on her hot dog, although she is feeling less awkward with the group. Maybe it's the beer—she's on her second. She adds to the conversation here and there, and admits that she hasn't had a hot dog since she was five or six.

"You're kidding? I bet we have hot dogs for dinner probably three nights a week at my house," one of the boys says.

"I think it's the only thing my mom can cook," says another.

"I only ever got them when I went to my friends' birthday parties," Annie says.

The discussion moves to talk about kids' birthday parties, and then to birthdays. Annie blurts out that her birthday is in early August.

"Yeah? What day?" Chris asks.

"The eighth," she says, feeling awkward again because she thinks she's called too much attention to herself, but no one else seems to notice.

Soon, with the stars glittering over the ocean waves, the conversation simmers down so that the crackle of the fire is the loudest noise around. Chris stands and reaches for Annie's hand. They walk away from the group, unnoticed, or at least unremarked upon. Hand in hand, they follow the crescent of the shoreline until they are far from the others, until the fire is the only marker back to the place from which they came.

Chris stops and turns to her. He traces an imaginary line from her temple to her chin with his index finger, then lifts her chin gently, leaning in to her, cheek to cheek. His face is warm and smooth against hers; his scent, spicy sweet, reminds her of that first kiss. It is so quiet she can hear their breathing. When their lips meet, it is simultaneous, like they both understood the exact moment they should come together. Annie understands the stupid cliché about the earth moving; she worries, briefly, if she will be able to keep her balance, but he holds her, his strength countering her own shaking knees. It is a soul kiss, out under the stars with God and the universe as their witnesses.

"I know a place we could go," he whispers as they break apart for a breath.

She doesn't have to answer. With her hand in his, they retrace their steps on the beach, neither saying a word. They walk up from the shoreline, straight to the turquoise truck, so that Pete and the others won't call out to them and disrupt the intensity of their connection. In the truck, there is only the blue glow from the dashboard, and Chris' occasional glance, his smile, his closeness, as they take off into the night. Ten minutes later, he turns the truck into the driveway of one of the grand estates that dots the coastline.

"They're away," he says, referring to the homeowners. "No one will see us, and besides, we're not going anywhere near the main house. Don't worry. This is where I was working last week. I know the layout."

He parks the truck in the darkened driveway and leads her past the swimming pool, beyond the expanse of the main lawn to a side yard. The first thing Annie sees is an elaborate swing set, but off to one side, there is a playhouse. It is more than an ordinary playhouse. It is the best playhouse a family of considerable means can possibly build for their perfect and wonderful children. It is a playhouse that would put to shame the first homes of most of the people who long ago settled this area. In miniature, the house has a working kitchen, a sitting room with child-sized wingback chairs, and a sleeping loft. Chris leads her up the loft's ladder and they settle together on the soft quilted bedding. When he kisses her, she melts into him with a raw desire that is way beyond her control, and he responds. Every touch is electric, every scent is a thrill, every new and unexplored sensation is a world in itself. In two hours, Annie learns a new language from beginning to breathtaking end, and when they are finished, she wraps herself in a cloak of new understanding, rejoicing in her love, and that she can feel such passion.

C3ED

ON HER BIRTHDAY, her parents take her to Prindle's for dinner. The evening seems endless, all the more because Annie has heard nothing from Chris since that magical night ten days earlier. Dr. and Mrs. Charles order a bottle of Veuve Clicquot in honor of having raised their second child to the brink of adulthood. By law still too young to drink with them, Annie begins by being patiently polite, smiling and tolerating familiar and banal stories of her parents' youth. Inwardly, she is counting the minutes until she can escape to her own new world, certain Chris will call her tonight. But dinner with her parents drags on and on. Feigning pleasure, she accepts their gifts of a rather hideous camel-colored cashmere sweater and a savings bond.

"Never too soon to start a retirement account," her father quips.

Only years of practice—years of playing her part—enable her to endure the long dinner. By the time her parents order coffee, she is inwardly seething. In the car on the way home, she pleads fatigue when her mother asks why she is so quiet, but she jumps out of the car almost before it is parked and races into the house. She can hear the Princess phone ringing as she flies up the stairs, but by the time she reaches it, there is no one on the other end.

Chris finally calls again two days later. "Sorry I missed your birthday," he says, "I did try to call that night."

Annie says she understands, and while she tells him all about the interminable dinner, one tiny corner of her mind is thinking, *You didn't try very hard. I've been home every other night this week. No one spends that much time at work.*

"Would you like to go out again sometime?" he asks.

"Tonight?"

"No, tonight's not good. We're working on a job that'll take most of the week, and I have to be on site at six in the morning.

Next Tuesday might be okay. How about if I call you that night after I get home?"

Annie says that would be fine, even though she's disappointed. It's only half-past eight. She also wonders exactly where "home" is for Chris. Except for the day at Beecham Woods, he's told her almost nothing about his life. Perhaps, she thinks, he's embarrassed. They talk for a few more minutes, but Chris sounds exhausted and Annie doesn't push. She tells herself to be content that he wants to see her again.

♋

IN THE NEXT few days, her parents expect her to spend all her evenings with them since she will be leaving for college soon. She finds it increasingly difficult to bear their attention, and they assume she can't wait to leave, find new friends, and begin her college life. On Tuesday night, when her mother reacts to Annie's sour temper by saying, "Never mind, dear, you'll be off to Tufts in just a few days," it is brought home to her with suddenness and clarity that her time with Chris is finite. She begins to shake. She retreats to her room without finishing dinner, and when the Princess phone rings, she grabs it.

"Hi," is all she says, the casualness in her voice completely fabricated.

"Hi, yourself," he responds. "What are the chances you can get out tonight?"

"Chances are good, but not until late. My parents are driving me crazy, but I think I can sneak out after they are asleep. I could meet you at the end of the driveway. Is midnight too late?"

They both understand without having to talk about it why subterfuge is necessary.

"Midnight it is. I'll be there."

Annie creeps down the back stairs at eleven-fifty, prepared with a story about leaving her book outside on the terrace if a parent should catch her. Chris' turquoise truck is already behind the screening arborvitae at the driveway's end; the lights are off, but the motor is idling quietly. She opens the passenger door and he reaches over to her, pulling her in close to him.

"Hey, sweetheart," he says, and her heart melts at being called "sweetheart." He kisses her cheek before putting the truck in gear and drifting noiselessly down the street. He seems to know where they are going. A few minutes later, he turns the truck into a church parking lot, sliding into the shadows deep in a tree-bordered corner.

"This is one of the few places in town where the cops don't come snooping around a parked vehicle," he says, shutting off the engine. Briefly, she wonders how he knows this, but she is distracted by his scent. Sweet and spicy at the same time, it is not store-bought cologne, but his natural aroma and completely intoxicating to her.

Maneuvering expertly around the steering wheel, he turns toward her. For a few minutes, they talk about things that Annie will never remember. Finally, he lightly kisses her hand, which he has been holding.

"You are beautiful," he says before his mouth moves to her lips. Again, they kiss, not lightly this time, but a deep, sensual kiss that sends shock waves through her body so that all she wants is for them to return to that playhouse of two weeks ago, or to go someplace, any place where they can make love.

"Okay, we'd better slow down," he says, pulling away from her. In the dim light from the street, she can see the wetness on his lips of their combined saliva, more erotic than repulsive.

"Hey, I got you a present." He reaches over her, opens the glove compartment, and takes out a small package wrapped in blue paper. There is a gold sticker on top embossed with "Once Upon A Time Antiques." Annie unwraps the box with shaking hands. Inside is a necklace, a small pendant. A stone of some sort hangs from a simple golden chain.

Chris turns on the truck's overhead light so she can see the stone is a deep red, the color of wine.

"It's a garnet," he says. "So you'll remember me."

Chris Garnet. She wouldn't have forgotten his name.

"It's beautiful. Thank you," she says. There's so much more she wants to say. He takes the necklace from the box and fastens it around her neck, then traces a line with his finger from where the chain rests on her shoulder to the stone resting against her skin two inches from the base of her throat.

"Whenever you look at this, think of me," he says.

"Do you think I might forget you?"

"You're leaving for college in, what? About three days?"

"Next week."

He nods, his lips pressed tightly together. Annie is desperate to hold onto him.

"Tufts isn't very far from here," she says. "You could come visit, you know."

He looks at her. "Mmm. I guess I could do that. You wouldn't mind?"

"I'd love it. I mean, it would be perfect. No parents keeping track of my every move, tons of stuff to do. We'd have a ball."

"Yeah, we sure would," he says, laughing. She picks up on the innuendo.

She laughs, too, giving him the naughtiest look she can manage. He ruffles her hair, kisses her again, and twists in his seat so he is once more behind the steering wheel.

"I'd better get you back home before we get into trouble here," he says. He starts the truck's engine.

Annie's elation crashes into disappointment. "So soon?"

"It's almost two in the morning."

She wonders what happened to two hours, how they could vanish so incredibly quickly. It isn't fair, but she knows he's right.

"Will I see you again?" she asks as they are approaching her house.

"Of course. I'm coming to visit you, remember?"

"I meant before I leave."

"I'm not sure what my schedule will be like. I'll try."

Annie's first reaction is anger. What can he possibly have on his "schedule" that's more important? Why did he waste so much time in the last two weeks? They drive back to her house in silence. Chris parks the truck in the street, keeping the engine idling softly.

"Do you promise you'll come see me?" she tries not to sound whiny.

"I promise."

Both of them know it would not be wise to linger, so one quick kiss, and Annie, who is fighting tears, opens her door.

"Hey, how do I find you at Tufts?" Chris asks. "It's kind of a big place."

"Hill Hall. Room 240." She closes the door as quietly as she can, then runs up the driveway. Half way to the house, she realizes that she has forgotten to thank him again for the necklace. She spins around to run back to the truck, but he has already pulled away, the sound of the engine fading into the night. Safely back in the house, she is in a turmoil of conflicting emotion: love and anger, hope and fear. Has she started something, or is it finished already?

⊗≫

IN THE DAYS ahead, these questions don't go away. They hide in her head, multiplying, running furtively through her conscious thoughts like bandits in the night. She tries to concentrate on the world in front of her, on the immediate and important considerations of her life. She finishes packing for college, helps her father load all her things into the station wagon, and sits quietly in the back seat of the car while her parents drive her to school. Nothing feels real. The journey from Bay River to Medford takes less time than she remembers from her visit last year because the questions take over. What has she done? What has happened to her? She tells herself she is not troubled by having slept with Chris, that she has no regrets. Quite the contrary, she thinks, reliving the night in the playhouse over and over in her imagination. She refuses to consider that she might never see him again; he has promised to come see her at school. She touches the garnet pendant at her throat. No, what troubles her is that she is caught up in something she doesn't understand, some powerful force of nature that will have its way with her. It reminds her of the time she went body surfing in California and got caught up in a huge wave that turned her over and over, disorienting her, scraping her knees and elbows against the rough sand on the ocean floor, finally washing her up on the beach, gasping and battered. She knows something will happen to her because of Chris, but she can't quite work out what it will be.

⊂⅋⊃

ANNIE MEETS HER roommate, Nelia Brown, a pretty, blue-eyed girl from Chicago, and they set up their dorm room, go to freshman orientation activities, learn their way around Medford, and find their way to their first parties and first classes in equal measure.

Nelia, who is even smarter than she is pretty, takes less than twenty-four hours in Annie's company to figure things out.

"What's his name?" she asks out of the blue on the afternoon of their second day together. They are sitting in the cafeteria; everyone else they were having lunch with has gone off to various activities.

Annie debates whether or not to divulge anything. "Chris," she says a minute later.

"Do you want to talk?"

"Not especially."

"Okay. Let me know if you change your mind." Nelia sweeps up her empty lunch tray, and Annie sits, poking her straw at the ice in her half-empty glass of cola, wondering what she could possibly say even if she did want to talk.

Classes begin and a rhythm of life is established. Annie finds her way in her new world, but much of the time she is thinking: *what if, what if?* She goes through each day feeling as though there is something she has forgotten to do, something she has misplaced, something she is waiting for. Over and over, she double checks to make sure she has the key to her room, her wallet, her student I.D. She triple checks her calendar to be certain that she hasn't forgotten a class or an assignment. She dutifully phones her parents every Sunday evening at eight.

Over the next few weeks, Nelia never asks about Chris, but Annie finds herself volunteering information: she likes hot dogs if, and only if they are cooked over an open fire, preferably on the beach; she knows how to play eight-ball, and once she almost ran an entire table; lavender grows best in sandy soil; Chris drives a pickup truck that's the wildest turquoise color.

"Turquoise? Not plain or blue or green?"

"No, it's definitely turquoise, like that bracelet you wear."

"Cool," Nelia says, twisting the turquoise and silver cuff on her left wrist. "My parents bought this for me when we were in Arizona last year. I've never ridden in a truck."

"I never had either, until this summer. It's not very comfortable, especially for making out," Annie giggles. "Oh, and speaking of jewelry, he gave me this." She pulls the garnet necklace from under her shirt. "I wear it every day."

Annie and Nelia become popular with the other girls in the dorm. Their room is often a gathering place, a social core, so that they have to close the door if they are trying to sleep or study.

The two of them sit cross-legged on their Indian batik print bedspreads. The Eagles' "Hotel California" emanates from Annie's cassette player. Strawberry incense burns in a thick glass ashtray, its heady odor wafting through the room in casual disregard of dorm rules. They're supposed to be studying, but the door to their room is open and soon Carol and Joannie stroll in, Joannie making herself comfortable on the beanbag chair, Carol on the floor, her back against Nelia's bed.

"There's a party over on Curtis Street. You guys want to go?" Carol asks.

"Sorry," says Nelia, "I have a paper due tomorrow that I haven't even started."

"No thanks," Annie adds.

"Come on, Annie," says Joannie, "Chris won't mind if you go to one little party."

It sounds odd to hear someone else say his name, but Annie likes the sensation of connectedness it gives her. Here, people link his name with hers. It's easy to pretend she and Chris are a couple.

CഏED

ON THE LAST Saturday in September, Annie and Nelia are sitting in their dorm room. It is early evening, and it has been raining all day. They are both working at their desks when the phone rings. Nelia saunters over, picking it up on the fourth ring.

"Hello?" Pause. "Sure, just a sec." She holds the receiver out to Annie. "For you."

Annie figures it's her mother again, so she's totally unprepared to hear Chris' voice.

"Hey, sweetheart. How's college?"

"Chris?!"

Nelia is smiling at her, giving her a thumbs up. She gathers her books and slips out of the room.

"The old dragon-lady down here won't let me past the lobby."

"What? What do you mean?"

"I mean I'm down here in the lobby of your dorm, hoping you will invite me up to your room."

"Here? You're here? Now?" Annie's glad she washed her hair that morning and bothered to put on makeup, but she's wearing her most hideous top and a pair of jeans that make her ass look really fat. "I'll be right down," she says. She sets a land speed record for changing clothes, cramming the discards into her over-stuffed laundry hamper.

The elevator takes forever. She's sure she could have run down the six flights of stairs much faster, but then the door finally opens, and she sees him in the lobby like some wonderful apparition she has conjured. His back is to her as he stands reading posters pinned to the wall. A shimmer runs through her whole body like an electric current.

"Hey."

He turns to her and his magic brown eyes draw her in. He looks so foreign in this space; it is taking her time to believe that he is really here, and not just some figment of her imagination. After all the zillions of times she has, in her longing for him, envisioned him with her, she is not sure she should believe her eyes. But then he wraps his arms around her. She sinks into him, into his spicy sweet scent. And in that first embrace, she understands that this is what she has been waiting for. In all the days and nights since she last saw him, she has felt off-balance, but now the world seems steady.

His first words are not the romantic declarations of her dreams but, "I'm starving. Is there any place around here we can grab some food? I didn't get off work until noon, and by the time I got cleaned up, I had to get on the road if I wanted to beat traffic and be here before you went out with some other guy."

Together, they run outside through the pouring rain to the familiar turquoise truck and Annie directs him to Gallarda's where they order a fourteen-inch pepperoni pizza. He wolfs down half of it in record time, but Annie can only nibble at the edges of one small piece. Her mind is racing, hoping the hours ahead will bring every wonderful thing she has imagined.

Back at her dorm, Hill Hall, she warns him that he might get a ticket if he parks in the lot reserved for upperclassmen, but he does it anyway. "I'll take my chances. It's still raining. Besides, we've got better things to do than spend twenty minutes looking for a parking place."

It occurs to Annie that she will have to sneak him into her room. According to the dorm rules, men aren't allowed past the main floor, and a graduate student is always posted at the reception desk, within sight of the elevator and staircase, to ensure no one violates the rules. The girls of Hill Hall have, however, mastered ways to get their boyfriends upstairs. More than a few times, Annie has helped by distracting whoever is at the desk while a young man quietly slips into the elevator.

Now, inside the building, she and Chris walk boldly into the main lounge, straight past reception, where the fat, pimple-faced grad on desk duty is nose-deep in a huge textbook. Nelia and three other girls from their floor are sprawled on the sofas in front of the television watching *Marcus Welby, M.D.* A half-empty bowl of popcorn and soda cans litter the low table between them. Annie takes Chris over to the group and introduces him.

"Anyone up for a convoy?" Annie asks a few minutes later. It is the code for the combination of distraction and usher service the girls use to get the boys past the residential proctor guarding access to the upper floors.

"You bet," says Carol. "Let's go."

Getting past the proctor, whose nose is buried in a book, is easy, and the corridor on Annie's floor is empty. No one sees the little group slip into her room.

Once there, Nelia looks pointedly at the other two girls and says, "Who's going to host the party?"

"What party?" Joannie asks, and Annie sees Nelia nudge her.

"You know what party. That slumber party that we all agreed we'd have when there are guests here from out of town. I think it might be Carol's turn."

"Sure. Everyone's invited to my room," Carol says.

"What are you guys talking about?" Joannie asks.

"Joannie, don't be so thick. We went to the same kind of party last weekend when Joe was here," Beth adds.

"Oh…yeah," Joannie says, "*that* party."

"Yeah, we'll definitely be out all night long," Nelia says. "I'm sure I won't get back here until, say, nine o'clock tomorrow morning. In fact, I'll just grab my stuff and we can go."

It is this night that will, for the rest of Annie's life, define love. It is the night when the darkness vibrates with color, candles fill the tiny room with starlight, and the rain drumming at the window is the music of the spheres.

Then, just before the light of the new day, she is wakened from a sleep of pure joy.

"I have to go, sweetheart," Chris whispers.

"What time is it?"

"A little past five." He is sitting on the edge of the narrow bed.

Annie props herself up on one elbow and brushes her hair out of her eyes. "Five? Why do you have to leave now? Nelia promised she won't be back until at least nine."

He cups her chin in his hand, kisses her lips lightly. "It's nothing to do with Nelia. I have to get back to work. Moretti asked me to head the crew at Beachfield House and we're supposed to start work at eight today."

"But it's Sunday."

"Doesn't matter. The job has to get done." He smiles at her.

"Look at it as just one more day for me to get a little closer to taking over Moretti's." He pulls his tee-shirt on. "Hey, I forgot to tell you that the boss has promised me a pretty good promotion. He knows I want to run the whole operation someday, and he's been giving me more responsibility. This job at Beachfield is a really good chance to prove myself. I can't blow it." He has finished dressing, and he stands, pulling on his jacket.

"I'm going to make this work," he says. Then he kneels at the edge of the bed and takes her hand in both of his. He is looking right into her soul as he says, "I have to make this work. I'm going to own that company and make tons of money, so when I go to your daddy and ask if I can marry you, he won't throw me out the door. And once we're married, I'm going to buy us a huge house, and we'll fill it with kids." He brushes a strand of hair off her face. "I want to give you the world, sweetheart. Go back to sleep now and dream about that." He kisses her once more. Then, before she can argue, he slips out the door.

9
ANNE

ANNE SAT BACK on her heels, surveying the newly planted lavender, then looked around and realized it must be quite late in the day. She was tired and she knew she looked a mess. Her hands were caked with dirt, there were smudges of earth on her face, and beneath her classic headband, her hair was in disarray. She stood, rubbing the pain in her back with her knuckles, stretching cautiously. Neither as supple nor as strong as she used to be, the physical manifestations of aging bothered her more than she would ever admit. Sometimes in her darker moments, she believed she had already lived far too long.

"'It is a tale told by an idiot…',," she muttered the quote to herself and used anger to push off the threatening blanket of depression. She picked up the shovel, gathered the empty black plastic pots, and headed toward the greenhouse in search of Mr. Tandy so she could ask him to water the new plants; she had had enough.

Late afternoon sun was cutting obliquely through the trees, casting the last of the day's light on the lavender. Anne sighed, a soulful sound on the edge of a cry, then straightened her shoulders. Tandy would take care of the cleanup. He was good at such things.

All those years ago, he had been the only one to recognize the wicked combination of youthful folly and capricious fate in which young Annie had been caught. Her parents, unforgiving and unrelentingly furious, had "arranged things," including the recruitment of Mr. Tandy to drive her all the way to Rainbow House, a discreet shelter for unwed mothers outside Akron, Ohio. Several months later, Tandy was sent once again to drive her back to Bay River. He had witnessed her grief and had kept her secret. For more than three decades, his unobtrusive presence remained her only connection to the past, and he understood better than anyone why the vivacious, winsome, young Annie was gone forever. But Anne, hardened to the very core of her being, had survived.

It was time to go back in the house. She would have a long, hot shower and a glass or two of wine. First thing in the morning, she would have to call Bella Dona Salon to see if she could get a last minute appointment for a manicure. Her hands were an absolute mess. She drew in one more deep breath of the sweet smell of the loamy earth and lavender before turning away.

10
SYLVIA

AT THE TEABURY Golf and Country Club, Sylvia pulled her Audi into the parking space across from her mother's Mercedes, and scanned the parking lot for Pier's car. He had a black BMW, almost identical to Jen's. It was the car Sylvia would have preferred, but her parents had bought the silver Audi S5 for her without bothering to ask what she wanted. They hadn't even asked what color she liked. Typical.

She and her parents were meeting Pier and his parents here for dinner to discuss the wedding plans. There were two country clubs in town, but this one was older, more exclusive, and much more expensive than the Eastside Club. It was referred to by its members merely as "*the* club," thereby implying a distinct superiority over any other sort of club.

So much for environmental green in this group, Sylvia thought, observing that among the seven of them, they had arrived in five cars. Pier had driven down from Boston, while his parents and sister came from their home less than a mile away. Henry Bennett had been at the club since early morning. It was customary for him to play a round of golf, have lunch in the Men's Grill, and squeeze in another afternoon round. Today, instead of going home, he'd simply showered and changed in the locker room before joining his wife and guests for cocktails. Sylvia had planned to ride with her mother, but decided at the last minute to stop in town for a few things, and now she was running late. Oh, well. She supposed, as the bride, she could get away with arriving after everyone else.

She tiptoed her way across the gravel driveway to the main entrance, trying to avoid getting pebbles caught in the thin-strapped, open-toed heels she wore. The August evening was still and muggy, and beneath the sheer silk of her dress, Sylvia was aware of an uncomfortable sheen of perspiration. She didn't want to be here tonight. All day, she had been wondering what would happen when the two mothers came face to face. Both sets of parents had lived in Teabury for years, and the women were acquainted, but they traveled in different social circles. Moira Kent made no secret of her eagerness to change that circumstance through this marriage, but she had no idea what she was up against. What Sylvia envisioned when she considered the possible outcomes was something akin to a small, ferocious terrier prancing straight into a tiger's cage.

In the last few weeks, Sylvia had seen her mother take an uncharacteristic interest in the wedding plans. The woman who had rarely concerned herself with any of her daughter's activities decided that the reception should be at the club. She booked dress fittings, cake tastings and meetings with photographers. She arranged tonight's dinner, ostensibly to provide a chance for the Kent family to see the venue. Unsure how to react to such attention, and indifferent to the wedding details, Sylvia allowed plans to be made for her. In her more cynical moments, she believed her mother's involvement was a deliberate attempt to undermine the event. With all the possible places for a reception, including Wheatley House, why would she choose the club? Sylvia was certain the decision was calculated to remind everyone that the Bennetts, not the Kents, belonged to Teabury.

She walked through the open door into the foyer, nodding an acknowledgement to the tuxedoed doorman, Fred, who was as standard a fixture in the place as the walnut paneling. She strode across the deep crimson carpet inlaid with the club's ubiquitous insignia of golf clubs crossed over the letter T. The third door on the right led her to the library, which contained no books but was the preferred place for small private parties to have a quiet drink before dinner. The room was decorated in a traditional New England manner: dark, uneven wood floors, chintz covered settees, and brass hinged butler tables.

"Sorry I'm late," she said, breezing in with her best attempt at looking cheerful. The rest of them—her parents, Pier, his parents and his seventeen-year-old sister, Lacey—were sitting around a small coffee table. This evening, they were the only group in the library.

"Darling. So glad you are here," said Sylvia's mother. Without actually saying it, she had clearly implied the word "finally" at the end of the sentence. As usual, Anne looked coolly elegant in a simple aqua-toned sheath dress and pearl choker. Sylvia chose to ignore her mother's tone, accepting instead a brief hug from her fiancé.

Both fathers, wearing nearly identical blue sport coats, stood up to greet her, and she dutifully accepted their embraces. She leaned down to kiss the air beside the cheek of her future mother-in-law. Moira Kent's midnight blue cocktail dress was so deeply cut that Sylvia, standing over her, could see her lace bra quite clearly. She was an attractive woman, but not as youthful as she tried to appear. Though her figure was still excellent, her skin had the leathery quality of too many hours on a tennis court. Her hair, shiny and cut in a fashionable bob, was raven black—several shades too dark for a woman of her age.

Sylvia took the empty chair next to Pier, and Clark, a waiter who had been at the club almost as long as Fred, appeared with a vodka tonic for her. Without having to ask, the staff of the club knew every member's cocktail preference.

"This is such a lovely room," said Moira. Her eyes gleamed as she scanned the room from its polished floors to its walnut paneled walls accented with soft-hued watercolors of fox hunting scenes. "Of course, we've been here before, but the last time was several years ago. John Cole's 50th, I think. Wasn't that it, dear?"

Pier's father, Pierson Kent III, swirled the scotch in his glass, clinking the ice cubes gently. "Haven't a clue. I was here last spring for a golf tournament. Chase Bank. Nice afternoon, but the back nine of the course here is a little flat for my tastes. I have to say, I prefer Eastside. We've been members there for twenty years."

"What's your handicap?" Sylvia's father asked, launching the two men into a golf conversation. The others pretended for a few minutes that they were interested in golf statistics, but soon Lacey took her cell phone from the small purse at her side, flipped it open, and transported herself to the world of texting. Anne made a face of disapproval that only her daughter saw.

"Sylvia, did we tell you that the bridesmaids' dresses arrived the other day?" Moira said, pulling her chair closer to the coffee table. She reached daintily for a cashew from the silver bowl in the table, the large diamond of her wedding ring flashing dramatically in the mote-speckled shaft of evening sunlight that slanted through the room. "Lizzie hasn't seen hers yet, because, of course, she's still in Italy, but Lacey modeled her dress for me, and it's just adorable."

Sylvia wasn't thrilled with the style or color of the dress. Her mother had ordered it straight from the newest line at *Saison D'Amour*, but the off-the-shoulder pink lace over an A-line gown of pink satin looked to her like something out of the 1980s.

Lacey, without interrupting her texting, echoed her mother's opinion. "I love it; it's *so* cute. It's like, wow, I might even wear it again after the wedding. And pink is so my favorite color."

"At least someone likes it," Sylvia said. She twisted the ruby engagement ring around on her finger; she was unaccustomed to its presence and found it slightly annoying. "Jen—she's my maid of honor—hates it."

"Did she actually tell you she hated it? How very rude," Moira said.

"It wasn't rude, really. She was just being honest."

"Well, I suppose you can't please everyone."

"I must say, I'm not surprised Jen didn't care for the dress," Anne interjected. "She is rather heavy, as I recall. The cut would not be flattering and pink will only make her look even more… well, porcine. Frankly, Sylvia, I don't know what you were thinking when you asked her to be in this wedding."

"Mother, she's my best friend. I want her in my wedding."

"But you hardly ever see this supposedly best friend anymore."

"That's not true. I saw her just a few months ago." With a flash of spitefulness, she added, "Remember, Mother? I told you all about that trip I took to Chicago." The satisfaction of seeing her mother flinch slightly gave Sylvia a delightful rush of power.

Anne recovered herself, offering her daughter a stiff little tightening of the lips that was nowhere near a smile. "Well, I suppose you felt you had to ask someone. After all, it's not as though you have a lot of friends."

Meeting Anne's granite eyes with a defiant glare, Sylvia replied, "You know, come to think of it, there *is* another other person I'd like to have stand up with me," she said.

"Another bridesmaid? How absurd." Anne understood and confronted the challenge. "It's such a small wedding; it will look ridiculous with more than half a dozen people parading down the aisle. As your future sisters, Lacey and Liz are certainly appropriate attendants, but any more than that and the bridal party will outnumber the guests."

"You're so right, Mother. I do like the idea of asking *sisters* to be part of the big day."

Anne glared malevolently at her daughter, then turned her back. To Moira, she said, "Tell me, when does your older daughter get back to the States? She must be having such a wonderful time. Florence is one of my very favorite places in the world."

"Liz will come home for the wedding, but she's spending the whole year in Italy," said Moira, putting her empty wine glass on the coffee table, along with her paper cocktail napkin, which she had twisted into a tight little wad.

"And I'm going over to stay with her right after graduation," Lacey added. She had closed her phone, but held it reverently in her lap with both hands.

"We're still thinking about that, dear," said Moira.

The girl sprawled in her chair, twisted her face into a pinched, belligerent expression, and whined like a two-year-old. "Mother, I am *so* going. Lizzie said I could."

"Lacey, please...." Moira began.

Anne, lifting her empty champagne flute toward Clark for a refill, interrupted, "Well, I hope you agree that having the reception here at the club simplifies everything. The food is generally acceptable, and there's quite a lovely view from the terrace. If the weather is warm enough, we can serve cocktails there before dinner, but of course, one never knows what the temperatures will be like in October."

Sylvia, bored, tuned out of the chitchat, downed half her drink in a couple of gulps and studied her groom, who also looked bored. In two months, they would be married. Pier was nice enough, she supposed, but she wondered what it would be like to actually live with him. Did she *love* him? After they got engaged, she had planned to move in with him, but somehow that hadn't happened. For one thing, even though she often spent the night at his place, he hadn't encouraged her to move her possessions to his apartment.

Pier was fussy about his space—he disliked clutter and got testy with her if she left her toothpaste on the bathroom counter or her coffee mug on the living room table. He also pointed out, and she agreed, that reverse commuting from Boston to her job here in Teabury would have been a colossal pain in the butt. Then, her father began talking about buying them a little house somewhere between Boston and Teabury as a wedding gift. Moving twice in the space of a few months would be silly, they agreed. Pier looked over at her and smiled. It was not an I-love-you smile, just a friendly acknowledgment.

Clark brought a second round of drinks for everyone and announced that their table in the dining room was ready whenever they cared to be seated.

"Shall we?" said Henry Bennett, rising. The seven of them meandered toward the dining room, the two sets of parents in the lead, Lacey trailing far behind, her attention focused once more on her phone.

"Now, let's think about seating," said Anne. "Pier Senior, you come sit beside me. Sylvia, you are on his other side. Moira, you take the place on Sylvia's left, then Henry, Lacey, and young Pier on my right. Lovely."

They all sat down to a dinner of roast lamb, rice pilaf, and green beans, all of which tasted like cardboard to Sylvia. Her earlier lethargy had evaporated, and in spite of the vodka, or maybe because of it, she was feeling a nervous energy, a kind of subdued tension. The various attempts at conversation amongst the two families sounded strained and were as bland as the meal. The Kents were remodeling their kitchen—such a headache, complained Moira, especially since the contractor was an absolute moron. Sylvia couldn't care less. Lacey was interrogated by the adults regarding her college plans, which she used as an opportunity to continue her campaign to go to Italy. Sylvia stifled a yawn. Henry Bennett ordered four bottles of wine for the table and launched into a long story about the trials of traveling through India and the difficulties of finding decent wine there. She'd heard the story before. The tight mask of polite interest on her mother's face indicated that Anne was also barely enduring Henry's tedious narrative.

"India's definitely not a place I'd ever want to go," Pier said. "Way too many people and absolutely filthy."

This was the only contribution he'd made to conversation all evening. It was such an obvious attempt to toady up to her father. Sylvia sipped her wine and wondered if Pier ever did anything without analyzing how the outcome would bring him some kind of advantage. She pushed her food around the plate without actually taking a single bite, and attempted to mollify herself by knocking back quite a bit of wine on top of the vodka she'd already consumed. Far from decreasing her restlessness, the alcohol only increased the edgy feeling until it began to ferment into full-blown frustration.

"India has its charms," Henry continued, "but a first-rate hotel and a reliable guide are essential. Anne, what was the name of that hotel we liked?"

"The Taj Lake Palace."

"Yes, that's it. Very nice. Two thousand a night, but the service was good and the views were spectacular."

Sylvia allowed herself a small smirk; she enjoyed watching her parents take the wind out of Pier's pandering. While her father droned on about the rooftop restaurant and the night lights of the Palace, her thoughts wandered back to Stone's Throw. She tried to imagine what Callie and Brad might be doing. Most likely, there were "regulars" gathered at the bar and tourists filling the tables, everyone clamoring to order food and drinks. She wondered, too, about Mike. When she'd traveled around the coastline with him, the world seemed full of endless and fascinating possibilities. Even the most mundane places and events—and what could be more mundane than a Holiday Inn Express breakfast?—were exciting when he was around. For a split second, she considered calling him to see if he would be available to take her wedding pictures, but that felt completely wrong. She wanted to spend time in his company, not hire him to work for her.

While the raspberry Pavlova was being served, Henry asked his future son-in-law if plans had been finalized yet for the honeymoon.

"They have," Pier answered, which was news to Sylvia.

"Well? Are you going to keep it a big secret or do we get to know where you two are going?" asked Moira.

"Hey, there are no secrets in this group," Pier IV said. "I've booked a week at the Gran Melia in Cancun."

No secrets? Pier was so clueless it made her want to scream. How could he not see all the pretensions, lies, and deceits that festered under the surface of her perfect, perfect family?

She was so focused on the irony of Pier's comment that it took a minute for the rest of the information to register. "Cancun? As in Mexico? I thought we were going to Fiji."

Casually scraping at a bit of raspberry glaze on his plate, Pier replied, "I know we'd talked about Fiji, but I like Cancun better. It's closer and it's half the price."

"But I don't want to go to Mexico. I hate Mexico. I hate the food, I hate the music, and you can't even drink the water." Sylvia's voice rose steadily so that she ended on an almost frantic note. Everyone at the table was watching her. Lacey's smirk was full of wicked delight; her father looked as though he was about to choke on his wine. Pier was stone-faced. Anne simply arched one slim eyebrow.

"Sylvia, dear," she said calmly and slowly as though she might be talking to a very stupid person, "you've never actually been to Mexico."

"I don't care. I don't want to go, especially for my honeymoon."

"Sylvia, I think we have to go," Pier said without making eye contact. "I've already sent the hotel a down payment. We're committed to the trip now."

Sylvia gazed around the table at the six people who were supposed to be her closest family. Clearly, each of them expected her to settle down and be a good girl, but just at that moment she felt something loosen and break inside her. It was as if a wall of ice that had been around the very core of her being shattered and fell away. She pushed back her chair, and stood, throwing her linen napkin with the embroidered Teabury Golf Club insignia down into the remnants of her raspberry Pavlova.

"No," she said, "*we* don't have to go. *We* don't have to do anything. I'm tired of all this bullshit. No one gives a crap about me or what I think; you all just go on your merry little way, doing whatever you want to do, making plans for me, and you expect me to follow along."

She pulled the ruby ring off her finger and tossed it onto Pier's plate where she noticed how its color clashed against the purer red of the raspberry juice.

"I'm out of here," she said. She turned and glared over her shoulder at Pier. "Oh, and by the way, you're dead wrong if you think there are no secrets in this group."

11
CALLIE

After Sylvia left Cedar Beach, the routine at Stone's Throw returned to almost normal. Business had picked up with the start of the tourist season. The tavern was still on shaky financial ground, but the bills were getting paid. Barely. There was still something screwy with the accounts payable. Callie would be the first to admit she didn't have the greatest head for numbers, but there were days when she couldn't come anywhere close to reconciling the balance sheets. Purchase orders were up, too, but the profit margin was down, which didn't make any sense. She made an appointment with Barry Lee, their accountant, without mentioning her concerns to Brad, since he'd just use it as an opportunity to bitch. Lately, she did whatever she could to avoid confrontation. Brad was stressed, too. The tight budget, long hours and late nights were taking their toll. She wished he'd talk to her, but in typical guy fashion, he just clammed up, becoming uncharacteristically snappish if pressed. Anything he couldn't fix immediately with a screwdriver and duct tape sent him off in a snit, which was exactly what Callie didn't need.

About the only bit of good news was that Ethan was back to his usual rambunctious self. On the morning of her appointment with Barry, he'd wakened her early by standing at the side of her bed demanding waffles for breakfast. She left Brad sleeping while she and Ethan went to the kitchen. The child zoomed around the kitchen doing his best Buzz Lightyear imitation while she stuck Eggos in the toaster.

"Wash your hands," she said.

"They aren't dirty."

"Wash your hands, Buster, and don't argue or there'll be big trouble." Callie tried to sound stern, but it was so good to see the boy active again. They both knew her threats were empty. He drank all his milk, ate three waffles as fast as she could put them on the plate, and made an unsuccessful bid for a Popsicle for "dessert."

"Go upstairs, get dressed, and don't forget to brush your teeth," she said, smiling as she watched the sturdy five-year-old stretching to climb the stairs two at a time.

Callie tidied the kitchen and fortified herself with toast and coffee. When she returned to the apartment, she began pulling together the paperwork she would need for her meeting with Barry, double-checking the figures from last year with those from this year, hoping she'd be able to pinpoint any significant differences. While she was working, Ethan found an old tennis ball and made a game of bouncing it down the back stairs, racing to try to catch it before it rolled in the kitchen. The racket drove her to distraction.

"Ethan! Stop it!" she yelled.

"I'm bored. I want to go outside. I want to go to the park. You said we could go to the park," he yelled back.

"Hey, what's going on here?" Brad stood, shirtless and tousle-haired at the bedroom door.

"Would you take this wild child out to run off some steam? I'm trying to get some work done."

"Yeah, Dad, come on! Momma promised I could go to the park."

"Okay, okay. Give me five minutes."

"One-two-three-four-five. Let's go," Ethan said, grabbing Brad's hand.

Callie stifled a giggle and refocused on her work.

An hour later, sitting across from the accountant, she was no longer smiling. Barry said he couldn't prove anything, but the P&L statements over the past six months showed a disturbing trend. The tavern was losing money in part because they were buying more liquor and dry goods than they were selling.

"Are you stockpiling for some reason?" he asked.

"No."

"Then, unfortunately, you need to consider employee theft. It's a huge problem in the restaurant business. Any chance someone's ripping you off?"

"Absolutely not. You know it's only me, Brad, and Alyssa working there," Callie answered.

"Callie, all I can do is tell you what the numbers say, but if I were you, I'd be keeping a close eye on that girl."

"It must be something else, Barry. Something we haven't seen yet. Are you sure there's not some way the computer could be screwing up? Maybe doubling expense entries? Or maybe the automatic bank charges are messed up?"

He gave her the same sort of look she gave Ethan when he was being particularly silly.

Oddly enough, as Callie drove along the flat rural road toward home, Alyssa Linn's bright red Miata flew past like all the demons of hell were after her. Speak of the devil, Callie thought, immediately feeling ashamed of herself for allowing Barry's suspicions to influence her. Alyssa had been with them for over a year. Callie trusted her with Ethan, for God's sake. Still, it didn't make sense that she'd be anywhere near Stone's Throw on a Monday morning. The past few weeks, the girl had a hard enough time getting to work when she was supposed to be there, let alone going near the place on her day off. Mulling it over, Callie determined that Alyssa must have stopped by trying to get an advance on her paycheck. She'd be out of luck on that one, especially since she'd have had to ask Brad.

Callie parked the car at the back of the tavern. It was good to see Ethan playing outside, scrabbling around in the muddy bit of grass that served as their backyard. She'd have some grubby clothes to deal with later, but it was worth it to see him acting normal again.

Inside, Brad was refilling the syrup container on the soft drink dispenser. "Hey, babe, what'd Barry have to say?" he asked without looking up from his work.

"Not much. We can talk about it later. By the way, was Alyssa here?"

"Today? I don't think so."

"What does that mean? Either she was here or she wasn't."

"The kid and I went to the park."

"All morning?"

He gave her a sheepish look. "We, um, went out for a bit. Little monster talked me into going to McDonald's for a second breakfast. Just got back maybe ten minutes before you."

"McDonald's? Are you kidding? He'd already had three waffles."

"That's not so much. He ran that off in ten minutes at the park. Besides, he's growing."

"Brad, you know I don't want him eating junk food, especially when he's been sick. What were you thinking?"

"I was thinking Eggos aren't exactly gourmet, and we were both hungry. One McMuffin isn't going to hurt us."

"I see," Callie said, altering both her tone and her expression to let Brad know he wasn't fooling her a bit. The trip to McDonald's was more likely his idea than Ethan's. "Only one McMuffin?"

"Yeah." Pause. "And a chocolate shake. But look at him. He's great. 100% back to normal, hungry as a horse again. Told you it was just some flu bug." Brad turned his attention back to the dispenser.

"We should still keep an eye on him. And no more crap food. For either of you." Callie figured that was a losing battle, but she had other, more immediate concerns now that Ethan was healthy. "Alyssa definitely wasn't here?"

"Not as far as I know. Why?"

"She was driving south on the main road about twenty minutes ago."

"Really?" He looked up from his work.

"It was probably just coincidence, but she lives all the way over in Bay Port, so I can't think why she'd be on the main road heading south unless she'd been here."

"I didn't see her," Brad said. Maybe it was because he wasn't looking her in the eye as he spoke, but Callie had the oddest feeling that there was more behind his words than he was actually saying.

By Friday, Ethan was complaining of yet another headache, and although the summer day was warm and sunny with gently cooling breezes wafting off the Lake, he spent the day curled on the sofa with his blanket and his thumb in his mouth. He didn't have a fever, but he refused to eat anything and had no interest in going to the park. Callie was worried, but Brad reassured her.

"Maybe he never quite kicked that flu. And the last few nights, he's been staying up really late. He'll snap out of it in a day or two," he'd added.

Late Saturday morning, Callie needed Alyssa to make an emergency run out to Wal-Mart for dishwasher soap. She'd thought she'd bought enough to last a couple of months, but there was none left in the basement supply room.

"Why don't you take Ethan along?" Callie said. "He's upstairs glued to that damn television again, which is probably why he has a headache. Take a five from the register and let him pick out some Hot Wheels. He loves those, and they're less than a dollar. No more than two, though. I don't want to be tripping over them all week long."

Two minutes later, Alyssa came back downstairs. "Callie, I'm worried about Ethan," she'd said. "He really doesn't feel well."

"Okay, leave him here. I'll go check on him in a minute, but I still need you to go get the soap."

As Alyssa went out the door, a group of tourists came in looking for an early lunch. For the next half hour, while Brad tended the bar and took food orders, Callie found herself dashing from tables to kitchen trying to keep up with an unexpectedly large but welcome lunch crowd. When Alyssa finally returned, the rush was over.

"I'm going up to check on the kid," Callie said to her. "Table five is just about done, check table three to see if they need anything. I'll be back down in a minute." When she reached the top of the stairs, she heard Ethan sobbing. Pushing open the door, she found the child standing by the ratty brown sofa, swiping at it with a bath towel.

"Hey, Buddy, what's going on here?" she asked.

"I'm sorry, Momma. I didn't mean to," he said through his tears.

Callie moved toward him and immediately caught the strong smell of urine. Ethan's jeans were soaked. "You wet your pants?" Surprise made her words sound harsher than she intended. Ethan hadn't wet himself since he was two years old. She cleaned him up, got him into fresh clothes, and sprinkled the sofa with baking soda, wishing that she could just throw the hideous thing out and get some decent furniture.

A new sofa would have to wait, but she decided she should take Ethan to the pediatrician right away, no matter what Brad had to say about it. She would call the doctor's office first thing Monday morning.

At eight o'clock on Monday morning, before she had a chance to call the doctor, the phone rang with more bad news: her mother, Peg, had been taken to the emergency room.

"She's fine now, dear," said Jack Hanlon, sounding anything but fine himself.

"It was just a little scare. Something the docs called a cardiac event," he explained with a strain in his voice that Callie had never heard before. "They're going to put in a stent, just to be safe, and they said she needs to take it easy. No stress for a while. You know how she is, always looking after everyone else. I guess now it's time for us to look after her for a bit."

"Do you need me to come down there to help out?" Callie asked, thinking as she said the words that the timing couldn't be any worse.

"No, dear. I know this is your busy season. We've got things covered here; it's one of the benefits of having a big family. And you're not to worry. Mama's going to be right as rain in no time."

His words made her feel ashamed that her offer of help was so reluctantly given. Long aware that the love and support that her parents and siblings provided was something she could always count on, Callie tried never to take any of them for granted. In the past, whenever she had felt things spinning out of control, someone had always been there to ground her. But maybe not this time. Maybe this time she had to keep her troubles to herself.

Less than five minutes after Callie hung up the phone, it rang again. This time, it was the woman from Harper's, the company that supplied all the meat and cheese they used in the restaurant.

"I'm sure it's just an oversight, but we haven't received full payment from you for the last two months," the woman said. She was pleasant but firm, reminding Callie that the company policy was to withhold all new deliveries until accounts were paid in full.

"How much do we owe?" Callie asked, shocked when the woman mentioned a sum far larger than they could currently cover. "Are you sure you've got the right account?"

Certain that there must be an error somewhere, Callie began going through the books herself. Nothing seemed out of place, except that the quantities that they had been ordering lately were larger than normal and didn't match her records. She knew there were a couple of times in the past few weeks when she'd run low on beer and soda, so she'd called in a special order, but she'd tried to be careful to record the extra purchases. Maybe Brad had called in some additional orders, too. Could she chalk that up to the hordes of summer tourists that had flooded the small town? Even adding extra hours to Alyssa's schedule, it was all she and Brad could do to serve up the requested drinks and food. That should have been good, she thought; they should be showing a profit, so something wasn't right.

In the afternoon, Ethan rallied a bit, or so it seemed to Callie, although later she would wonder if she either imagined him to be better, or if she just was too busy to notice his condition. It was another three days before she got around to calling Shoreline Pediatrics.

Thursday morning, she sat with her son on her lap in the pediatrician's office. Normally in the summertime, the place was deserted, but today there were four other children in the waiting room. They were busy playing with the collection of brightly colored toys while they coughed wetly and wiped their running noses with their hands. For once, Callie was glad that Ethan sat quietly in her lap unwilling to join the fun. If children weren't sick when they came in here, they surely would be by the time they left.

"Mrs. Collins?"

Callie carried Ethan when the nurse led them to an examining room. The air conditioning had cooled the room too much and all the hard, sterile surfaces seemed uncompromisingly icy and impersonal. The sound of crying children echoed through the walls, making Callie tense and uncomfortable. She undressed Ethan and held him, droopy and lip-chattering, as he sat on the white papered table. They waited in the small room for almost an hour. Dr. Kapoor, when he finally breezed into the room, was as cool and impersonal as his surroundings while he tapped and prodded and peered at his small patient.

"We will take some blood, and I will telephone you in the morning," he said in a melodic, syncopated accent before he vanished out the door as briskly as he'd entered. Callie dressed Ethan quickly. When the nurse returned to stab his tiny finger, squeezing it hard so the blood ran not just into the pipette, but down the side of his hand as well, he hardly whimpered. That, more than anything, alarmed Callie.

At the reception desk, she balanced his weight in her arms while she wrote a check to cover the visit. One hundred twenty-five dollars for what amounted to seven minutes in the doctor's care. She tried not to get upset by the nurses' scowls when she explained she had no health insurance, or take offense when the receptionist made a small, contemptuous *tsking* sound. As long as they got their money, what the hell difference did it make to them?

Two days later, when Callie got the doctor's phone call, his words made her dizzy with fear.

"Mrs. Collins," Dr. Kapoor began, his clipped accent more pronounced over the phone than it was in person. She struggled to understand what he was saying. "I am thinking we might have a bit of a situation here. There seem to be a great many white cells in your son's blood at the present moment. We would like to see him for further evaluation. Today, if possible. Would you bring him 'round to the hospital in Cross City, please?"

Cross City Hospital was small and sparsely equipped. Callie had never set foot in the place before. For Ethan's sake, she pretended they were on a grand adventure as she bundled him into the car. Ushered into Dr. Kapoor's office at the hospital with frightening promptness, Callie asked the doctor to explain just exactly what he'd meant by "a situation." Kapoor skirted the question with vague references to more tests before asking the one question that Callie always dreaded: what could she tell him about the family's medical history? She explained that Brad's parents, both still hale and hearty in their late eighties, lived in Florida, but her biological parents were an unknown factor.

"Ah, this is too bad. We have a notion that your son might be suffering a hereditary disorder, which is rather difficult to detect. It would be somewhat easier to merely inquire of the family, but as that is not the case, we will continue with our testing."

Callie was holding Ethan on her lap, her arms wrapping around him tighter and tighter as though to shield him while the doctor spoke. She felt tears stinging her eyes and her throat was too tight to talk. Here was yet another injustice in the long list of unfair things, a list that Callie thought she had buried long ago. "These tests—are they expensive?"

She saw the doctor raise one heavy eyebrow, a look that conveyed his astonishment that she would even ask such a question.

"Not to worry, Mrs. Collins. I am certain your insurance will cover this, yes?"

Again, Callie had to explain that they had no insurance, and again, she had to ignore the fleeting look that told her he considered people without health coverage to be slackers, part of an unworthy underclass. "But we can pay for whatever Ethan needs," she assured him.

The nurse returned to take more blood from her son before Callie was allowed to carry him, sobbing, to the car.

Back at Stone's Throw, there were still customers in the dining room, even though it was almost three in the afternoon. The summer tourists paid little attention to the clock. Brad and Alyssa had been on their own slinging cheeseburgers and French fries since ten in the morning, and they were tired and snappish, resentful that Callie had been away from the work.

"What'd the doctor say?" Brad asked, pulling another round of beers for a four top. He didn't even look up from his work.

"We can talk about it later," Callie replied, juggling her purse, car keys, and Ethan's limp weight in her arms. Brad stopped what he was doing and looked straight at her. She watched the color drain from his face. "I need to get Ethan settled upstairs."

Thirsty summer sailors and shoppers had drifted into the tavern all through the afternoon and into the evening so that Callie and Brad had no chance for an uninterrupted conversation until after the place closed for the night. Alyssa, predictably, left immediately after the last customer was out the door. Callie gave the kitchen only the fastest, most basic clean up, while Brad put the bar to bed, but still it was well after midnight before the two of them made their way upstairs.

Callie went to the file cabinet beside the desk, opened it, and tucked the evening's cash and receipts under the bar ledger where they could wait until morning. She picked up the bankbook, flipped through a few pages, glancing once more at the uncooperative numbers, but her eyes burned and the figures blurred.

"Okay, so what exactly did this doctor say?" Brad asked, dropping wearily onto one of the mismatched chairs.

"All he told me was that they need to do more tests," she said.

"Yeah? What kind of tests? How much will this set us back?"

Callie closed the bankbook and glared at Brad. She couldn't explain exactly what sort of tests the doctors were planning, nor could she answer his questions about how much all of it would cost. She purposely did not tell him about the call from Harper Foods or the check she had already written to the pediatrician that morning.

"He's our son. We have to do everything we can, Brad," she said, moving from the desk to the battered brown sofa. "We really don't have any choice."

"There's always a choice."

Exhausted, Callie snapped.

"How can you possibly think that? This is our *son*. Money is not the issue."

"Yes, it is." Brad paced the floor between the sofa and the big table. "I don't know what the hell you're thinking, but you know we don't have the extra dough for all this shit right now."

"Well, I'm so sorry it's inconvenient for Ethan to be sick. I'll mention that to him first thing tomorrow, and I'm sure he'll feel better right away." She narrowed her eyes at her husband. "What the hell are *you* thinking?"

"Look, don't take it out on me. I'm just giving you the facts. The money isn't there, and without insurance, well…"

"Well, what? Are we supposed to just ignore what the doctors say?"

"No, but if we don't have the cash…" Brad pulled out one of the chairs at the dining table, flipped it around so he could straddled it backwards, resting his arms against its back, his hands folded prayer-like before him. "Look, all I'm saying is maybe we can wait a while. Maybe he'll get better on his own. I'm not so sure those doctors know what they're doing anyway."

"Oh, right. That's a good idea. We'll just sit back and watch Ethan suffer. Jesus, what kind of a cold-hearted bastard are you, anyway?"

Brad glared at her for a minute. Finally, his body sagged so that his head was resting on his hands. He half-sobbed, "I don't know, Cal. I just don't know what to do."

Across the darkened room, in the middle of the night, the two of them recognized the fear in each other, the fear of parents feeling powerless to protect their child.

Brad rallied first. "Speaking of cold-hearted, maybe there is one thing we could do," he said tentatively. "Why don't you try asking your dear mother if she would come up with a little money?"

"Peg doesn't have any money, besides— "

"No sweetie, your other mother."

Callie's eyes widened. "Are you joking?"

"Absolutely not. If she could give you the money to buy this place, she can goddamn well cough up a bit more for her sick grandson. Ask her."

Callie looked down at her hands, twisting her wedding band around and around as was her habit when she was worried or upset. "I can't. I promised I would never contact her again. That was the deal."

"Screw the dumb-assed deal. That's bullshit. Tell her it's a loan. We'll pay back every cent. Besides, we're not asking for us; it's for Ethan."

He came over to her, sat beside her, put his arms around her. "Look, baby, we both want what is best for Ethan, but I don't want to lose Stone's Throw, and we could. You know the state of the economy as well as I do. There's no way in hell we'll get a bank loan right now, and the medical bills could kill us. Christ, even trying to sell everything we own to pay them off would be tough. But that's our last ditch. We need to do anything we can, explore every option, before we mess around with selling our home and our livelihood, and if that means groveling to your birth mother, well, let's do it. It's not like we care what she thinks of us."

Callie snorted. "I know what she thinks of me."

"Hey, don't go down that road."

"I'm not, really. I'm just trying to figure out why, in her world, it's all about the money and what your friends think. Family doesn't seem to count for much."

Brad released his hold, pulling away so that his hands were on her shoulders. He looked into her eyes. "Well, it counts big for us, and Ethan and I are your family," he said. "We need you to do this for us."

Callie tipped her head back, letting her gaze wander over the collection of family photos on the bookshelf. Family. She had always believed she would do anything for her family, but she'd never thought she'd have to go back on her word or go begging. The irony wasn't lost on her that Stone's Throw represented the sole thing Anne had ever provided to her. She didn't want to lose it for many reasons, but her child's needs came first. She bit her lip, slowly shaking her head back and forth. She rubbed her face with open palms, wiping away tears that she hadn't realized were streaking down her cheeks.

"I don't know," she said. "I just don't know…"

Brad ran both his hands through his hair. "Okay," he said, "if you won't call your mother, will you at least talk to Sylvia? Maybe she can help us out."

Callie, feeling as though she had been beaten with sticks over every inch of her body, closed her eyes. She tried to get her bearings. On some level, she knew this very same thought had been in the back of her mind, but it was not what she wanted to do. She had toyed with the idea of keeping in contact with Sylvia, getting to know her a bit. After all, it wasn't Sylvia's fault that Callie had been tossed aside, and from what Callie had gathered, Anne wasn't much of a parent to the child she *had* kept. It might do them both good to develop a bond of some sort, but not like this. She wanted to approach her half-sister from a position of strength. She'd like to invite Sylvia to visit them again, but only so she could show her how nice life was for the Collins family. Callie needed to prove to her mother and Sylvia and everyone else in the world that she could take care of herself. She didn't need them or their goddamn money.

The only trouble was that she had already accepted money from Anne. Callie had always tried to rationalize the arrangement by telling herself that she had no choice; the big-city lawyer who'd met with her had made it clear he wouldn't take no for an answer. At the time, Callie had readily agreed that the money was to be a one-time, one-way deal. Cash the lawyer's check. No further contact between mother and daughter. Ever. Which was fine, because

Callie didn't need her birth mother. She wasn't fool enough to say no to the cash, but she sure as hell didn't need or want anything else from Anne Bennett. She could do just fine on her own.

And now she hoped to hell that was true. Maybe it wasn't. Her brain scrambled for answers, but there were only questions and problems. But now, the most critical problem wasn't about her. It was about Ethan, and he needed something that Callie and Brad, for all their love, couldn't provide.

"Okay," she said, answering herself as much as Brad.

"Okay, what?"

"I'll talk to Sylvia. But I'm never going to ask Anne for one cent. Sylvia mentioned that she has some kind of trust fund, so maybe she can help. But if she can't, that's it. We'll have to sell Stone's Throw."

Two weeks later, Callie still hadn't gotten around to calling Sylvia. It was easy to put it off; there was always something else more pressing going on at the tavern. Business was going strong. The tavern was packed every night; it was all that the three of them—Brad, Callie, and Alyssa—could do to keep up with a lunch crowd that ballooned each afternoon to an evening dinner rush. All the merchants in Cedar Beach agreed this was the best summer in years, and Stone's Throw was the most popular place in town for tourists to stop for a rest after they docked their boats at the marina. They browsed through the small town gift shops and pseudo-antique dealers, working up an appetite. Day after day, customers filled the tiny dining room and bellied up to the bar, ordering burgers and beer at a steady pace that ran from eleven in the morning until eleven at night.

In the midst of the chaos, three times the following week, Callie had had to leave Brad and Alyssa on their own all day while she drove Ethan fifty miles to the hospital in Bay City. She signed documents, release forms, and dozens of papers pledging to pay all Ethan's medical expenses out of her own pocket. Each time she signed, she swore to herself that she would find the money somehow, whatever the cost. It would all work out. It had to.

Ethan, exhausted by the doctors and nurses and the long car rides, was perfectly content to stay out of trouble. He spent hour after hour on an old rattan settee that Brad had dragged to one corner of the kitchen so that during the day, Callie didn't have to race up and down the back stairs to check on him. Each night after Callie tucked him into bed, he would sleep until she roused him the following morning. Though his inactivity made it easier to take care of business, she would, in an instant, trade his listlessness for the obstreperous little boy he used to be.

Friday was always the busiest day at Stone's Throw. People who had been in town all week hadn't left for home yet, and the new vacationers usually arrived mid-afternoon, hungry and thirsty. By five o'clock, the place was jammed and it was almost impossible to keep up with orders. Callie and Alyssa rushed back and forth from the kitchen to the tables, each keeping an eye on the burgers left to cook by themselves on the griddle. This Friday, the dining room was completely full and the people waiting for tables were crowded so deep around the bar that it was hard to carry trays stacked high with food from kitchen to customer. Often, the patrons would take it into their own hands to pull tables together or add extra chairs for their friends, further blocking the servers' way.

Hustling to the bar, Callie saw two families, each with young kids, take over the big circular table in the corner. A minute later, a heavyset blond man blustered through the door, his wife and two teenaged sons tagging behind him. He saw the people in the corner, shouted greetings across the room, and pushed his way through the crowd toward them. Callie was too busy to object as the guy commandeered chairs from other tables, eventually jamming a dozen people in the tight corner.

"Miss?" a man in an ugly orange Hawaiian shirt stopped her as she passed his table. "Is our food ready? We've been waiting half an hour. And we need more beer."

"Coming right up." She faked a cheery smile.

Callie dashed back to the kitchen just in time to whip four overcooked burgers from the griddle, slap cheese on two of them and fling them into buns waiting in paper-lined, red plastic baskets.

"You okay, Ethie?" she asked, glancing at the small figure scrunched under a blanket on the settee. She tossed pickles on the burgers, and added a handful of potato chips to each basket.

Ethan nodded without taking his thumb out of his mouth. Callie carried on with her work, her attention focused on getting all the food baskets on one tray while still having enough room for the drink orders.

Leaving the kitchen, she maneuvered through the people clustered around the bar where Brad added four bottles of MGD to her tray before she headed to the dining room.

"Hey, doll, how 'bout some service over here?" the heavy blond man at the corner table bellowed at her as she was handing baskets of burgers to Mr. Hawaiian shirt and friends.

"With you in a minute," she replied, clearing a slew of empty beer bottles from the burger table. With all the tables she had going already, this next one ought to be Alyssa's. Callie spotted her on the other side of the room standing by a four-top of good-looking twenty-something guys. Apparently, Alyssa was too busy goofing around, giggling, and acting coy to notice her help was needed elsewhere.

Callie threaded her way back through the crowd, balancing the tray of empty bottles over her head. She tried to catch Alyssa's eye, but she was no match for the four GQ's who had the waitress' undivided attention. With the place as busy as it was at the moment, Alyssa should be working, not socializing. This wasn't the first time in the past few weeks Callie had noticed Alyssa being way too flirty with the men. Lately, she'd developed a pattern of going for the tables where there were no women, spending too much time and energy being chatty. Callie wouldn't ream out the girl in front of her customers, but later the two of them would have to talk about her keeping her mind on her work instead of trolling for boys.

She handed out bills and ran credit cards for two tables, flew back to the kitchen to pour cups of milk for two toddlers, then reluctantly returned to the creep in the corner who had called her "doll."

"What can I get for you?" she asked, digging an order pad from her apron pocket.

"What's on tap?" he asked.

"Miller, Leinenkugel, Bud…"

"Let's go with the Leinie," he said. "We'll need six, no, make it eight, and two regular Cokes. Wait, one of those is diet Coke, and…what? Four root beers?" The four younger kids began pounding the table and chanting, "Root beer, root beer, root beer!"

Ignoring the racket, the man began rattling off the food order for everyone at the table. "My wife here and the lady next to her in the pink hat want chicken salad sandwiches. These two kids'll have grilled cheese, and…what else we got? The rest of you guys want cheeseburgers? Sally, you want a burger or a sandwich? Okay, that's eight cheeseburgers. Cheddar. None of that Velveeta crap, right? Give me the double bacon burger, no cheese. And split the tab three ways. That oughta make it easy for ya."

Callie wrote as fast as she could, sorting out who wanted fries, who wanted potato chips, clarifying wheat or white for the sandwiches. She didn't bother to ask how they wanted the burgers cooked.

"Got it," she said. "I'll be right back with those drinks."

"And bring us a new bottle of ketchup. This one's disgusting," the man added, pointing at the half-empty plastic bottle.

On her way to the kitchen, Callie dropped the drink orders at the bar and asked Brad to have Alyssa take them to the table. She raced to the kitchen, pulled the pre-formed burgers from the fridge, put them on the grill and set up sandwich baskets. She got the fries started, took the tub of chicken salad from the fridge and double-checked that it should go on wheat bread. She put together the sandwiches, flipped the burgers, and checked the fryer basket, all the while thinking that they might have to hire a part-time cook if the rest of the summer stayed this busy.

Alyssa zipped into the kitchen. "Hey, can you slap a couple more burgers on? I need two for table seven," she said. She looked into the plastic tub holding chicken salad. "Shit, is this all that's left of the chicken salad? I just got three more orders."

"Damn. I should have called the supplier on Wednesday, but it got away from me. How many sandwiches do you need?"

"Three. I just said that."

"Sorry. My mind's on fifty other things. Would you run back out there and grab the drink order for the corner table? Brad'll have it up by now. While you're doing that, I'll figure out a way to stretch what's left in here to make up three more sandwiches."

Keeping an eye on the burgers, she artfully filled three sandwich rolls with piles of iceberg, chopped the chicken salad finer so that it would spread farther, and tossed a double layer of sliced tomato on each sandwich.

"Mommy, can I have some water?" Ethan called softly from his place on the settee. Callie rushed to fill his plastic Elmo cup with water. "Do you want something to eat, baby? You haven't had anything all day."

He shook his head as he sipped at the water, curled back under his blanket, and returned his attention to his thumb. *He should be better by now*, Callie thought, running her hand over his forehead. They had heard nothing about the test results, so was that good news? Or did it mean the doctors just didn't know what was wrong?

The smell of meat burning drew her attention, and she raced back to the burgers. Some of them were more than a little overdone. She slid the charred meat onto buns, absolutely certain the obnoxious blond guy would complain, but she'd worry about that later.

Alyssa's timing was perfect as she swung through the kitchen doors just in time to grab the food for her table. "Hey, you know that big group you've got at the corner table?" she asked.

"Yeah. Are they complaining already?"

"No, but did you check the kids' IDs?"

"No. Why? Aren't they just drinking Cokes?"

"Nope. The women have the Cokes. The two older boys are drinking beer and they sure as hell don't look twenty-one to me."

"They've got beer?"

"You'd better check it out."

"Shit." Callie picked up her tray of food and headed to the dining room. Serving alcohol to minors violated one of her most basic principles, and not just because it was against the law. Callie could feel the equal proportions of rage and despair rise in her, as they always did, when she thought of Steve. Peg and Jack Hanlon's seventeen-year-old son, smart, handsome, top-of-his-class, and favorite of the Hanlon family, had been killed by a drunken teenager flying down a country road at 110 miles an hour. Kids and booze were a combination that Callie vowed never to allow on her watch. Running a tavern, she'd seen her share of adults with a few too many under their belt, and she'd learned how to deal with them, even if it meant calling Sheriff Walton. Beyond fines, lawsuits, and other horrible things that could happen, she never wanted anyone to experience the pain that her family had had to endure, especially if the drinker was underage.

At the corner table, she could clearly see empty beer glasses in front of the two pimple-faced boys. There wasn't much she could do except get these awful people out of Stone's Throw as fast as possible. She slung down the food orders in front of each person, without asking if they needed anything else, turned to walk away. The blond guy called out to her. "Hey, hold on."

She looked over her shoulder.

"You forgot the damn ketchup," he said, his mouth full of bacon cheeseburger. He made a circular motion with his index finger, "And bring us another round here, okay, doll?"

"I'll need to see some IDs for the boys first," she countered. The two boys looked at each other with an unmistakable "busted" expression.

"I don't see why that's necessary," the man said, "I'm their father."

"Sorry, sir. It's the law. I can't serve to minors. I'm sure you understand."

"No, actually, I don't understand. What the hell does it matter in this hick town if they want to have a beer or two? It's not like they're gonna be driving." He reached in his pocket and pulled out a thick roll of cash. "This make it easier?" he asked, peeling a twenty dollar bill off the roll with puffy sausage fingers.

"Sorry, sir," Callie said, contorting her face into a contemptuous grimace. "The law says—"

"Ah, for Christ's sake," he huffed, "don't go righteous on me." He shoved the twenty back in his pocket and turned to the boys. "So, what else do you guys want? Coke? Root beers?"

"Nothing, Dad, it's fine," said one of the boys. Everyone else at the table looked uncomfortable, which made Callie feel slightly better, but confirmed her long-standing observation that in a large group, the most uncivil person often assumed control.

"Okay, then. Bring me a shot of Dewar's. This friggin' beer's so weak it's like drinking water."

"In a minute," Callie said. It would be a long minute and a short shot.

"Miss, I asked for white bread, not wheat," said Mrs. Blond Man.

Biting her tongue, Callie apologized and removed the offending sandwich. In the kitchen, she scraped the chicken salad from the wheat bread onto white. She thought about all the waitresses she'd worked with who would spit on someone's food for the kind of treatment this table was giving her, but she couldn't bring herself to do such a thing. She enjoyed thinking about it, but she would never actually do it.

After the table from hell left, the rest of the afternoon and evening sped by in a normal cadence of mayhem. The usual parade of tourists came through the door displaying every sort of attitude from disdainful snobbery of the big money Grosse Pointe crowd to the frazzled young families weary and grateful to have someone else cook for their cranky, sunburned children. None left as big a mess at their table as the blond man and his crew who, naturally, left no tip whatsoever. Dog-tired and short-tempered by the time the last patron left, Callie locked the doors for the night.

"What was the deal this afternoon with that big table in the corner?" Brad asked as they trudged upstairs to the apartment.

"They were a total pain in the ass," Callie answered, pulling keys from her pocket. She unlocked the file cabinet and put the night's cash and till receipts in the drawer.

"Alyssa said the kids were drinking beer."

"She told you right. The table was a nightmare. The guy actually got pissy with me because I wouldn't bring another round."

"How the hell did they wind up with beer in the first place? Jeez, Cal, you of all people know better."

"Hey, I told you it was the dad who ordered," Callie said, slamming the file drawer shut. "Son-of-a-bitch ordered for the whole table. I had no idea who was getting what. I just assumed the beer was for the adults and put the order in. Alyssa's the one who took the drinks to the table and never carded the kids."

"Hmm. That makes it even weirder that she would tell me." Brad was quiet for a minute before adding, "It bothers me that she was so, like…almost excited about something that could bring this place down. Seriously, you should've seen the look in her eyes." He paused again, giving inordinate attention to one of Ethan's crayons that he'd picked off the floor. "There's something going on with her, and it ain't good. We can't trust her."

Whatever was going on with Alyssa, and Callie was beginning to think Brad had a point, she was not in a mood to discuss it. "Whatever. I'm going to check on Ethan."

Brad crossed the room and put his arms around her. "Look, we're both whipped right now, and everything seems like it's going to hell in a handbasket. We need to talk about this, but it can wait until tomorrow. Let's make sure the kid's okay, then get ourselves to bed. Everything'll look better in the morning."

Exhausted as she was, Callie couldn't sleep. While Brad snored beside her, she lay awake, staring into the dark. All the demons of the day danced in her head, made even more monstrous by night when there was nothing left to be done except fret. She worried about the bills and if she could bring herself to ask Sylvia for a loan. She worried about Stone's Throw and wondered for the zillionth time how the hell the accounts had gotten so screwed up. Tossing from her back to her left side, she tried not to wake Brad as she battled her frustration. Maybe she wasn't any good at running a business. Obviously, she hadn't planned for supplies very well for this summer, since they kept running short of things. No chicken salad on a hot summer day. Down to the last case of ketchup in mid-July when she'd thought she had enough for the whole summer. Damned if you ordered too much, damned if you ordered too little. Her father had warned her that the restaurant business was always a tightrope walk. Even if Sylvia bailed them out now, what would happen next year? You could never tell how things were going to go, even without the myriad factors that could take you down any time: crazy, drunken customers, the Health Department, suppliers who couldn't be flexible with billing, and nit-picking accountants.

Alyssa was troubling her, too. One minute, she was Little Miss Super-server; the next day she didn't come to work or even call in sick. Something didn't add up. Plus, it had been her fault those kids had been given beer. Alyssa took the order to the table; she was the one who should have checked the IDs.

Callie remembered one night back at the beginning of the busy season when the cash drawer had been short by fifty bucks. Brad swore he hadn't taken any money out, and she knew she hadn't taken it. At the time, they'd chalked it up to someone double-keying in an order, although the computer was supposed to catch those kinds of errors. She'd checked over the receipts the next day as usual, but couldn't find the mistake. Then time had slipped away, and she'd forgotten about it. Until now. It was an ugly notion that came sneaking into Callie's head under the cover of darkness, but nevertheless, it made sense, and once she began to dwell on it, there was no turning back.

Callie sighed into the night, turning on one side, then the other. She willed her mind to be quiet, steadied her breathing, tried to relax her tightened shoulders, but peace still eluded her. Beyond all else, beyond her conflicted feelings about Sylvia and Anne, her worries about Peg, and the headaches about money and bills and insurance, beyond her fears about losing Stone's Throw, she was scared to death for her child.

12
SYLVIA

SYLVIA SHOT OUT of the club parking lot, screeched around corners, and tore down the quiet streets of Teabury ridiculously over the speed limit. On the freeway, she zigzagged through traffic, pressing the accelerator to ninety miles an hour. This was what freedom felt like. All chains broken.

On the outskirts of Providence, she took the exit for Danfield, driving only slightly more carefully through the less familiar territory. She found her way to Tom's storefront office at the edge of town and parked in a small lot across the street. In this part of Danfield at eight-fifteen on a Saturday evening, there were only two other cars in the lot, both old, rusty Chevys. Her sleek silver Audi looked out of place. The dismal street was quiet. No other cars drove past, no pedestrians walked along the littered sidewalks.

Sylvia got out of the car, telling herself it was unlikely Tom would still be at his office. Frankly, she wasn't sure why *she* was at his office. Whatever deep force within that had compelled her to throw a temper tantrum at the club was still enticing her to behave badly. Coming here was like a dare she couldn't resist. She crossed the street knowing she would knock on the office door, but hoping he wouldn't answer. If he didn't, she would go someplace else. She wasn't sure exactly where, but it would not be back to the club. Nor would it be back home. Maybe she'd go to a movie. Or to Michigan.

Dusty olive drab curtains were drawn across the front windows, the only privacy from the street offered to anyone consulting Tom Harvey in the large, open room that served as his office. She remembered sitting in the hard wooden chair across from his cluttered desk when she first approached him about finding Callie. He'd exuded an aura of confident charm that she found comforting. "As long as I have a birth certificate, there's an 80% chance of finding her," he had said.

The office door, its center an opaque milk-colored glass with T. Harvey Investigations stenciled in black letters, was locked. Sylvia was about to turn away when she saw an intercom buzzer to the left of the door. She pushed the black button.

Shortly, she heard Tom's voice, barely recognizable over the scratchy speaker system. "Sylvia?" He sounded surprised, but not unpleasantly so. "Are you all right?"

Looking above the door, she noticed the discreet eye of a CCD camera jutting from the lintel. Of course, a detective would have his own front door under surveillance.

"Hi, Tom," she said. "I don't suppose you'd believe that I was just passing through the neighborhood?"

"Not for a second. Hang on, I'll be right down."

Less than a minute later, lights flicked on beyond the curtains, then Tom was unlocking the door.

"Come on in," he said, holding the door wide.

"I wasn't sure you'd still be here."

He ushered her into the room, which was as shabby and dreary as she remembered. He looked fairly shabby himself. His weathered jeans were worn thin at the knees, and the logo of a 1998 "Run for Fun 5K" adorned his faded green tee shirt. He gestured to the uncomfortable chair in front of his desk.

"Unless I'm out on a case, I'm always here. I live at work. Literally," he explained. "There's an apartment upstairs. Makes my commute to the office pretty reasonable. Besides, given the nature of this business, I tend to keep all kinds of crazy hours. And I never know when a client might show up," he said, offering Sylvia the slightly arrogant smile that they both knew held just a touch of flirtatiousness. "Which leads me to ask, how can I help you?"

Moment of truth. How could he help? Standing in the dingy office in her silk dress and stiletto sandals, Sylvia couldn't come up with any reasonable answer. Instead, she stammered, "Um. I'm not really sure. I had sort of a blow out with the family. I mean, I guess I probably shouldn't have come here. I just got in the car and, well… here I am."

She tried to smile, but her face felt thick with shame.

"Let me guess: Mom wasn't so thrilled that you found Callie?" If Tom had noticed her discomfort, he was ignoring it, pretending that it was perfectly normal for a client to appear with no warning on his doorstep.

"Hardly. But it's more complicated than that."

Tom waited silently for her to continue.

"I should go," she said. "I…I really don't know why I'm here and I'm sure you've got plans. Things to do."

His eyes held more the look of amusement than annoyance as he replied, "Actually, my only plans for tonight were to go foraging for some dinner. There's a place across town that does a decent steak, and their wine's not bad. If you give me ten minutes to change clothes, I'll buy you dinner and you can tell me the whole story. You up for it?"

Sylvia's better judgment told her it was not a good idea to accept the offer, but she was not in the mood for good judgment. The wildness that had gripped her earlier in the evening flooded back, warming her blood like strong drink. Tom was an unknown quantity, different from anyone else she had ever met, and there was definitely some chemistry between them. "Sure. That sounds nice," she said.

∽≪≫∾

HER CELL PHONE was ringing. Slowly, Sylvia opened her eyes, took in her surroundings. Sour smelling sheets, dingy walls, the thick smell of stale air in a dirty room. Tom's bedroom. Her mouth tasted like a cat box, her eyes were gritty, and the sound of the phone's incessant ring tone was splitting her head. It had been a long time since she'd had a hangover, and this one would be world class.

At least she was alone.

Groaning, she sat up in the tangled bed sheets. Even if she could figure out where the damn phone was, she wasn't going to answer it. It was probably either her mother or Pier.

The cell phone chirped, signaling that someone had left her a message, and she figured out the sound came from her purse, which she saw lying beside a lumpy chair. Someone's clothes were on the chair. Her clothes. Stumbling from the bed with a sheet wrapped around her, she dumped the contents of her purse on the floor, pushing items aside until she extracted her phone from the heap. She looked at the caller ID. Pier. Ugh. Three messages from him, and one from her friend, Jen. She'd deal with them later. Then, she saw there was a fifth message from yet another number. Something about it was vaguely familiar, but she was too muzzy-headed to care at the moment whom it might be. She would listen to the messages later.

The time and date on the phone told her it was Monday. Almost two o'clock on Monday afternoon. A day and a half completely lost, to say nothing of two entire nights. She shoveled her wallet, keys, various containers of makeup, and the phone back into her purse. Scanning the room, she saw several empty wine bottles lined up beside the waste basket, a mostly-empty bottle of Stoli on the

dresser, and a crumpled bag from Dunkin' Donuts on the floor beside the bed. No wonder she felt like shit. There was nothing else in
the room except a cheap television on a tray table and an ugly floor
lamp. She crept over to the dresser where a note had been taped to
the mirror: *Out on a case. Coffee in kitchen. Back by 3.*

First things first, she thought. The first thing was to pull herself
together and get the hell out of here before Tom came back. What
in God's name had she been thinking to come here, anyway? She
remembered being out-of-control angry with Pier, her mother, and
everyone else who had plans for her. No one ever asked her what she
wanted, they just told her what to do, and she was tired of it. *Guess I
showed them.* The thought was immediately followed by self-disgust.

She had been down this road before. Too many of her teenaged years had been spent on this road. Weekend after weekend in
boarding school, and often entire weeks in college, she had spent
in a stupor, loading herself to the gills with booze, crawling around
unfamiliar apartments or hotel rooms. Her pathetic attempts at fun
had never accomplished more than almost getting her kicked out of
boarding school, and definitely causing her to flunk out of college.
She'd made a promise to herself to stop this kind of behavior and,
until now, she'd been pretty good. But here she was, once again,
waking up in some guy's apartment feeling like total trash.

"Stupid girl," she said aloud while she pulled on her clothes
and gathered her things. She desperately wanted a shower, but not
here. Not another minute here. This apartment was filthy; it made
her skin crawl. Mercifully, she couldn't remember much of Saturday night or Sunday, but a general revulsion overwhelmed her now.
"Goddamn it." The foxy little flirtation that she'd thought such a
cute diversion had turned ugly. Disgusting. Once she was out of
this place—and escape couldn't come fast enough—she'd pull herself together once and for all. Tom was a huge mistake. Something
she'd never let happen again.

What she couldn't shrug off quite so easily was the whole scene with Pier and the parents. Sylvia groaned just thinking about trying to straighten out that mess. The more she thought about it, the more she realized there would be no "straightening out." Spending the weekend slumming in Tom's bed had burned that bridge.

In spite of how horrible she felt physically, a new notion settled over her: no matter how hard she tried or what she did, her happiness could never come from someone else. On the heels of that thought, she realized her anger had nothing to do with Tom, Pier, or even her mother. It was hers and hers alone to deal with, and she could let it own her—or she could pull herself together and move on.

On the off chance that Tom might be in his office, Sylvia crept down the stairs and slipped silently through the back door. Outside, the August air was hot and thick, and though she was relieved to have made her escape from the apartment, the humidity made each step an effort. Crossing the street, she heard her cell phone beep again. She fumbled in her purse for the phone, feeling dizzy as she checked the caller ID. What was it that was so familiar about that fifth number? She couldn't quite place it.

The parking lot, full now on a Monday morning, was larger than she remembered. It took her a few minutes to locate her car. Once she was settled in the driver's seat with the air conditioning on full blast, the fog in her head cleared a bit. She looked again at the phone, this time recognizing the Michigan area code. Stone's Throw Tavern. Callie was calling her.

Great.

Did that mean she'd changed her mind and had decided to come to Teabury after all? Perfect timing. Sylvia rested her forehead on the steering wheel, letting the cold blast of the A/C blow directly on her. She had no idea what to do next, but she did know that there would be no wedding. Pier should count his blessings—he'd dodged a bullet.

As much as she wanted to shower, change her clothes, and sleep, going home was not an option. In her present condition, she didn't want to risk seeing her parents, especially since she'd be forced to deal with the fallout from Saturday evening. The thought made her stomach roil.

Home. Interesting concept. If at any time in the last five years she'd been thinking straight, she would have found her own place. As it was, she'd screwed around, making up one excuse after the other, always hoping Wheatley House would feel like home some-day. But home was about the people, not the place. Which might go a long way toward explaining why she'd never moved in with Pier. Maybe somewhere in the depths of her being, she'd known all along they weren't meant to be together.

Whatever.

She punched in the code to retrieve her messages, deleting the three from Pier without bothering to listen to them. The fourth, from Jen, was short. "Call me the minute you get this." Sylvia's head was throbbing too hard to think straight. She'd return the call later. A couple of hours wouldn't make that much difference, and whatever was on Jen's mind would be easier to focus on after coffee and aspirin. She hit delete and played the fifth message.

"Sylvia? This is Brad. I'm, ah, sorry to bother you, but I was wondering if you could maybe give me a call back. When you can. I mean, only if you feel like it. Thanks."

His voice sounded strained and weary, making it obvious something was wrong. Images of car crashes, fires, and crazed drunks with guns flashed through her imagination. She glanced at the dashboard clock: two-fifteen. That meant one-fifteen in Michigan. The lunch crowd would still be there; not a good time to call, Sylvia reasoned, though she knew she was stalling. Why would Brad be calling her? She was curious, but her head felt like mush, and she wanted to have her wits about her when she talked to him.

Looking across the parking lot, she saw Tom's dark green Toyota turn in and head toward the south end of the lot, away from her. Still, she ducked below the dashboard, waiting a few minutes before rising up just enough to catch a glimpse of him walking across the street to his office. He was carrying a large bouquet of flowers, and for a fraction of a second, she felt guilty. She'd thrown herself at the man, behaving like a spoiled, drunken slut, and he'd responded exactly as she predicted. Maybe in some part of his guy-brain he'd thought he was in control of the situation: the older man bedding the distraught young woman, but Sylvia knew better. She might have been black-out drunk, but she'd been the one who'd used him. Badly.

"Oh, get over it," she said aloud, not sure if the comment was meant for Tom or for herself. As she watched him disappear inside the office, her cell rang again. Jen's number was on the ID. She wasn't in the mood for idle chatting, but Jen had called twice now; she decided to take the call.

"Hey, what's up?" Sylvia answered, hunching behind her steering wheel like a character in a low-grade television cop show. She tried to sound normal despite a sudden, unpleasant wave of dizziness.

"I broke up with Dan."

"Are you serious?" Sylvia's surprise was genuine, but she was having trouble responding. Her head was pounding and sitting in the hot car was making her feel nauseous.

"Totally serious. The guy's been cheating on me for months. I can't believe he's such a complete asshole, and I never had a clue."

Sylvia felt pre-barf sourness rising in her throat. She wished she hadn't answered the phone.

"I stopped by his place unexpectedly yesterday," Jen prattled on. "He'd had a cold, or at least he'd said he did, which is why we didn't go out last weekend. After work, I decided to go by his place to see if he was feeling better. Come to think of it, I bet the rat bas-

tard was lying like the dog that he is about that, too. Anyway, I walk
in, and *she's* there. And I'm like Miss Florence Fucking Nightingale,
bringing him orange juice and cough medicine, and—"

"Jen, I need to call you back. I can't talk now."

"But I—"

"I'll call later. I promise." Sylvia snapped her phone shut, tossing it on the passenger seat. She leaned back against the headrest,
willing herself to take deep, even breaths and not puke. Closing her
eyes made the nausea worse. She stared across the lot at the dingy
buildings wanting only to get away from this crummy neighborhood before Tom came back outside looking for her. Steeling herself against her physical misery, she put the car in gear, pulled out
of the lot and headed for the highway.

Twenty minutes later, she took the exit for Springdale Mall.
Her first stop was Starbucks. At the table farthest from the door,
she sat curled around a double shot espresso, sipping cautiously
until she was feeling normal enough to wonder again why Brad
would call her. She finished the espresso, bought a grande bold,
a blueberry muffin, and a bottle of water. After downing a couple
of Motrin that she found in the bottom of her purse, she picked
cautiously at the muffin, considered her future, and waited for the
wool blanket-hangover to lift.

When her head was clear again, she went to Sports Authority
and bought running clothes, two pairs of socks and new Nikes.
At Macy's, she purchased underwear, jeans, and a plain white polo
shirt. Then she drove back to Teabury, straight to the fitness center,
where she bought a new membership and carted her purchases to
the ladies' locker room. Two miles on the treadmill, thirty minutes
with the weight machines, and an hour in the sauna sweated out
the last effects of the weekend. By the time she had showered and
changed into the new clothes, it was late afternoon and she was
ready to return Brad's call.

At this time of the day, the health food café adjacent to the fitness center was almost deserted. She bought a grilled veggie and goat cheese wrap, a huge bottle of spring water, and a cup of green tea. After this past weekend, taking better care of herself was at the top of her list of resolutions.

The conversation she had with Brad didn't last more than ten minutes, but it underscored everything she'd been contemplating since that morning. Or perhaps it was because of what she'd been contemplating that morning when she heard what he said and knew beyond any shadow of doubt what she would do.

First, she called Lisa Carney and quit her job, effective imme-diately. Lisa sounded more relieved than surprised. Sylvia tried to apologize for not giving more notice, but Lisa brushed her off with a cheery, "Not to worry, dear. We'll be fine." Sylvia cringed inward-ly, remembering what an unreliable employee she had been, but the truth was that she had never really cared about creating the flawless corporate luncheon or bride-zilla's perfect day.

If she were honest with herself, she'd have to admit that she had never really cared about much of anything. Material possessions had always been handed to her so casually that their worth meant nothing. Friends—except for Jen and Pier—were only the transient relationships of boarding school or summer camp; everyone moved on or away, making deep ties pointless. And why should she give a crap about school? It wasn't as if the kind of grades she got would change her life one bit.

It was in Michigan, though, that a glimmer of honesty found its way into her sphere of self-indulgence. For the first time, she'd encountered people who didn't measure each other's value in terms of clothes, cars, and club memberships. Callie and Brad had given her proof that there was more to a party than place cards and table arrangements. Seeing how they cared about each other, even cared about her, had made a deep impression. And Mike. She couldn't stop thinking about the freedom she'd felt when she was with Mike. He was so in control of his life. She envied him that, and she couldn't recall any time when she'd envied anyone so much.

Sylvia decided she had go back to Wheatley House. She had to try one more time to talk to her mother, even though it was the last thing in the world that she wanted to do. Their so-called conversation at Oceanaire still stuck in her craw. Why was it so hard for her mother to be a normal human being? Someone who could admit to past mistakes, someone who had problems and imperfections? What could possibly be her reasons for being so cold, so… impenetrable, especially now that the secret, as far as Sylvia was concerned, had been discovered?

A flicker of suspicion darted through her head. A terrible thought. Terrible in that it made perfect, crystal-sharp sense, a hard-edged indelible truth. It wasn't just the shocked reaction of her daughter or that her club friends would be scandalized by Callie's presence that kept Anne Bennett from acknowledging her firstborn child. Sylvia would bet her inheritance that Henry Bennett knew nothing of his wife's past.

Henry was a benignly neglectful father. Assuming he was a similarly innocuous husband was not a grand stretch of imagination. He played golf; he went to the office once in a while to make sure the family money was still earning sufficient interest to maintain the Bennett lifestyle. He was not the kind of man to look for trouble, and such a deep deception would be beyond his line of vision.

The insight redoubled Sylvia's determination to confront her mother once more. To feed her courage, she brought forth every memory she could conjure of the times her mother had belittled her, ignored her, or waltzed over her triumphs and terrors with equal disregard. Birthdays unacknowledged; school events ignored; behaviors both good and bad brushed aside.

It was time for a reality check.

Whether or not Sylvia could break through her mother's wall of denial and arrogance, she had already decided that she would fight with everything she had to not become the person her mother was, and the most direct way to do that would be to return to Michigan. Brad had called her twice, detailing exactly what the situation there was, so that Sylvia understood what needed to be done. It was the first time in her life that she could remember feeling needed, as if what she did made a difference to people she cared about. This was about so much more than just the money. It was about being part of a family who came together when there was trouble instead of putting up fortresses of self-defense. Sylvia flashed back to the day Callie had told her the story of the Hanlon family camping trips and how they all worked together at their restaurant. She remembered the anniversary party that Callie had thrown for Peg and Jack, and how the celebration had flowed beyond the two of them to encompass the entire gathering. And Ethan. She had saved all the pictures he had colored for her. Knowing that he was not just some cute little kid, but actually part of her family—her nephew? half-nephew?—gave her a rush of pleasure. Family—a group to belong to, a place to fit in—was what Sylvia had always wanted more than anything.

Ethan had trusted her, innocently and uncritically accepting her as someone who belonged in his world. After Brad's second phone call, she saw there was a reason—a desperately important reason—for everyone to come together. It wasn't fair that the smallest, most fragile of them all should be the one to set change in motion, but fairness was a rare commodity.

The timing was good, Sylvia thought as she turned down the tree lined-avenue leading to Wheatley House. This was the week that her father was always away for his annual boys-only golfing trip to Gleneagles. At half past five in the afternoon, her mother would likely be home alone.

The streets were quiet; the summer sun pooled in languid patches across the sweeping lawns on this side of town where real-tors referred to properties as estates rather than houses. Wheatley House, arguably the most impressive of all, was set in the midst of six acres of velvet lawns and showcase gardens.

Sylvia turned down the driveway and the familiar sound of the gravel crunching under the wheels of her car made her stomach tighten. Though she'd always taken it for granted, now she thought about how much her parents spent to maintain Wheatley House. The driveway alone—yards and yards of deep pink Desert Rose gravel that her mother insisted on having replaced every spring— probably cost more to maintain than Callie and Brad needed to pay off their creditors. Who the hell cared that much about a driveway? What was wrong with blacktop? She nurtured her rage, stoking the fire of her fury with every notion of injustice she could muster. Wrath might be effective; nervous quibbling her mother would dismiss with contemptuous disregard.

Sylvia ran through her tactics once more. First, she would be clear that she had made up her mind: she had no intention of marrying Pier. Then, she would take her mother's favorite ap-proach and simply ignore any further questions about her behav-ior at the club. She was only a little nervous when she pulled up in front of the house and parked the car in the area reserved for guests. Steeling herself, she went to the front door and rang the bell like a total stranger.

After what felt like hours instead of minutes, Anne opened the door.

"Sylvia. What on earth have you been doing?" her mother asked, expressing no pleasure at the sight of her daughter.

"Hello, Mother. Nice to see you, too. May I come in?" She tried to elbow her way past her mother into the front hall, but Anne stood firm.

"Are you going to explain your appalling behavior? You left your father and me in the most awkward situation. And what about Pier? Have you apologized to him? I can't imagine what possessed you...."

"I told you Saturday, the wedding is off. I don't want to marry Pier, and that's all I have to say about it." Already, the words to justify her actions, the lines she'd been planning to deliver, had come out sounding all wrong. She forced herself to look her mother in the eyes without flinching. "Are you going to let me in the house, or would you prefer to just brawl out here on the driveway?"

"Don't be ridiculous." Anne hesitated for just a fraction of a second. "Of course you can come inside."

Sylvia followed her mother into the house, down the hall to the west sitting room, then through the French doors to a small terrace. Nearby stood a small bar trolley holding glasses, an ice bucket, and a variety of bottles.

"I was just about to fix myself a small cocktail. Would you like something?"

Hair of the dog. Liquid courage. Too tempting to resist. "Okay, but only a small one."

"Gin and tonic?"

"I'd prefer vodka."

"Really?" Anne's tone making it sound as though her daughter had asked for a shot of cheap whisky and a beer chaser.

"So," Anne began while she delicately transferred a few cubes of ice from the silver bucket to two crystal highball glasses, "since you haven't come here to explain yourself, to what do I owe the pleasure of your company?"

Sylvia watched her mother pour two fingers of vodka in one glass, and a more substantial portion of gin in the other. As revved up as she had been in the car on the way over, now that she was standing in her mother's presence, her brain felt scrambled. Coherent thoughts dissipated like wisps of smoke in the wind.

"I quit my job," she said, keeping her eyes on the tonic water bubbling to the top of each glass as Anne stirred each drink with a silver swizzle stick.

"Why am I not surprised?" her mother replied, handing her a drink. "Running out on commitments seems to be your theme for the week."

Casually, as though there were no one else with her, Anne turned her back. She removed the tongs from the ice bucket, placing them carefully on the black lacquer tray. She settled the lid on the silver ice bucket and plucked two linen cocktail napkins from a stack beside the ice bucket. Strolling casually to the patio table, Anne perched herself gracefully on one of the six chairs surrounding it. She placed one of the napkins across the table, indicating where her daughter should sit. Purely from belligerence, Sylvia chose a different chair, sliding the cocktail napkin six inches to the left before putting her glass beside it.

Anne brushed an imaginary strand of hair away from her face. "Have you come here to tell me what is behind all this drama with Pier and your job and God knows what else?"

"Not exactly." Sylvia was transfixed by the crimson smear of lipstick left on the edge of her mother's glass.

"I'm sure you'll be delighted to know that the club is all abuzz with tales of your little show," Anne continued. "I can understand why you would change your mind about the wedding—Pier is dull and his parents are ghastly—but couldn't you have been a bit more discreet? And did you quit your job, or were you fired?"

"I wasn't fired. I'm moving."

"I see. Well, that isn't exactly earth-shattering news," Anne replied, sounding bored. "You're far too old to still be at home. I believe your father had plans to buy a small house for you. It was meant to be a wedding gift because, God knows, we didn't want the pair of you roosting here, but I'm sure he can be persuaded to put the title in your name."

"I'm not staying in Teabury."

Anne raised one perfect eyebrow. "All right. You have your trust fund. As long as you aren't too stupid, you should be able to manage. However, that account is not a bottomless pit. Both your father and I felt that you would manage the money poorly, so you only have access to a small portion of it until you are thirty-five. If you're planning to follow the crowd and go to New York or D.C., you might have to think about getting a job, although heaven knows what you would do. "

"I'm not going to New York, and as for a job, I'm sure I can find something. I worked for Lisa for three years."

Anne sniffed. "She only hired you as a favor to me. You do realize that without your degree, you are simply not qualified for anything, and working part-time planning parties hasn't exactly given you a top-drawer résumé."

Sylvia felt the familiar tension between herself and her mother ratchet higher. She folded her linen napkin, focusing on trying to make the crease follow part of its embroidered design.

"I suppose I could put in a call to Buffy St. John," Anne said. "Her art gallery seems to be doing well, but I'm fairly certain she only hires college graduates. Maybe you should think about going back to school. No one in New York—"

"You weren't listening. I said I'm not going to New York. I'm going to Michigan," Sylvia blurted out. "I'm going to Callie." She heard the intake of Anne's breath, the involuntary rattle of the ice cubes in her glass.

"Oh, for God's sake. Leave that alone. Leave the whole thing alone. I told you that subject is off limits." Anne's lips were thin, pinched, and the pupils of her eyes had become pinpoints of anger.

"Callie is a person, not a thing or a subject, and she needs our help."

"Our help? What does that mean? She wants our money more likely," Anne huffed, raising her glass to her lips.

"Perhaps," Sylvia acknowledged, shrugging. "But so what? Her son—your grandchild—is sick. They don't have health insurance."

"That's not my problem. There's nothing I can do."

"Come on. You know that's not true." Sylvia barely got the words out of her mouth before Anne exploded, slamming her glass on the table, splashing gin.

"Goddamn both her and you straight to hell. I don't want to hear another word about her. Do you understand that?"

Sylvia, shocked, raised her own voice in defense. "What is it with you? How can you be such a bitch? This is your daughter you're talking about. And your grandson. How can you not care? He's sick. He might even die and they need our help and you act like it's nothing to do with you."

Sylvia looked at her mother, sitting primly in her summer linen yellow skirt, her Dior blouse, her standard daily accessories of gold necklace and assorted rings and bracelets that would pay Callie's mortgage for months. "I don't understand why you won't even talk to her."

Anne's eyes narrowed as she said, "Maybe you'll understand this: I named you Sylvia because I detest that name."

"What?" The non sequitur left Sylvia disoriented.

"I wasn't going to waste a good name on a child I didn't want. And I most certainly didn't want you. Do you understand that?"

In the heat of the August evening, Sylvia shivered at the viciousness of her mother's declaration. Their eyes met. Sylvia looked away first, the bitterness of rejection creeping over her like a blanket of thorns.

"You were a mistake, just like her," Anne continued, disgust and loathing clear in her voice. "When I found out I was pregnant with you, I couldn't believe it. How could I have been so stupid twice?" She paused just long enough to toss back a significant portion of her drink.

"The first time was understandable. Regrettable, but under-standable. I'm sure you've done the math. I was quite a bit younger than you are now. Foolish. In love. All of those tiresome clichés. But you. That was different." Anne paused, her words hanging like glass shards in the summer air. From somewhere nearby, a bird whistled melodically, its delicate, sweet song incongruous in the moment.

"I should have known better, especially after that first debacle," Anne continued. She looked out toward the gardens and spoke soft-ly, as if only to herself. "I was so naïve. I ignored what I didn't want to believe until it was too late. Another child was the last thing on earth I wanted, but everyone, including your father, assumed that children were part of our plan, so I pretended I was happy."

Anne opened her tightly clenched fists, and Sylvia could see where her rings had left purple marks on her hands. She tossed her crumpled napkin on the table, and took another large swallow of her cocktail before continuing.

"Once you were born…" Anne paused, and Sylvia wondered if she had heard just the slightest catch in her mother's voice. "Once you were born, I couldn't bear to be near you. You think you are so clever, but you have no idea what a mess you have made."

Sylvia sat very still, absorbing this new information. It shouldn't be a big surprise, but hearing her mother tell her outright that she was unwanted made her feel changed from the inside out. The woman sitting across from her, the woman she called Mother, had suddenly lost her power. All the years Sylvia had tried to win her mother's love and approval dissolved into meaninglessness. Now, her decision to leave Teabury made even more sense; it was time to move on. Move away.

The empty, silent space between them stretched out like a Si-berian plain. She wondered if her mother, who had withdrawn to some inner place of her own, was going to reveal anything more. Anne retrieved her mangled cocktail napkin, toying with it distractedly, plucking at the embroidered edge of the wrung out, twisted cloth with one perfectly manicured fingernail. The diamonds of her wedding rings glinted in the last rays of the evening light, her bracelets struck dulcet notes in the silence. With a perceptible shudder, Anne sat straighter, raised her chin, and drew the impenetrable barrier of her customary haughtiness around her like a cloak.

"I will not have the unfortunate incidents of my past dredged up and mauled by you or anyone else," she said. She swirled the ice in her glass and took a final swallow, then stood.

Sylvia put her hand out, grasping her mother's wrist. "But this isn't about you," she said. "It's about your daughter. And your grandson. Don't you care about him? And what about my father? Does he know about Callie?"

Anne shook Sylvia's hand from her arm. The flashing in her eyes matched the tone of her words. "Stop it! How many times do I have to say that?"

"He doesn't know about her, does he?" The minute the words were out of her mouth, another thought occurred to Sylvia. "What about Callie's father? I bet you never even told him you were pregnant."

For the first time in her life, Sylvia saw her mother's perfect posture sag. Round-shouldered, her head bowed, she said, "Oh, Sylvia, you silly, silly girl. Don't you understand that was impossible?"

"Nothing is impossible, especially telling someone if they are going to have a child."

Anne looked up, pain and defeat in her eyes. "You don't know what you are talking about. Please just go. Go away."

13
CALLIE

"LET'S MAKE THAT six dozen." Callie pinned the phone to her ear with her shoulder and punched numbers on the calculator, figuring exactly how much she was spending for the food order.

"Okay. And what about bread?" the woman on the other end of the line asked.

"Yeah, we'll need—" She was interrupted by a crashing thud from the other side of the room. Ethan had rolled off the sofa, taking down a tower of plastic blocks he'd been stacking on the coffee table. Callie glanced over, annoyed by his antics.

"Ethan…"

He was thrashing on the floor. Legs and arms flailing wildly. His face was contorted.

"Ethan?"

A guttural, choking sound was his only response.

"Ethan!"

◌৪৩

IN THE HOSPITAL waiting room, Callie wondered how much more she could take. Things were definitely going from bad to worse. What was that old saying? God doesn't give you anything you can't

handle? What if that wasn't true? What if there was no God? What
if she just went completely crazy here in the hospital waiting room,
trashed the place, pushed over the stupid aquarium and threw chairs
at the old couple huddled in the corner? What if she body-tackled
the fat, complacent nurse at the reception desk and scratched her
eyes out? Callie shook with the effort of trying to hold herself together. She alternated sitting, then standing, pacing the small waiting area adjacent to the more clinical part of the hospital, not noticing the floral wallpaper that was meant to be cheery or the soft green
carpet that was meant to be soothing. She checked her cell phone for
the umpteenth time. No messages. No missed calls. Where the hell
was Brad? He was supposed to have been meeting with Barry, their
accountant, but when he didn't answer his cell phone, she'd called
Barry's office only to be told Brad had left an hour earlier. Grabbing
a magazine from a tidy stack on the side table, she flipped through
its pages without seeing a thing, impatiently tossing it aside a minute later. She allowed herself one quick, vicious kick at the leg of the
chair, but it didn't help. Nothing helped. She envied the fish in the
aquarium, floating in their artificially controlled oblivion.

    Too many troubles were crowding her thoughts. First and fore-
most, of course, was Ethan, but she forced herself to think about
something else, something less scary. There sure was a shitload of
things to choose from. Money, or lack of it, was right up there at
the top of the list. What had been looking like a solidly profitable
summer had disintegrated to a bookkeeping nightmare. Barry had
showed her where the numbers didn't add up, but hadn't offered
any solutions. Their suppliers were clamoring for money and were
indifferent to her pleas for more time to pay the bills or to create
some kind of staggered payment plan. In tight times in the past, she
had managed to skitter around credit problems, but Stone's Throw
was in deep trouble now. The banks were no help. She'd been to
six of them in the last three weeks. Half the country and most of

the state of Michigan were in debt; Stone's Throw was just another statistic to them. Callie wracked her brain trying to come up with a plan but, so far, nothing was working. She'd done everything she could think of, including making a complete fool of herself trying to suck up to the manager at Stateview Bank. He'd been her last, best chance, and she'd set up the meeting, hoping to get a loan that could buy them some time, but the minute she'd walked into the guy's office, she knew she had made a mistake. The moral superiority of the guy had hung like an odor in the air. The plaster Madonna and Baby Jesus figure on his desk right next to the photo of his frumpy, pious-looking wife should have been her first clue that he'd be some ultra-conservative jerk. Two minutes into their conversation, he made it pretty clear that he considered taverns in general and liquor consumption in particular to be signs of low morals and loose behavior. Terrific. She'd pleaded with him, even tried offering him free cheeseburgers, but the weasel-faced bastard was not even remotely interested in helping her out. Self-righteous twit.

"You idiot!" she muttered just loud enough so that the old couple in the corner looked at her, their expressions more fearful than pitying. She glared back at them. They looked like twits, too.

She stood again and picked up another magazine, flipping through pages of home decorating tips that struck her as beyond ridiculous. Who the hell has time to grow their own lavender for handcrafted drawer sachets? *La-di-dah.* Who the fuck even uses drawer sachets? Not someone whose unconscious kid had just been rushed to the hospital. Callie threw the magazine back on the table. *Bet Sylvia uses drawer sachets,* a little voice in her head sneered. The notion carried its way to a more rational part of her brain, reminding her that she had promised Brad she would call Sylvia, which she still hadn't done. *No time like the present.*

She retreated to one of the fake leather chairs and dug her cell phone out of her purse. She contemplated Sylvia's name on her contact list. What, exactly, was she going to say? She couldn't just ask for the money, and she sure as shit wasn't in the mood for a pleasant chat about wedding plans. No way would she go near that conversation. And she didn't want to tell Sylvia about Ethan. That would make what was happening too real.

This whole damn Sylvia thing was so confusing. There was a part of her that wanted to like her half-sister. It couldn't have been easy for the kid to walk into Stone's Throw the way she did, all alone, not sure what awaited her. It also couldn't have been easy growing up with the Ice Queen for a mother, being shuffled off to boarding school, no brothers or sisters…well, none available.

But Sylvia was set for life. No money problems. No sick kids. No feeling like no matter what she did, how hard she worked, it was never enough. There was nothing the two of them had in common—except a mother with all the endearing qualities of a viper. Jesus, probably even a viper took better care of its young. In all her life, Callie had never been envious of anyone else, even other children who had their real parents caring for them. But now, somewhere deep within her, she had to admit that in meeting Sylvia, a small spark of "what if" had been ignited.

Callie thought back to her parents' anniversary party. Peg and Jack had accepted Sylvia, no questions asked. They never judged anyone by where they came from, or by their clothing or appearance, and they weren't going to start with Sylvia. Sylvia, in turn, had relaxed with them until Callie could see that underneath all the layers of bravado and bullshit there was a lonely, insecure little girl looking for her sister like the lost child of a fairy tale. Maybe there was something to all the crap about money not buying happiness. Given what she knew about her birth mother, Callie figured it was a pretty sure bet that the Bennett family gatherings weren't much fun. She pictured a long dining room table, loaded with crystal and silver. A tuxedoed servant poured champagne while Sylvia and her parents silently picked at caviar and roast beef. Definitely not fun.

Maybe one day, she wouldn't mind getting to know the kid a bit, but not now. She didn't want to ask for money, and she didn't want to be anywhere near the damn wedding, and she sure as shit didn't want anything to do with Anne.

But she'd promised Brad that she would try. For Ethan. In the maelstrom of her emotions, there was still that promise. Callie looked down at her cell phone, which had shut itself off. *Okay, that's a sign. I shouldn't make this call right now.* Easy to justify when she still had no idea what she would say. Even if Sylvia could help them out with a loan, the last thing Callie wanted was for her half-sister to feel that she had to, or even could, buy her way into Callie's life.

Another notion surfaced: Sylvia might refuse to lend her money. Maybe now that they had met, that was enough. The mystery was over; the discarded child had been found. Maybe like their mother, Sylvia would much prefer to pretend Callie just didn't exist. Especially if there was money involved. She put the phone in her purse and sat glaring at the glimmering, tranquil fish drifting peacefully in their blue-green world.

At the far end of the long, gleaming white linoleum corridor, the swinging doors parted and finally, Brad was there, jogging the distance between them, his face almost as white as the surrounding walls. His presence filled the acrid little waiting room with familiar security, and Callie rose so that he could catch her in his arms. Immediately, she disintegrated into a weeping hysterical mess, much to the further alarm of the old couple in the corner. She tried to tell him what had happened, but the sounds that came out of her mouth were only incoherent blubberings. What would they do about money when no one at the goddamn banks would give them the time of day, and where was Alyssa because she hadn't shown up for work again, and—shit, she had been trying to call him for hours and where the hell had he been, anyway?

"Shh, honey. It's okay. Everything's going to be okay," Brad chanted softly in her ear until she quieted, caught her breath in a final sob and pulled back slightly from his grasp. She wiped her face with the backs of both hands, and allowed Brad to lead her to the small, fabric-covered sofa, the only piece of furniture in the waiting room on which they could sit side by side. While he held both her tear-soaked hands in his, she took a deep, ragged breath and told him what had happened.

"It felt like hours before the ambulance got to us," she said, "and then the ride here…I couldn't do anything. I felt so helpless. I'm his mother, goddamn it. I'm supposed to be able to protect him, and I couldn't do it. I couldn't help him." Callie dissolved again. Brad held her, shushing and cooing until her sobs reduced themselves to whimpering.

After a few minutes, she lifted her head from his shoulder. Her eyes felt terrible. Swollen and red, mascara smeared. "I tried to call you."

Brad looked away. Before he had a chance to answer, the swinging doors opened again, and a doctor in green scrubs strode toward them, making eye contact as he drew near. They both stood as he approached.

"Mr. and Mrs. Collins? I'm Dr. Voss. I've been seeing to Ethan, and I appreciate your patience. Right now, let me assure you that he is resting comfortably. I'll take you to see him in just a few minutes," he said. Callie searched his face for the things he might not be saying. His expression was an equal mix of kindness and concern. Were they trained to look like that in med school, she wondered?

"Your son has had a seizure, as I'm sure you are aware. That event, combined with the recent medical history, suggested that an MRI needed to be ordered to evaluate the situation. I have the results." The doctor paused, glancing for the first time at the older couple still huddled in the corner like terrified mice.

"Shall we sit?" asked Dr. Voss, gesturing for them to return to the sofa. Like obedient children, Callie and Brad sat down. The doctor pulled another chair near so that he could sit across from them, his back to the older couple.

"What's the verdict, Doc?" Brad asked.

Dr. Voss sat on the front edge of the chair, his feet apart, his elbows resting on his knees. In his hands he held a closed manila file folder. He looked straight at the two of them as he said, "The MRI revealed that Ethan has a small meningioma—a brain tumor."

Callie heard a small cry and realized it came from her own mouth. Brad was sitting so still he might have been made of stone.

"The good news is that these things are usually benign and, in this case, it is operable," the doctor said. "The not so good news is that any brain surgery is a very tricky business, as you can imagine."

Callie couldn't imagine. She couldn't imagine her little boy lying on an operating table while someone with a saw cut through his skull.

"We'd like to schedule this relatively soon; time is a factor. There is an excellent neurosurgeon, Dr. Edward Clifford, who works out of Children's Hospital in Bay City. I've contacted him and called an ambulance to transport Ethan there as soon as possible."

CB&CO

LATER, CALLIE WOULD remember the next few days as nothing but waiting for endless, unbearably tense hours in rooms that smelled too strongly of floor wax and antiseptics. The first twenty-four of those hours were the worst. She and Brad hadn't been allowed to ride in the ambulance, so they made the drive from Cedar Beach to Bay City in Callie's Mercury Mountaineer, both of them silently encased in their own worries for the hour-long journey.

Once the ritual of paperwork had been completed, a waifish girl in scrubs, looking far too young to be a nurse, led them through the maze of corridors to the pediatric ward. Ethan, sedated to a deep sleep, was unaware of his parents' presence. Brad paced; Callie sat in a green vinyl chair beside his bed.

He was so quiet under the white blanket. His dark chocolate curls had been cut down to the scalp which was now speckled with monitors like tiny metallic Cheerios. One arm lay outside the covers, taped to a plastic plank so both his arm and the IV would stay in place. Callie avoided looking at the point of intersection between the tubing and Ethan's delicate skin. She focused instead on his perfect little hand. Perfect. That was the right word, she thought. When he had been born, she, like most mothers, had admired, wondered, thrilled at the ability of her own body to create this living being who, though just a child now, would grow one day to become a man. It was the exquisite treasure of motherhood to know that this person would always be a part of her. Not that she felt he owed his life to her; if anything, she felt a bit of the reverse—she owed her life to him. His smile; his delight in the wonders, both large and small, of the world; his potential for all the years to come made her, even on the darkest days, know that she was privileged beyond measure. That her own birth mother had never felt this was tragic.

Because they couldn't just ignore Stone's Throw, late that night Brad drove back to Cedar Beach. Someone had to put up signs saying, "Closed due to family emergency." Someone had to tell Alyssa not to bother coming to work. Someone had to throw out food that would spoil. And someone had to get Ethan's blanket and favorite books so that Callie could read to him even though he would be lost in a twilight world of medication for...who knew how long?

After sitting motionless too many hours, Callie finally stood, stretching the stiffened muscles of her back, her legs wobbly beneath her. She brushed the backs of her fingers across Ethan's pale cheek, kissed his brow. It was meant to be a guardian kiss, a kiss to stay with him despite the blood and bandages that soon would cover his small head. She prayed, words from memory spliced with her own pleas, and chanted her supplication over and over as she settled once more in the green chair. The nurse brought her a thin blanket, which she pulled to her chin and, unable to keep her eyes open, Callie slept.

Brad returned just before five the next morning, dark circles under his eyes, his cheeks freshly shaven, but hollow. Callie noticed for the first time that he had lost weight. When had that happened? He brought two cups of coffee and two egg McMuffins with him. The sandwiches sat untouched and congealing in the paper bag and the coffee grew cold in the silence of the room as they sat side by side, Brad's strong hand holding hers, occasionally stroking her hair lightly, brushing a stray strand back into place.

Just past six in the morning, two nurses came in the room to wheel Ethan away. One of them turned to Callie as he maneuvered the gurney out the door. "You should go on down to the cafeteria, get yourselves a hot meal. It's going to be a long day for ya'll," he said, his softly accented words resting lightly in the air. For no reason that made any sense, it was reassuring to know that Ethan was being looked after by these two young men who seemed so much more present, more substantive, than the aloof Dr. Clifford.

Callie tossed the soggy McDonald's bag in the trash. "Let's go," she said to Brad. She shouldered her purse and headed out the door, not bothering to wait for his answer, not caring that they had just wasted good money on bad food.

In the cafeteria, the smells of overripe bananas, bacon grease and industrial coffee mingled unpleasantly. Brad pushed a tray along the stainless strips of metal, collecting plates of scrambled eggs and toast that would be only marginally better than what had been in the McDonald's bag. Callie's stomach was burning from too much stress and coffee and too little food. Impulsively, as they approached the cashier, she put a carton of chocolate milk on the tray, thinking how much Ethan would like to have chocolate milk for breakfast. Silently, she promised him that if only he would get better, she'd make certain there would always be plenty of chocolate milk in their refrigerator. The "if only" made her stomach roil. If only prayers and promises were enough to make a difference.

Brad paid for the food and carried their tray to a crumb-speckled table, Callie following leadenly behind him. He took the plates and their drinks off the tray and went back to the service counter for silverware while Callie sat staring at nothing. He returned to the table, sat down, and buttered his toast. He was talking to her, but she wasn't focused on his words. She barely registered any information until she caught something he said about Alyssa.

"What?"

"She quit." Brad scooped a forkful of scrambled egg onto his toast, balancing it carefully as he lifted it to his mouth.

"She quit?"

"Yup. Left a note on the bar saying she was headed out of town."

"She's gone?" Callie repeated, once his words registered through the wooly heaviness surrounding her. "Why?"

"Beats me." Brad reached for the salt shaker and liberally sprinkled his food. "She's a flake," he added. "I'm glad she's gone."

It troubled Callie that Brad didn't look up from his food as he mentioned this. Something was going on, something she couldn't see.

"I don't get it. Last week, she was asking for more hours. She said her rent had gone up."

"Well, there you have it. She obviously decided it would be easier to just move away." Brad pushed his half-eaten food away and stood up. "I need some air. I'll be back in a minute." He turned and left without another word. Physically and emotionally drained,

Callie couldn't summon the energy to be angered by his abrupt departure. Still, she had no idea how she would stay grounded if she couldn't count on Brad.

Ethan's surgery took twelve hours. Twelve hours that Callie spent in the dismal waiting room, pacing the floor or scrunched in a chair, where so many others had waited and worried before her. She tried to envision positive outcomes for all those other people, as if by association Ethan's surgery would then also be successful. Except life didn't work that way. Tears of grief had been shed in this room.

Callie scowled at everyone within eyesight, warding off all docile expressions of sympathy before they were offered. It took all her effort not to think about what was happening to Ethan. Brad was even less able to sit still. He made multiple trips to the coffee shop, rarely buying anything. He stepped outside for air half a dozen times an hour. He insisted on going off to the hardware store because he'd forgotten to buy batteries for his flashlight last weekend.

"You forgot *what?*" Callie asked.

"Batteries. D cells. We might need that flashlight. I'll be back in half an hour." She figured it was his way of coping.

Occasionally, a nurse would come in to give them an update and offer them more bad coffee from cardboard cups. Toward the middle of the afternoon, a matronly volunteer assigned to look after the comfort of those in the waiting room suggested Brad and Callie go get something to eat. Although food was the last thing on Callie's mind, she obeyed because in her mind, if she did exactly as she was told, if she followed every instruction she was given, well then, everything else would be all right, wouldn't it? Her way of coping.

Brad persuaded her to leave the hospital, but she panicked the minute she left the building. She would only go as far as the Burger King across the street, and then she refused to stay more than fifteen minutes.

When they returned, and there was still no news, she called her brother, Bill, holding herself together long enough to tell him what was happening. She assured him with words she didn't quite believe that everything was going to be fine. Ethan was in the best of hands.

"How's Mom doing?" she asked, purposely changing the subject. She listened, but ten minutes later, couldn't remember a word Bill had said.

Her sense of time blurred. The doctors and nurses came and went, going about their ordinary, daily business. Inwardly, she was screaming at them, "Just make this nightmare go away! Please!" Trapped in the climate-controlled, fluorescent world of the hospital, she felt time become a new dimension, each minute seeming more like an hour, the hours like eternities. Finally, while Brad was off wandering yet again, Dr. Clifford strode into the waiting room, still wearing his surgical scrubs, and for the first time in what seemed like forever, Callie allowed herself a flicker of hope. Surely he wouldn't look so smug if he had bad news.

14
SYLVIA

THE TROUBLE WITH the long drive from Teabury to Michigan was that it gave Sylvia too much time to think. She wanted action now, not the psychological gymnastics and mental handwringing she'd incessantly put herself through for the last ten years. She'd had enough of that. Driving fast and pumping high-volume rock—Phish, Metallica, Journey—helped.

The miles drifted by, and as she drove on, pictures of her parents, Pier, Callie, Brad, and Ethan wove through her mind while the background of music provided a cinematic effect.

She'd never known anyone who had the sort of troubles Callie and Brad were facing. In hindsight, she could see that from the beginning it had been part of her fantasy to not only find her sister, but to rescue her, although from what exactly Sylvia had never been quite sure. She had blithely assumed that wherever her half-sister was, she couldn't possibly have the advantages Sylvia had been raised with; Callie would need rescuing and it would be no less than Sylvia's duty to restore her to her birthright of privilege.

With an ingrained sense of entitlement and superiority that had never been questioned by anyone, including herself, it had been easy to dream about bringing her sister back to Teabury, back to her rightful place in the world. Occasionally, Sylvia fantasized that everyone, including her mother, would praise her and call her a hero because they'd be so incredibly grateful that the family was finally united.

Reality, however, wasn't quite working out the way she'd planned. In spite of Callie's financial difficulties (and there, at least, was something Sylvia could offer), who was rescuing whom was questionable. Sylvia thought of the old "be careful what you wish for" warning: she had desperately wanted to find Callie for so long, but now everything had become as distorted as an image in a fun house mirror. Still, the choice was clear. She had to go to Callie now or the delicate bridge they had forged would be broken forever.

It was Brad's second call that had galvanized her. The first time he had contacted her, that horrible Monday after she'd left Tom's place, Sylvia had been in rough shape, unable to sort out her own wretchedness, let alone anyone else's. The guy had clearly been asking for help, but all she could think about was herself and her own misery. Poor, pitiful Sylvia who'd just dumped her fiancé and her wedding plans and didn't know what to do with her life, which of course, *must* be more important than anything he had to say. It was humbling to recall that phone call.

But Brad had compassion as well as a brain in his head. He'd phoned again, forty-eight hours later, with a plan. After giving her an update on Ethan's condition, he again detailed the problems they were having at Stone's Throw, but this time he proposed a solution that added a new twist to Sylvia's participation. She listened and quickly determined that the plan was not only feasible, but nothing less than brilliant for everyone. *Including dear Mother,* Sylvia thought.

After his call, it had taken her less than an hour to pack the few things she cared enough about to take with her; there was so much that she didn't want. For the immediate future, her computer, a few clothes, and credit cards would be enough. The lightness of her possessions was exhilarating. Twice, while she was packing, her cell phone rang. Both times it was Tom. She ignored the calls.

Her parents weren't home when she left. No big deal. They wouldn't exactly have done some grand huggy-kissy farewell in any case. Besides, if they wanted to talk to her, they had her cell phone number. Not that they would use it. Sylvia couldn't actually remember a time when either of her parents had ever called her; it had always been she who called them. She'd tossed one small suitcase and her computer in her car and spun out the Desert Rose driveway without a backward glance.

By the time the sun was slanting low across the horizon, Teabury and the confines of her old life had been left far behind. With every passing mile, the sounds of the road both comforted and excited her. She felt stronger, less like someone who had been walking around in a trance, totally absorbed by forcing herself to be what her parents wanted or absolutely didn't want, depending on the day. Finally, now, she was free of all that, and finally, she understood what had kept her in her parents' house until today. She had been waiting. For years, she had been waiting for something that would never happen. All this time, in everything she had ever done, she had been standing in front of them, hoping to be acknowledged as worthy and deserving of her parents' love. Whether she was being good as a young child, acting out as a teenager, drinking too much, getting kicked out of college, or still living under their giant roof, long past time to leave, it was all about trying to get them to notice her, to pay attention to her, to care for her. The more she thought about it, the more she realized even her engagement to Pier was about getting their attention. She cringed, remembering how smug she'd been, believing that Pier was pleasing his parents by marrying her. Ha. Whatever his motives might have been, hers were worse. And it had almost worked. For a while, her mother had been moderately interested in producing a wedding, as long as it reflected well on the Bennett family.

Sylvia considered what might have happened if she had just shut up and behaved herself on Saturday. (Was that really only three days ago?) Hard on the heels of that thought, she wondered what she would be doing now if she'd never gone to Michigan. What if she had never known about Callie in the first place? But those "ifs" were merely ancillary to the big question: if she'd never felt like part of a real family for just those couple of hours, would she have accepted Pier as a suitable life partner? It terrified her to realize that she might have gone through all the motions of happily-ever-after until she was so resigned to her fate that she never bothered to think about anything more important than the color of her nail polish. Far down the road on the dusky, distant horizon, the first star of the evening appeared. *A good omen*, she thought, breathing a sigh of relief.

The music, nothing more than background noise, was beginning to grate on her nerves; every track sounded the same. She reached to shut the damn thing off just as a new tune began: "Mike's Song."

Mike Kowalski. She couldn't stop thinking about him. Since that day when they had driven around the Michigan Thumb taking photographs, she had looked at his website more than a few times. By now, she knew each of the images by heart, and his passion for his work was obvious. Some of his newer pictures were from the places they had been together; she remembered watching him take the shots and when she saw the images on his website, she couldn't help feeling an intimate rush of adrenaline knowing she'd been with him to share a moment that he had captured forever. The last thing in the world she wanted right now was another complication in her life, but she promised herself that someday when she was more settled, it would be nice to see him again. She hit the stop button, content to drive in silence for a while, reliving the sense of freedom and infinite possibilities she had experienced with Mike.

As the darkness rose around her, fatigue set in. The day had started rough, hadn't improved much over the last eight hours, and she'd had enough. At the next exit advertising food and lodging, she pulled off the highway. Her first order of business was food. McDonald's, for which she'd developed a taste, was half a block farther on her right. She parked the car, walked into the restaurant, placed her order, and sat as far as possible from the other diners while she wolfed down a chicken sandwich, a large order of fries, and a strawberry shake. She was back in her car in fifteen minutes.

Next, she followed the signs to one of the ubiquitous Holiday Inn Express hotels. Suitcase and computer in tow, she stepped up to the front desk only to be told by the middle-aged clerk that there were no single rooms available.

"We've got a convention here this week, hon. Bunch of *ins*urance fellows," the clerk added unnecessarily.

"Really? You don't have any rooms at all? This place is in the middle of nowhere," Sylvia hadn't meant to sound so testy, but when the pleasant expression on the clerk's face hardened, she modified her tone. "I'm sorry. I'm just really, really tired. I've been driving all day."

"You could try Day's Inn, up the road about three miles," the clerk said.

Ready to cry at the thought of getting back in the car, Sylvia picked up her suitcase. "Thanks anyway," she said, offering a weak smile. She should have planned this better. In all the craziness of the day, her rush to flee Teabury, she hadn't given a thought to booking accommodations for the night.

"Of course, if you're only staying here one night, there is another option," the clerk added.

Sylvia looked up hopefully.

"We don't have anyone in the Grande Honeymoon Suite tonight. It's a lot more expensive, but you'd be real comfy. There's a

Jacuzzi and a fully stocked mini-bar. Comes with a complimentary bottle of champagne, too."

Done. Sylvia handed over her credit card.

Room 4224 was a tacky Valentine card. The king-sized bed was covered with a deep red synthetic coverlet and embellished with half a dozen lace-edged pillows stacked against the pink satin headboard. A heart-shaped box of chocolates sat on the dresser between two vases of slightly dusty-looking fabric roses. In a corner of the room, just a few feet from the bed, stood a sparkling white Jacuzzi tub (at least it was clean) large enough for two and flanked with mirrors that rose to the ceiling. How convenient. Further investigation revealed an average bathroom with a conventional shower, a television inside the giant armoire, and a mini-bar, stocked with beer, Perrier water, and the promised champagne, a bargain brand that Sylvia had seen in grocery stores for $5.95 a bottle. Only in her worst drinking days would she ever have touched that crap. The chocolates, however, were another story. She ate four while she waited for the tub to fill and another two as she soaked away the day's tensions in water as hot as she could stand. The remaining two chocolates she decided to save for the road the next day. It was still a good seven hours to Cedar Beach.

Charged up on a sugar rush, her next order of business was calling Jen. Whatever the deal was with Jen and Dan, chances were good that the two of them were already back together. Jen wasn't above being a drama queen when it suited her. Pulling on flannels and a fleece top, Sylvia turned down the coverlet, grimacing at the pink satin sheets. She settled herself on the bed, stuffing a bunch of the lacy pillows behind her back for support. When she was comfortably nestled in, she picked up her phone. Jen answered on the second ring.

"Hey, sorry it's taken me so long to get back to you. Lots of stuff has been going on here," Sylvia said.

"No big deal," Jen replied.

"So, what's the story?"

"I told you. I caught Dan with some little slut who looked about fourteen. I threw a carton of orange juice at them and walked out."

"What do you mean—'with'?"

"She was over at his apartment in the middle of the day, *supposedly* bringing work from the office, because he was *supposedly* too sick to go to work."

"But they weren't, like, in bed or anything?"

"Well…no."

"Then maybe she *was* just dropping off work. Just because this girl was at his place doesn't mean he was cheating on you."

"You're defending him? Are you serious?"

"I'm just trying to help…"

"Look, Syl, what I'm trying to say is that maybe Dan isn't right for me. I mean, I loved the *idea* of Dan—who wouldn't? He's good-looking and successful and he'll probably make junior partner in the firm this summer, but I'm not sure I see myself as Mrs. Czerwenka. God, that name is so…plebe. Besides, he's really into his job right now, and I don't want to wait around for him. There're a lot of guys out there. Dan's not the only fish in the sea."

"Wow. I don't know what to say. I'm sorry."

"Don't be. I mean, it's like, kind of amazing how things can change when you least expect it. What's that old saying? 'When one door closes, another opens', right?"

This was not what Sylvia expected to hear, but Jen's solid, confident tone made it clear that if she had sounded like she was in crisis mode earlier, she'd now found some way to put it all behind her and move on. Sylvia had always admired that quality; it wasn't something she herself could do.

Jen was so clever at analyzing situations, carefully calculating the best possible outcome in any circumstance, no matter what crazy thing either of them did. Whatever she did—either moving on or figuring out how to patch up her relationship with Dan—she'd land on her feet.

"I have some news, too," Sylvia said. She related a detailed story of her tantrum at the club, finishing off by telling Jen of her decision to go to Michigan. She drew the line, however, at confessing anything about her binge weekend with Tom.

"Wow. It's true then," was Jen's reaction.

"You knew already?"

"Umm, I saw something on Facebook a couple of hours ago."

"What? What did you see on Facebook?"

"Lacey Kent posted that you and Pier broke up."

"You're Facebook friends with Lacey? How do you even know her?"

"Hey, I flew out for your birthday party at his parents' house last summer, remember? No, probably you don't because that was the night Pier gave you that gorgeous ruby. Too exciting."

Sylvia had forgotten. Jen had stayed in Teabury less than twenty-four hours, there were a lot of Pier's friends at the party, and Sylvia's general recall of that night was sketchy.

"What did Lacey post?" Sylvia asked.

"Not much really. Just that you threw Pier's ring at him and walked out."

"That's about as much as Lacey would know, but trust me, the whole thing is a lot more complicated than that."

"It must be," Jen said, "because, frankly, I think you are out of your mind. Pier's such a sweetie, and as far as I can see, he's never done anything to deserve being humiliated like that in a public place."

Stung by her friend's words, Sylvia was speechless. There was some truth in Jen's criticism. Pier was who he was; he'd never done anything particularly good or bad. About as exciting as cold toast, but not bad, mean, or even completely stupid. Maybe she had been thoughtless to create such a big scene at the club. Pier was guilty of nothing worse than benign conformity to a predictable existence.

"I just felt like I was being programmed by everyone around me. I need some freedom."

"To do what?"

"I'm not sure. My only immediate plan is to go to Michigan for a while. Brad called me to say that Ethan is really sick and they have a ton of bills they can't pay, so I'm going out there to help them out. I'm half the way there now, somewhere in Pennsylvania."

"Help out? How?"

"They need a little money…"

"Oh, there's a big surprise. Are you insane?"

"No, no. Brad and I have it all figured out. I'll lend them some money, which they'll pay back in a year, and while I'm there, I'll stay with them and work at Stone's Throw."

"Hold on a sec, you're giving them money so you can *work* there?"

"It's not really like that. They're going to teach me how to run a bar and restaurant. Kind of like an apprenticeship. Maybe I could even have my own place someday."

"You're kidding, right? I mean, working in a bar, for God's sake?"

"You're the one who just got done talking about changes. Besides, I want to help Callie any way I can, and working in a bar might be kind of fun."

"Hey, suit yourself. But you of all people in a bar?"

"I don't drink like I used to." Okay, that was true as of right now. No one needed to know about this past weekend. Sylvia chose to block it from her mind, and as far as she was concerned, it never happened.

"Yeah, we'll see about that," Jen said. "Hanging around some hick town in the middle of nowhere is going to get old pretty fast. I'm thinking seriously awful after about two days, by which time I'd bet good money that you'll be nipping at the vodka every chance you get. I guess I can understand if you want to get away for a while, but why don't you go to New York or L.A.? At least you could have some fun, meet some cool people."

"Maybe my ideas of fun and cool have changed."

"Since when?"

"Since I...I don't know. Things arc just diffcrcnt now."

"This sounds like a really bad idea to me, but if you're so into being Susie Trailer-trash, I'm sure you'll have tons of fun. What could be better than working with a bunch of losers in a sleazy bar?"

Sylvia was about to argue, but something shifted in her perception of her long-time friend. Had Jen always been so judgmental of people she didn't even know? Had Sylvia herself been like that? The answer was painfully obvious. They'd both been notorious at boarding school for being catty and rude to anyone they considered inferior, which meant most of the student body and all of the teachers.

The conversation had started strangely and got progressively weirder. Now, although neither of them seemed to have much more to say, Sylvia sensed something traveling just under the surface of Jen's words, something she couldn't quite decipher. The silence between them grew so long that Sylvia wondered if the connection had been dropped.

"So..." Jen began cautiously. "Are you sure you and Pier are done? Any chance that after a few months in the backwoods, you'll be begging him to take you back?"

"Not a chance in hell. That bridge is burned to the ground. Besides which, I'm pretty sure Pier totally hates me now."

"Hmm."

"What?"

"Oh, nothing. Just wondering."

The undercurrent that Sylvia had detected rose to the surface, clarifying in a flash why the timing of Jen's attitude adjustment made perfect sense. *Really? You want to go after Pier?*

"Oh, my gosh, I've gotta run, hon. Let me know if you're ever in Chicago."

This time the connection was broken. Sylvia looked at the phone's incandescent screen. Twenty-three minutes and seventeen seconds. That's how long it took for the last person in Sylvia's familiar world to disappear. She had to hand it to Jen for figuring out pretty quickly that if Pier needed a bit of consoling, who better than she? It was a classic Jen Gardner move. Check out the situation, size up the angles, make a plan. No doubt she was on the phone to Pier right now. Checkmate.

Sylvia threw off the covers and went for the last of the chocolates. She picked up the box, then put it down again as it dawned on her that she didn't really *care* if Jen and Pier got together. She returned to the bed, burrowed under the covers, and fell into a deep, untroubled sleep.

◔◑

IN THE MORNING, she took a long shower, washing her hair twice, letting the past run down the drain with the soapy water. In the hotel's self-serve dining room, she helped herself to scrambled eggs, toast, juice and strong black coffee, pleased with herself for making a more responsible meal choice than last night's junk food and chocolate chaser. She rarely bothered with a real breakfast; dashing out the door with coffee and a handful of Cheerios had always been good enough, but from now on, she vowed to take better care of herself.

Several of the other tables were already occupied: four businessmen in dark suits, white shirts and striped neckties shuffled papers amongst themselves as they ate. An overweight, middle-aged woman and her equally overweight daughter spoke in low tones while they bent their heads over the iPad between them. Each had a plate at her side from which they devoured great chunks of sweet roll without bothering to look at what they were eating. At the table nearest to her, a gangly boy with a protruding Adam's apple sat with a round-faced blond girl, ignoring the food on their plates. Neither looked old enough to be out of high school. Sylvia, aware suddenly of how much older she was, looked away, unsettled.

In the far corner, parents with three small children did their best to keep the kids under control. The dad opened three miniature cereal packets and let the children eat with their fingers while the mother poured milk into sippy cups.

Sylvia pretended to be looking at the complementary newspaper on her table, but the *Allentown Times* didn't feature much she was interested in reading about, and her thoughts were preoccupied by the adventure that lay ahead. This feeling of freedom was a better buzz than she'd ever gotten from booze. Maybe this was what she'd been trying to find all those times in the liquor. She did not need Pier or Jen or even her mother; her sense of self wouldn't come from other people any more than it would come from a bottle. That one last, shameful weekend with Tom must have been the price she'd had to pay before she could tear herself from her old ways, but she was free and clear now. Jen was wrong: working in a bar would hold no temptation. She was wrong, too, when she called Brad and Callie losers. Jen was the kind of person who viewed people the same way she viewed her clothes: easy to acquire, and just as easy to discard when something better came along. If Jen was chasing Pier, Sylvia could almost feel sorry for the guy. She didn't hate him, but she didn't love him, either.

Pier was comfortable. He was familiar with the framework of her life, the substructure of boarding school, the club, the rules of behavior that were part of her world. She recognized that the two of them could have grown old, settling carelessly into those same habits and customs with no qualms at all. But love? That had to be something else entirely.

Sitting at the little table, identical to the one at the Holiday Inn Express in Michigan, she sipped her coffee and let her eyes wander around the room, eavesdropping on the conversations around her. The mother and daughter spoke too quietly to hear, and the businessmen were droning on about profit margins, sales, and customer complaints. More interesting was the young couple at the nearest table.

"We should be home by four or five, depending on traffic," the girl said.

"Should we tell them right away?" the boy asked. "It's kind of a lot to drop the minute we walk in the door."

"They're going to figure it out anyway," the girl replied. "Dad might be a little upset at first, but at least he likes you. He'll come around, especially when he realizes he won't have to shell out for a big wedding. And Mom will cry, but then she'll run out and buy baby clothes right after dinner."

There are a million stories, Sylvia thought. All these people and all their separate lives, each of them engrossed in their own world.

The round-faced girl caught Sylvia's eye and glared at her with a mind-your-own-business expression. Embarrassed, Sylvia made a show of fumbling through her purse for her phone. There was no one she wanted to call, but she could mess around with it and at least look as though she were doing something important.

She had some of the shots she'd taken in Michigan on the phone's album. There was a nice one of Mike leaning against the textured bark of a silver birch, his head cocked slightly so that he looked as if he were saying, "So, what are you going to do next?"

She wondered if he ever thought about her. Was he out along the shoreline right now, taking pictures again? Had he been back to Stone's Throw? He'd asked her to email him sometime, which she hadn't done. She'd never even thanked him properly for the day out. Or the dinner. She should do that. Just send a quick email to say "thank you." And, not for the first time, she thought it would be nice to go out with him again.

15
CALLIE

"AMEN." CALLIE LOOKED up after Bill finished the prayer. The oldest of the Hanlon siblings, Bill had always taken it upon himself to be the leader. Four of them—Bill, Molly, Brad and Callie—stood in a circle holding hands in the waiting room near ICU. Ethan had come through the surgery well, but Callie was still angry, and anger made her contemptuous of piety. The idea of being subservient to a God who would treat her child so badly enraged her. Still, she knew Bill's intentions were good; prayer was the best he could offer, so she quelled her fury.

The minute Callie had told him about Ethan, Bill had contacted the rest of the family. He and Molly rearranged their own lives and made the three-hour drive from Ann Arbor to Bay City. Unfortunately, there wasn't much they could do beyond offer hugs and prayers. Ethan's surgery had been on Tuesday. Was that yesterday or the day before? Callie wasn't sure; she tried to think clearly, but stress and fatigue had taken a toll. She felt as though she'd been in this stupid hospital forever. The doctors kept telling her everything was looking fine, but what did that mean? How could anything be fine while Ethan was still in intensive care, still hooked up to too many machines, still merely a fragile, broken-looking shell of the little boy she loved so dearly?

Hours after the surgery, when she had finally been allowed to see him, she was only permitted in his ICU cubicle for five minutes out of every hour. Now, she could stay longer, but there was still nothing more she could do than stand beside his bed, touch his small hand where it was not swathed in gauze and adhesive tape, and try not to think about the unfairness of it all. Why had this happened to him? Why did anything bad happen to kids? What if the doctors were wrong and the Ethan she knew never returned? Nothing else in her life—not even the way Anne had treated her—had ever rocked her sense of security, her trust that happy endings were possible the way the last few days had done.

After the prayer, Callie watched Brad return to the spot he had staked out on one of the waiting room sofas where he sat watching the Weather Channel. She couldn't grasp his fascination with a river flood in Missouri until she realized he wasn't actually paying any attention to the images on the screen. She wandered to a window, looking out on the bright summer day, while Molly cleared up clusters of empty coffee cups.

In her bleakest hours, when anger and depression overruled positive thinking, when it was too easy to see only life's woes, she spiraled back to wondering why she had been tossed away not once, but twice, by her birth mother. What possible reason could the woman have for being so heartless toward her own child?

Rape. Incest. Callie could only imagine that her biological father must have been an even worse monster than her mother to make Anne so violently opposed to any contact. Such thoughts made a road too dark and scary to venture down.

Now, just like all the other times when that darkness threatened, Callie forced herself to focus on the good things. She did have good things, wonderful things in her life—her family, Brad and Ethan, Stone's Throw. Aware that her ability to steel her mind against unpleasantness was the strength that kept her going, she also wondered if, ironically, this was exactly the same trait that allowed Anne to dismiss her so casually.

"Cal, I wish we could stay with you, but we need to get back on the road," Bill said, breaking into her ruminations.

Tamping down the embers of her inner bitterness, Callie managed a fragile smile. Bill and Molly had dropped everything in their busy schedules in order to be here offering love and support. They didn't deserve her black mood.

"You guys have been great. Thanks so much for coming up here." She hugged them both. "Tell Mom and Dad I love them."

"They really wanted to be here for you, too," Molly said.

"I know." Callie understood that the only reason Peg and Jack weren't with her was because Peg was under strict orders to rest after having a stent threaded through her blood vessels the day before Ethan's surgery. Why were so many awful things happening at once? *I should be in Ann Arbor helping to look after Mom,* she thought. *It isn't fair. Neither of them did anything to deserve this. I didn't do anything to deserve this.* She felt frustration and rage start to boil up once again, and the effort it took to override it was increasingly exhausting. Forcing herself to keep up the façade of calm control, she said, "You guys are the best."

Once again, a whiplash of emotions shook her, but this time, despite her best efforts, she felt the corners of her smile quiver. An unaccustomed sting of tears burned the backs of her eyes. Rage and anger were familiar. She could subdue those feelings. But helplessness overwhelmed her.

Refocus, she told herself. *Bill and Molly sacrificed their time to drive up here to hold your hand in this awful room.* These people were her family. Blood ties mattered less than the ties that kept people together through thick and thin. To hell with Anne and Sylvia and whatever kind of dirtball her biological father might be.

After Bill and Molly left, the room seemed to grow larger and scarier than it had been moments before. Callie wrapped her arms around herself, shivering.

"I need some air," Brad said. "I can't just sit here. This place gives me the creeps."

"Fine," Callie replied, turning her back to him.

"*What?*" he asked.

She glowered at him over her shoulder.

"Cal, it's three-quarters of an hour before we can see him again, and it's not like we can even talk to him. He doesn't know we're here. Hell, he doesn't know *he's* here."

"So go. Get out of here. Do whatever it is that you do when you leave every ten minutes."

"What's that supposed to mean?"

She turned and faced him. "You tell me. What does it mean?"

He held her gaze for a moment, then dropped his eyes and muttered, "For Christ's sake." He tipped an old, battered Michigan State cap on his head, pulled the bill down low over his eyes, and walked out of the room.

Left alone in the dismal waiting room, Callie felt the tears build behind her eyes again, and this time she let them flow, swiping at them with the backs of both hands. She sat on one of the ugly orange chairs, pulling her knees up so that she was curled in a protective ball, and let the misery wash over her. She closed her eyes, tried to let her mind go blank, if only to get some peace, but hospital sounds—the dinging of the intercom, nurses paging doctors, phones ringing, the clang of carts being wheeled down long corridors—kept the nightmare real. The clock on the wall read just past two in the afternoon; it would still be the better part of an hour before she could see Ethan again. Suddenly, she couldn't sit in the horrible room any longer. She had to get out of this dreariness. Just for a few minutes.

Not consciously aware of where she was going, she turned corners and followed corridors and found herself at the door of the hospital chapel. Anger and the harsh realities of life had taken a toll on the remnants of any faith she'd ever had, but nevertheless, she opened the door and entered the dimly lit space. As her eyes adjusted, she noticed another person sitting in the shadows, head in hands. *Brad?*

Silently, she slid in next to him.

He lifted his head, and the pain in his eyes made her heart contract.

"Whatever it is, you'd better tell me," she said, knowing she didn't want to hear.

He sighed a deep, soul-rending sound. "There's a couple things to do with Alyssa that I haven't had a chance to mention, what with all Ethan's troubles. I've been meaning to, just the time was never right."

"Oh, God, Brad…" Callie felt dizzy. She willed herself not to faint.

"No, it's not what you think, Cal. Well, not really." He ran his hands through his hair and Callie waited, afraid to say anything.

"She didn't quit; I fired her."

"What? Why?" Given what had been going through her head a few seconds earlier, this wasn't bad news.

"I should have told you a while ago that she'd been acting… weird…around me lately. Couple times, she cornered me, got way too close. Said some really inappropriate stuff."

"And?"

"She got pretty pissed when I wouldn't take her up on any of her, um, offers. There was this one day when we were down in the basement. I had to tell her to keep her hands to herself, that there was nothing going to happen between us. Ever. She got real ugly. Said something like, 'You think you're hot shit, but I'll get you for this.' She looked crazy, and the way she said it really spooked me, so I started paying closer attention to what she did while she was supposedly organizing the stockroom.

"Cal, she was stealing from us. Left, right and center, every chance she got she was walking off with stuff: booze, ketchup, bar towels, even the goddamn toilet paper. It kind of figures, too, that the little bitch was under-ringing sales and pocketing cash, too. Like the stuff she was hauling out of the basement wasn't enough?"

Callie didn't realize that tears had been running freely down her cheeks until Brad reached over and gently brushed them away. "I'm sorry, babe. I should've told you sooner."

"Yeah." Callie raised her eyes to the ugly sound-proof tiles of the chapel ceiling, sighed deeply, and brushed her hands over her tear-streaked face. "Yeah, that would've been good."

"But there was so much going on. Sylvia showed up. Ethan got sick. You were working so hard to keep everything together. I thought I could take care of it. I didn't want you to have to deal with one more thing."

Their eyes met. Callie could see the truth in Brad's eyes, that he'd been trying to do what he thought was best.

"Jesus, Mary and Joseph. I can't believe it. I can't believe she'd do something like that to us. Did you call the cops?"

"I thought about it, but honestly, I just want her gone."

Callie looked at her husband and asked the question that had been worrying her for weeks. "So are we—you and me—are we okay?"

Brad drew her into his arms. "Yeah, babe. No doubt there. Ever. We might still have a rough road ahead, but we'll take it on together."

Later, after they'd both seen Ethan, and he'd been moved out of ICU to a regular room, Brad returned to Stone's Throw to spend the night. He'd tried to persuade Callie to come with him, but she refused. "I can't leave Ethan here all alone, Brad. I just can't. There's a sleeper chair in his room. I'm staying with him."

"Okay, babe. I get it. I'll be back here first thing in the morning."

Callie was roused from an unsettled sleep when two orderlies came in at eight the next morning to take Ethan for testing. He murmured a bit as they moved him to the gurney, but he was so groggy, Callie wasn't sure he knew where he was or that she was there with him.

"We'll bring him back in thirty minutes," the orderlies promised cheerily as they wheeled him away. Stiff from hours in the lumpy sleeper chair, she was still exhausted and sorely in need of coffee. In the tiny adjoining bathroom, she splashed water on her face and combed her hair, weaving it back in a French braid to keep it off her face.

She was just ready to head to the cafeteria when Brad slipped into the room.

"Morning, babe." He greeted her with a kiss. "Hey, I've got great news. Look who's here." He pointed, and there, standing in the half-open doorway was Sylvia.

Confused and disoriented by Sylvia's appearance, Callie could only say, "I don't understand. Why is she here?"

"I called her," Brad replied.

"You did *what?*" Callie pushed herself away from Brad. "Why in hell would you do that?"

"Because she can help us."

"I don't want her help."

"Cal," Brad began, but he was interrupted by Sylvia, who had stepped tentatively into the room.

"Callie, I'm so glad Ethan's surgery went well," she said. "I... I'm sorry you've had to go through all this." She glanced around the room, looking nervous.

Callie knew that look, knew how it felt to be beyond the comfort zone and all alone. For a split second, she flashed back to the day Anne's lawyer had put her in a similar position. Just as quickly, she pushed the memory away. "Yeah, thanks. But I don't think there's much you can do to help."

"Actually, she's already done quite a bit," Brad said. He pulled a check out of his pocket and held it in front of Callie.

"Oh, my God."

"It's more than enough to take care of the medical bills and keep Stone's Throw afloat," Brad said.

"That's really nice of you, Sylvia, but we can't take this money," Callie replied instantly.

"Yes, you can. First of all, it's not like I'm just giving you the money. It's payment in advance for my apprenticeship."

"Your *what?*"

"Yup." Sylvia's demeanor, which had shifted from nervous to nearly confident, grew bolder. "You and Brad have just agreed to hire me and teach me everything you know about running a bar and a restaurant."

"Oh, I don't think so." Callie glared at her husband.

Brad pushed his glasses higher on his nose. "Actually, Cal, it's a great idea. With Alyssa gone, we'll need the help. You've always said you can't do everything."

Brad folded the check carefully before tucking it in his shirt pocket. He crossed his arms over his chest, and Callie decided the gesture was as much from a place of authority as self-preservation. He continued, "After all the stuff with Alyssa, I got to thinking not only were we seriously short-handed, but it looked like Stone's Throw would go belly-up if we didn't get some cash real fast."

Seeing the look on Callie's face, Brad hesitated. "I know you did everything you could, baby, and I really didn't want to go behind your back, but I took a chance and called Sylvia to see if she could help us out."

"It was Brad who figured out how to make it work for all of us," Sylvia added before Callie could get a word in. "You guys need an extra hand, so I'll take over Alyssa's job—minus the embezzlement, of course—and you can teach me how to earn a living."

Callie stared at her. "Are you completely out of your mind? You have no idea what you are getting into."

"So teach me."

"It's not that simple, and it sure as hell isn't society-girl kind of work. Besides, don't you already have a job? Planning fancy parties?"

"I quit."

Callie studied her half-sister, and this time Sylvia matched her gaze with equal self-assurance. There was something else different about her, too. She reminded Callie of herself years ago when so many things seemed possible. When the world wasn't such a scary place.

"Are you sure you want to do this?" Callie asked, gesturing toward the check in Brad's pocket. "I mean, if you've got that kind of money, you don't really need to work. And then there's your wedding. What are you going to do about that?"

Sylvia took a step toward Callie, putting her hand gently on her sister's arm. "We have a lot of catching up to do. What do say we get out of here for a while, grab a cup of decent coffee? Brad can stay with Ethan for an hour or two, right?"

Brad smiled at them both. "No problem."

"But I…"

Brad put his hand on her shoulder and looked deep in her eyes. "Cal, it'll be fine. I promise. You've been here for days, sleeping in chairs, eating nothing. It's time to give yourself a break, get away from this place for a while. Go with Sylvia, have a decent lunch. Relax. Ethan and I will be here for you when you come back."

Callie was still afraid, but she knew he was right. She turned to her half-sister. "Let's go," she said, hoping some of the younger woman's courage would find its way to her.

16
ANNE

O N THE EVE of their voyage, Anne sat across the table from
Henry at Les Pierres. The chic new restaurant, named for
the chef, Pierre Alain, and the owner, Pierre Guichard, boasted a
night vista as spectacular as its cutting edge cuisine. Anne, whose
still spoke and read French quite well, supposed that the name was
also in reference to the jewel-box views. Through floor-to-ceiling
windows, the lights of New York City glittered in all their finery.
Feeling wrongly dressed for the surroundings, Anne wished that
she had chosen something less understated than her simple, winter-
white suit adorned only with pearl earrings.

They had finished dinner during which conversation had been
blessedly minimal and exclusively to do with either their meal
(poached lobster on spinach, veal in morel sauce, strawberry and aru-
gula salad with foam citrus dressing) or the trip to South Africa, on
which they would embark at a revoltingly early hour the following
morning. While Henry examined the bill and fiddled with his credit
cards, Anne sipped her espresso. The tiny *demitasse* would likely keep
her awake most of the night, but she fervently hoped that the ensuing
fatigue along with a dose of Ambien would enable her to sleep for
most of the ridiculously long flight to Cape Town. She hated flying.

The journey to South Africa had sounded so pleasant when they first discussed it last summer. Now, except for providing an escape from the dreary winter weather, there was nothing about it that appealed to Anne. It all seemed like too much work. Dragging around day after day, taking in the scenery and occasional glimpses of wild animals, was exhausting. If she found the myriad peoples and cultures interesting, the searing poverty and squalor of so many lives depressed her. The trip had been Henry's idea, of course. He adored this sort of thing. The grand adventure—traipsing through market places, riding in those terrible rattle-trap vehicles, dust and mud and flies everywhere.

To keep herself entertained, she would take photographs, as she always did on their trips. She had recently purchased a new digital camera, now securely stowed in a merlot-colored leather travel case. Studying its intricacies would provide her with something to do during the long flight, and Henry was always complimentary about the albums she put together after their various travels. Even though each album took several weeks to assemble, compiling them was something she enjoyed, often a great deal more than the trip itself. After they returned home, she could spend weeks and weeks immersed in sorting through the pictures, writing captions, adding mementos until the entire journey was permanently captured in a thick album. There was something comforting in the preservation of the experience, in knowing she could open any one of the numerous albums that lined the music room bookshelves and be transported to another time and place. Henry would occasionally look at them when he needed to remember the name of their favorite restaurant in Hong Kong, or the guide who had led them trekking through the Andes, or which operas they had seen on their various trips to Vienna.

Anne glanced at him now, sitting across the table. He was gazing out toward the city lights, his mind placidly wandering in its own direction. More than likely, he was mentally reviewing a recent golf game. She often thanked God that the man was able to keep to himself so much of the time. To be married to someone with whom one could be comfortably silent was something Anne considered essential. He was also getting better looking with time, she noticed. His hair, still thick, was silver now, and the less taut skin around his owlish eyes lent him a dignified maturity. If, in her heart of hearts, she thought him to be irretrievably stupid, at least she could find no worse faults in his character. He conducted himself with dignity and innate social grace at all times. And for some unfathomable reason, he loved her. He had proven that.

"I heard from Sylvia today," Anne said.

"Oh? I wondered if she would call before we left," he replied.

"She didn't call. She sent an email."

"How is she settling in?"

"Rather well, I believe. Apparently, she has a boyfriend."

"Really?" Henry paused to sip his coffee. "I suppose it's about time. It must be over a year since that incident with Pier. I hope she treats this one a bit more kindly than she did poor Pier. Is the fellow anyone we know?"

"Of course not. She's in Michigan."

"There are a few people we know in the Grosse Pointe area."

"I'm quite certain she's not in Grosse Pointe." Anne didn't mention that there were three rather well composed photos attached to the email. One was of Sylvia laughing, wrapped in the arms of an attractive blond fellow. The second picture showed a different man and woman posed in front of a clapboard house with a neon sign for *Miller Lite* in the front window. Anne had stared at the image on her computer screen until her eyes stung and the woman's face was burned indelibly on her mind. The final photo was a close-up of a small boy sporting a brightly colored button that read, "Now I Am Six." His short hair and gap-toothed smile gave him a mischievous look, and his deep brown eyes reminded Anne of someone she'd once known.

"Oh. Well." Henry dabbed his napkin to his lips. "I've never actually ever been to Michigan. Have you?"

Anne, taken aback, wondered for the briefest moment if Henry was deliberately baiting her, then decided he was simply being obtuse.

"No. And I have no intention of ever going there." Anne raised her eyebrows to emphasize her point. "Surely, you of all people should understand that."

"Mmm. Yes, I suppose so." He went back to examining the dinner bill.

Anne hadn't meant to sound so sharp with her husband. He was trying to do what he thought best, but God, sometimes a conversation with him felt like attempting to communicate with a two-year-old child. She considered apologizing for her tone of voice, but dismissed the idea when she saw him looking at her once more with the annoying expression of sympathy and concern he had developed after learning about Callie.

This is all Sylvia's fault. If she wanted to make a tabloid story of her own life, so be it, but she had no right to poke around in things that were none of her business. Anne still felt a sharp twinge between her shoulder blades when she thought of that evening at the club and the subsequent mayhem. Having her daughter behave so poorly in public was a profound embarrassment and one of the few times, perhaps the only time, that Anne had been completely unable to control the situation. For weeks, the gossip mills had been busy. Even Henry noticed groups of people at the club would stop talking when he came into a room, and Anne refused to go near the place. The Kents were not important to her, but they had left the Teabury Club in a huff, and people in the dining room had noticed their abrupt departure. Moira, narrow-eyed with fury, had stormed out the door muttering discernible obscenities, followed closely by

Pier III, who had turned an unhealthy shade of red. Pier IV had been calm by comparison. He'd stood watching his parents leave, wiped a splatter of raspberry juice from his jacket, then turned to Henry and shook his hand. "Thank you for dinner. Goodbye, sir," he'd said, before striding from the room.

Perhaps the boy had been relieved, Anne thought.

"This place certainly isn't modest about its prices." Henry looked up from the black leather folder embossed with the logo of Les Pierres. "I understand the lobster, but $185 for veal is a tad high, don't you think?"

"They can charge whatever they please after the last review. *Everyone* wants to eat here."

Henry mumbled something else, but Anne was distracted, still thinking back to that last episode at the club.

She remembered the night had been uncomfortably warm, the air thick with moist, fetid odors as she walked through the parking lot. She and Henry had driven to the club in separate cars, which meant she had to drive back to Wheatley House alone, wondering all the while what on earth had precipitated her daughter's unconscionable behavior and what might happen next. Unlikely as it seemed, Anne had been certain that the events of the evening were somehow connected to Sylvia's unhealthy obsession with ancient history.

Sylvia hadn't come home that night. Or the next night. When Henry had expressed concerns, Anne dispelled them as quickly as she could.

"Sylvia is twenty-two years old and completely capable of taking care of herself," she'd said. "Weren't you independent at that age?"

"Yes, but…"

"Henry, she's fine. Obviously, she needs some time alone to think things through. Perhaps she's embarrassed by her behavior; she certainly should be."

The whole mess became much more complicated after Sylvia left town. Henry took it upon himself to call his daughter's cell phone on which he left three messages before she returned his call. She told him only that she was safe, and had found a place to stay in Michigan. Henry was completely flummoxed and began to pursue his daughter's motives with maddening firmness of purpose. He bombarded Anne with questions.

"Why in the world would she be going to Michigan?" he had asked over and over. "You must know something about this."

Anne had stonewalled.

A week later, returning from an evening in the city, he had said, "I'm worried. I don't care how independent she thinks she is. Who, or what, is in Michigan?"

Trapped in the car, Anne had no escape. She was exhausted. *Please, just let this go,* she had pleaded silently.

"She might be in some sort of trouble, you know," Henry had said. "Perhaps we'd better phone the police."

Defeated, Anne had put her hands over her eyes. She had lied and Sylvia had called her bluff; Henry knew nothing of Callie's existence.

"There is no need for the police. I know where she is and who she's with in Michigan." If the truth were going to come out—and it seemed Sylvia was hell-bent on it—Anne wanted Henry to hear the story from her.

Explaining her past to him in the confines of the car had been terribly awkward. There were no distractions; there wasn't even the crutch of strong liquor. Henry, forced to keep his eyes on the road, took the news quietly. She apologized for not having told him sooner.

In keeping with his character, Henry remained silent most of the way home. After some minutes in which Anne had feared that her carefully constructed world might come to an abrupt and igno-

minious end, he had calmly asked if she wished to establish any sort
of relationship with her first-born child.

"God forbid," Anne had answered, looking away from him,
out the window.

"But she is your daughter," he said.

She turned to him. "Henry, dear, I'm well aware of that. However, both she and Sylvia are grown women. We are not talking
about some wretched little waifs who must live on the streets begging bread from strangers. If Sylvia, for God knows what reason,
has decided to make this unfortunate incident in my life her own
pet project, well, that is her choice, but as far as I am concerned, I
would think it is abundantly clear that I have no wish to wallow in
my past mistakes."

Anne's voice had been strong and confident as she spoke. It
was a façade, a practiced role that she had perfected over the years.

Now, over a year since that night, she regarded Henry across
the table at Les Pierres. It was true she had no desire to remember
the past, but sometimes in spite of her best efforts, the past stole
her away. Sometimes she still flashed back to that morning after
Chris had left, when Annie had gone to the main floor lounge in
Hill Hall, radiant with the night's love, eager to tell Nelia and the
others how romantic it had been—Chris driving all this way to see
her, telling her he loved her, swearing to find a way for them to
be together always. It was almost like they were engaged. And she
couldn't wait to hear from all the girls that he was the cutest guy
they'd ever seen. But it all turned out wrong when she danced into
the dorm lounge and found everyone silent, staring at the dusty
television. Nelia, sitting on the sofa, her legs drawn up under her,
turned to Annie. "Big crash on I-95."

"The names of the injured have not yet been released, pending
notification of the families." The announcer's wooden words cap-
tioned the image on the screen: A school bus had narrowly missed

a head-on collision with a semi that jumped the median. Two other vehicles hadn't been so lucky.

"Oh, my God, look at that mess," Carol had said. Annie had looked again at the television screen and saw the piled up cars littering the highway. The semi had plowed straight into a now unidentifiable white vehicle. As the television camera panned the scene, she heard the announcer say there were no survivors from the two smaller vehicles. In the twisted wreckage, she could also clearly see the crushed cab of a turquoise pickup truck.

From the time that Sylvia had revealed her knowledge of Callie's existence, Anne had had to relive that moment too many times. What she much preferred was forgetting. She told Henry only that she had made a terrible mistake her freshman year in college, and yes, she had had a child, whom she had given up for adoption the moment it was born.

"It is all rather complicated, isn't it?" Henry had said that evening in the car.

"No, actually," Anne had replied. "It isn't complicated at all. It's quite simple—it happened a long time ago. It's over, and there isn't anything more to discuss."

Since that night, neither of them ever made mention of the incident or of Sylvia until this evening. Tomorrow morning, they would be off on another adventure, and when they returned eight weeks later, they would resume their normal routine. That was the way of the world.

Henry retrieved his credit card from the leather billet and folded the receipt carefully into his wallet. His actions, slow and deliberate, at once annoyed and calmed Anne. Henry Bennett was perfect for her.

Anne sipped the last dregs of her espresso. "Are we finished here? It's past ten and we have an early flight tomorrow."

ACKNOWLEDGMENTS

MY FATHER, WHO generally found fault with everything I did, always said I could write well; therefore, the last thing I wanted to do was write. I got a late start, but eventually I figured out that there was a certain sense of power in creating fiction, and I was hooked.

My father was my first, and arguably my best critic and editor. I wish he could have helped me with this manuscript.

Help, however, has come from many others. My husband, Jerry, is second only to Dad in his laser-sharp analysis of a manuscript, and he's #1 when it comes to moral support. I literally could not have done this without him.

Even with Jerry's constant encouragement, *The World Undone* would not exist without the help of many other wonderful, knowledgeable people. Mr. Fred Shafer, writing teacher *extraordinaire*, has taught me much about the writing process and has somehow managed to persuade me that revision can be fun and exciting even the eighth time around.

Special thanks goes to my early readers: Carol Harrison, Mary Helgren, Patricia Danch, Deb Daly, Diccon Lee, Tom Bradfish, Betsy Driver, Ceil Barrie, Rolanda Derderian, Camille Prindle, and Gabrielle Prindle. Also thanks go out to Katie Bibbs, Shari Brady, Susan Bearman, and Cindy Serikaku for their encouragement during this process. To Weezie and Bink, thank you for the weekend at your lovely Cape Cod house where the seed of this story grew into a working concept.

Once I had a finished manuscript, I realized that publication was going to be even more challenging than writing. Without April Eberhardt's enthusiasm, guidance, and depth of knowledge, this story would be stuck in a drawer. I'm equally grateful to Nathan Everett and Lynn Bell for their professionalism and patience with my endless questions.

A huge thank-you must also go to my three writing groups: Off Campus Writers' Workshop, The Writers of Glencoe, and Forest Writers' Group in Lake Forest. I have learned so much from all of you, and I so appreciate the friendships I have made in each of these groups.

Finally, to my three fabulous daughters and their wonderful husbands—Betsy and David, Sarah and Nick, Kate and Bill—and the extended Driver family, for all of the stories we share, thank you.

AUTHOR

MARY DRIVER-THIEL holds a B.A. in Fine Art and a Master of Arts in Teaching. She divides her work time between writing and private tutoring. In her spare time, she enjoys running, cooking, and spending time with friends. *The World Undone* is her first novel; she is currently working on the sequel. She lives in the Chicago area with her husband, Jerry, and Woki, the Wonder Dog.